As Silver Is to the Moon

A NOVEL

R. A. Watt

TER
PUBLISHING

AS SILVER IS TO THE MOON
Copyright © 2019 R. A. WATT
All rights reserved.

Cover Designed by Damon Freeman

www.ryanawatt.com

ISBN 978-1-9990009-0-5

Printed and bound in the United States
First Edition

*For my wife Sarah, my three children,
my sister, and my father. Without your
encouragement this book would
still be unfinished.*

ly·can·thrope

noun

1. A werewolf.

2. A person affected with lycanthropy.

-THE AMERICAN HERITAGE DICTIONARY, 5TH EDITION

It is madness for sheep to talk peace with a wolf.

-THOMAS FULLER

Prologue

Ancestral Roots
Calais, France
1773

The hulking figure of Thibault Lalaing stood motionless at the edge of the warehouse roof. He scanned the wharves for any movement as the rain pounded incessantly on his hat, the wide brim shielding his eyes from the onslaught. The air had a cold, penetrating dampness that chilled to the bone, but he was oblivious to its effects in his quest to find the traitor.

The younger and much smaller Sabine Martin stood silently beside him. She was fierce, and had killed before. But this would be different. This was one of her own kind.

She trembled as she contemplated the plan she was committed to. There was only one outcome possible tonight: her death or his.

Sabine looked up at Thibault. "Are you confident this is the correct dock?"

He nodded. "Yes, he bought passage on that boat." He pointed to a weathered trading vessel tethered to the docks. "It leaves in the morning, but I'm told he will attempt to board before dawn."

Sabine squinted in the darkness but saw no movement, save for the odd scurrying wharf rat. As they surveyed for activity that didn't belong, the deluge continued.

Thibault scowled. "Let us find this wretched traitor, dispose of him, and be gone of this filthy place. I wish to be home with before noon on the morrow."

The port city of Calais was a major trading hub with England, and the gateway to the English settlements and beyond. Leaving France was unthinkable for their people, and those who chose to were dealt with severely. Even fatally.

Thibault was a powerful man, unlikely to need assistance from Sabine. But she needed to learn and move up in the ranks, and so she had volunteered to assist him on this mission. This hunt. She glanced at his thick, corded neck as it pulsed in the moonlight with each beat of his heart.

This would be no easy task.

Dawn was approaching and time was running out. Sabine shifted uneasily.

He peered down at her. "Quit squirming. Your movement will alert him of our presence."

She shrugged. "My apologies . . . I need to urinate."

He shook his head in frustration. "Go then. Over there. Be quick."

Sabine crept as quietly as she could on the graveled rooftop to the exhaust stacks, crouching down behind them for privacy as she pulled out her short sword and laid it beside her. She could see Thibault between the stacks, completely still as he kept watch on the docks. As usual, he seemed dismayed at her *weakness*.

But that attitude was his weakness.

Sabine disrobed hastily and stood naked in the near-freezing rain. She couldn't risk damaging the only clothing she had with her.

She brought forth the familiar, painful tingling from the center of her being, forcing it to the outer limbs of her body. Her fingers extended and the joints expanded as coarse black hair grew out from each digit—each arm. Her nails lengthened and grew sharp as the pain she fought to keep quiet overtook her whole body.

Awkwardly—on her hind legs—she now stood a foot taller in her humanoid wolf state—her *lycan* form. Her surroundings were now highly defined to her lupine eyes, and her sense of smell incalculably improved. Adrenaline coursed through her veins; the power of ten men at her will. In this half-transformed state, she grasped the short sword as best she could in her claws. Her thinking and motives were less clear now, and she had to focus. She had to move forward and ignore the hunger that chewed at her.

Thibault stood guard, facing away, still searching for the traitor they'd come for. Not realizing he—*she*—was standing behind him.

If he turned before she made her move, it would be her end. His considerable frame gave no hint as to the speed and viciousness it was capable of.

The pads on her feet made less noise than her shoes, and she crept up behind him, holding the sword in her claws.

His perceptive ears heard her approach, and he hissed without turning. "Stop moving so much, you—"

Thibault never finished as her deadly sharp blade inflicted it's mortal damage in one fell swoop of Sabine's powerful lycan arm. As a human, she hadn't the strength to cut so cleanly in one swing, so it had to be as a lycan. It would have been a painful, traitor's death for her had she failed.

His lifeless body slumped to the roof gracelessly.

The instinct to fully transform and hunt was almost overwhelming, but she willed herself to return to human form.

The cold rain was refreshing on her exposed body. The heat produced by the transformation was immense, and she welcomed the frigid water on her steaming skin.

She leaned over Thibault's body and rummaged through his pockets for any bits of gold or silver she could find, then returned to the stacks where her clothing lay. Before she dressed, Sabine gently rubbed the newly-formed bump on her stomach. "Not to worry, we will be safe in England," she said, more to herself than the budding life inside. "They won't stop us."

She waited at the dock for the ship's captain and crew to arrive, eager to ascertain who had given her travel plans away before their journey to England was complete.

At least Thibault hadn't been told whether the lycan traitor was male or female.

It was his loss to assume.

As she stood steadfast, Sabine gazed up and was transfixed by the almost-full moon. It called to her, like it always did. The urge was there, buried deep . . . but there. She longed to transform—*all the way*— and simply run.

Chapter 1

Santa Isadora, California
Present Day

Though I didn't realize it at the time, the trajectory of my life was drastically altered that Friday in early March. Well, arguably it was the move to Santa Isadora that changed it.

My first week in ninth grade at Redwood High School passed almost without incident, which seemed like a win. Until Friday afternoon. It was March ninth, and we had just moved to California. My new math teacher asked me to stay after class for a few minutes, as he wanted to give me some worksheets for the weekend to assess how much I knew of their curriculum. Usually, that would ruin a weekend, but math came easily to me. And honestly, I had nothing else to do.

I exchanged books in my locker and hobbled outside to find a small crowd around the racks where my bike was locked up.

Everyone was gathered around two kids. I couldn't see who they were, but one was insulting the other. My bike was locked up in the middle so I couldn't leave.

I whispered to an Asian guy I recognized from my class. "What's going on?"

Warily, he eyed me up and down. "Bruno Vincent and his

buddies from Baker are here. Luckily it ain't me he's picking on. But sucks for Jermaine." He motioned to the black kid that I could now see was getting pushed. "As long as Jermaine doesn't lip off, Bruno won't do much. He wants guys to fight back."

The bigger kid, Bruno, looked a year older than me and wore a dirty white shirt and jeans. He had spiky blond hair and his pock-marked face had the look of a permanent scowl.

Though athletic in his own right, Jermaine was a little shorter and looked to be shaking.

"Come on, Wilkins, ain't you gonna say something? Anything? I insult your mom, and you don't care? Don't you have any family honor?" Bruno shouted as he cornered Jermaine up against the bikes in the rack.

I recognized Jermaine; he was also in my class. He was arched backward over the seat of a mountain bike. "B-Bruno, I don't want any trouble," he stammered. "You know that."

Bruno paced back and forth with a hateful grin, surveying the kids in the front row of the expectant crowd. "Now, Jerk-Off—I mean, *Jermaine*—you sure seemed pretty cocky at our last soccer game when you scored against us. I think you need to back it up now. Don't you worry these kids will think less of you if you don't stand up for your mother's honor? Doesn't that bother you?"

Jermaine shook his head.

"You look worried. Are you going to cry? Surely you won't cry in front of so many kids?"

The crowd closed the circle, hungry for a fight.

My temperature rose, muscles tensed. Where were the teachers?

Bruno leaned closer and faked a punch. Jermaine flinched and covered his face. When Jermaine's hands came down, his eyes were glassy.

"Oh, oh, there's my Cry Baby. Right on cue. See, I figured maybe by this point in life I couldn't make you cry without actually hurting you. But look at that, tears from Jerk-Off!"

Jermaine swallowed hard and wiped his eyes with the sleeve of his shirt, still bent backward awkwardly over the bikes.

Rage boiled up inside me. I looked at Kevin. "Why don't you help him? Isn't he your buddy?"

"No point, bro. If I step in, I'll accomplish nothing except getting a beating. Bruno's two goons are waiting for someone to be a hero. Best if nothing happens."

I considered saying something, but Bruno was big and menacing and I was skinny and weak. Not to mention I was the new kid and pathetic at fighting. *Keep quiet and blend in.* That was always my motto. So I just I stood there, shaking, adrenaline rushing through my veins, hoping for someone to help him.

"Come on, Pansy, do something. Push me. Hit me. Anything." Bruno kept leaning his face in close to Jermaine's.

Jermaine tried to look brave, but he was trembling. I couldn't take it and stepped forward.

"Hey!" I yelled. "Jermaine is plainly scared of you. I think you've proved that to everyone here. Why not just leave him alone?"

Bruno turned and his eyes lit up to hear someone call him out. He looked at me and squinted. "Huh?"

Everyone was staring at me. "I'm just saying, clearly you're way stronger and he doesn't want to fight. Let's just say you win, okay?"

He gave me a funny look. "Are you new here? Is this a joke?"

"Yeah, I'm new. I'm just saying . . ." I limped over to the center of the crowd.

Bruno started fake laughing. "Wait. So you want to take his place. That's what you're saying? You want me to break your other leg?" he asked, referring to my limp. I'd been born with LLD, a leg-length discrepancy. My left leg was an inch shorter than my right, so it was almost impossible to walk without a limp.

I shook my head. "No, not at all. Just saying you win. Jermaine gives up. I give up. Everyone hears it, loud and clear."

Bruno eyed me. "Where you from? What's your name?"

"Does it matter?"

"It does if you don't want a fist in your mouth," he said.

Not that I cared; my history was public. "My name is Teavan and I just moved here from New York. Are we good now?"

Bruno smiled an unfriendly smile. "New York? Oh, all fancy-like, aren't ya?" He circled me. "What's your last name?"

I figured if I could get him talking I could chat my way out of this. "Laurent."

Bruno's eyes went wide, a look of surprise on his face, and he stopped pacing to stare at me.

"Laurent?"

"Yeah."

He shook his head, whistling. "Are you serious? Please tell me you're related to Hub Laurent?"

I sensed we were making progress. Maybe our families were friends.

"Yeah, that was my grandfather. We just moved into his place."

Bruno smiled. An ear-to-ear, genuine smile this time. "You have seriously just made my day. My week. My *month*."

Chapter 2

It was my turn to smile. Things were looking better. I noticed Jermaine had used the opportunity to quietly leave the scene.

"So, we're cool?" I asked.

Bruno came over, still grinning, holding his hand out like he wanted to shake mine. Only as I stretched out my hand, his other arm swung under and his fist rammed into my gut, knocking all the air from my lungs.

Bruno laughed. "I didn't say we were cool, City Boy. I said you made *my month*. You don't know how happy I am to know you live here."

Gasping for air, I doubled over, trying to catch my breath. From behind me, I heard, "Come on, Bruno, end this guy. Just do it. He needs a lesson. Hit him!"

The crowd was getting restless. Bruno Vincent and the new guy who couldn't even breathe. I held my hands up in defeat, and oxygen finally fed my hungry lungs. "I give up."

He lunged and pushed me. I stumbled but didn't fall.

"Oooohhhh," the crowd said at the same time, backing up

to make more room.

"Bruno," I coughed. "I don't want to fight, I concede defeat," I said. Why would he want to fight me because my last name was Laurent?

"Oh, you 'concede'? You think you're a smart city boy?" he asked, circling me as I just stood there. He slowly reached forward to put his palm on my chest, but I slapped it away out of instinct.

"Oooohhhh," went the crowd again.

"So you do have some feistiness, City Boy. Come on, kid, let's do this," he said. "This is something I have dreamed of."

Dreamed of? "You don't even know me."

"Oh, but I do," he said, grinning.

He slowly went to lay his hand on my chest again, but this time I gently grabbed his wrist to remove it. Except at that moment, his right palm came out of nowhere and slapped me hard on the cheek.

WHAP!

A sudden sting spread through my face. I could feel the burn and heat on my cheek as everyone stared.

"Fight, fight, fight!" the crowd chanted.

I felt like I was going to wet my pants, and my cheek stung.

How did I get myself in this position?

Life had been sweet in New York just six months earlier. Well, maybe not great, but relatively good compared to Santa Isadora.

I had a couple decent friends, and that seemed like enough. My older sister, Suzanne, didn't talk to me much, but I assumed that was normal.

My dad started to drink a little too often in the last few

years as the publishing house that had once described him as an 'up-and-coming thriller author' was no longer purchasing his books. I wasn't sure if his drinking was ruining his writing or the other way around. Either way, he didn't pay us too much attention since he was usually lost in his writing or his research.

But our once-stable world flipped upside down last November when we got word that Grandpa Hub (short for Hubert) had passed away. His lawyer in Santa Isadora, California had called and informed Dad that Grandpa died of a heart attack. He and my dad had never seemed close; something happened before my time that had put a riff between them.

The lawyer informed us Grandpa wanted his ashes dumped in the forests around his acreage, and there was to be no funeral. Made things easy for us, I guess.

Until he explained the will.

Grandpa left the house and two hundred acres to Dad, on the condition that he couldn't sell or rent it out for at least ten years. My dad cursed and shook his fist, at first thinking Grandpa had gotten in the last laugh. But later he reconsidered and wondered if it was a blessing. A blessing for his writing career, anyway; not for Suzanne and me, that was for sure.

Despite our protests and threats to live on the street, Dad sold the old apartment. The three of us were California-bound by March of the following spring.

"Relax, you guys," he had said. "Maybe I can write a couple bestsellers and get enough money to move back to New York, whether we can sell Grandpa's place or not. Look on the bright side—there's no traffic or pollution in a small town."

Yeah. Or anything else, for that matter.

It took me all of a week at my new school to find myself cornered and about to be beat up.

My normally non-existent temper flared. I felt cornered.

There was no way out.

My inner hostilities from the last six months, the forced move from New York, and the humiliation of being slapped boiled up to the surface. I charged Bruno, gritting my teeth, ready to knock him back. Hoping for him to stumble and go down.

It didn't quite work.

Instead, he expertly stepped away, grabbed my head, and threw me in the dirt. There was lots of chanting now. I felt tears welling up that needed to be held back; I couldn't let him or the other kids see.

"Is that seriously all you got?" he asked and laughed. "Tough Laurent kid from New York, and that's it? I slapped you because I was getting the feeling it might be like fighting a little girl. So far I was right."

The crowd started laughing uneasily. I was still on my hands and knees, staring at the dirt and blinking my eyes as quickly as I could to hold back the tears that were squirming to escape.

Bruno leaned over and picked something up from the ground. He examined it from the corner of his eye. "These your keys, kid?"

I looked over. My keychain must have fallen out of my pocket when he threw me.

I nodded. "Give them back."

"Make me," he said as he slid them into his pocket.

I stood.

He grinned, nodding. "Maybe you do have some honor. But this time, it's gonna hurt."

My fists rose up, ready for whatever was coming.

"Stop!" a girl yelled, stepping out from the circle with her hands out. She had long, espresso-colored hair, pushed back with a hair band, perfectly in order and silky smooth. Her eyes were round and green, and her skin was an olive tone. She was beautiful.

"Bruno, come on," she continued, looking back and forth between him and me. "Give him his keys and go home. Please. Do the right thing, you've proved your point."

Bruno rolled his eyes. "Oh, *Churchmouse*. Why you gotta stick your nose where it don't belong?"

She shook her head. "If something here doesn't belong, it's you. Are you really so insecure that you stoop to picking on people smaller than you? Or better at soccer?"

Bruno's face reddened, and he stepped toward her with his open palm lifted. "I don't normally hit girls, but you want a slap, too?"

Before she could respond, there was a flash from the crowd, and then someone darted out and pushed Bruno from behind—hard. He hadn't been expecting it, and stumbled and fell.

The crowd went wild.

I looked up but couldn't quite see who did it, just his silhouette. The sun was behind him. But I could tell that it wasn't Jermaine.

The unknown savior had a ponytail. He had freckles.

Only now I could see it wasn't a he—it was a she.

Chapter 3

Her name was Sybil; she was in my homeroom.

"Bruno, if you even *pretend* to touch Rachel I will make you regret it for the rest of your life. You made your point, you pathetic, inbred, piece of crap. Now go home!" she yelled, sweeping her arm toward the street.

Bruno stood up, making a point to dust off his hands and shirt. "Oh, oh, who do we have here? Little Orphan Annie, coming to the rescue of her cousin and the new kid?"

Her freckled face twisted at the comment and her green eyes opened even wider; I could almost see her pulse quickening. She had wild red hair that was long, tangled, and jammed in a ponytail with random strands poking out. "You want to test out what it feels like to hit a girl? Hit me then, Loser." She stepped forward with the challenge, both of her fists clenched at her sides.

The crowd whispered and shuffled around.

Bruno seemed unsure, scratching the back of his neck.

"Listen, Sybil, this doesn't concern you or her." He

gestured to Rachel.

She stepped forward again, aggressively. He stepped back. She was smaller than Bruno, but she appeared wild-eyed and formidable.

"Whatever. I'm done here. These two wimps could probably learn a lesson from you in at least standing up for themselves," he said, then looked at me. "You hear that City Boy? And Jermaine, wherever you've scurried off to? This isn't over, boys. Trust me. Annie only bought you some time."

Despite Bruno backing down, Sybil stepped forward once more. This time Bruno's back was up against the bike rack.

"You call me *Annie* one more time, just once, and I will do my best to make sure you never father any children."

"Oooohhhh," went the crowd again, hungry for excitement.

Bruno looked around, uncertain, but covered and protected himself *there*.

"You would do that, wouldn't you? Is that the best your drunk-bum-of-a-father has taught you? Fight dirty like a street rat and stick your nose where it don't belong? "

She bristled, and her green eyes went dark in anger. "I will do whatever it takes to win," she threatened. "And give him his keys back. *Now*."

Bruno shrugged and sidled his way from the bike racks, holding his hands up in mock defeat. He grabbed my keys from his pocket and threw them in the dry dirt.

"Come on guys, let's leave these losers," he said, speaking to his two buddies. The three of them walked over to a Jeep in the parking lot and jumped in. Bruno sat in the open-top passenger seat. "See you soon, Laurent." He winked at me before they squealed out of the lot.

Jermaine came through the crowd as they drove off, and everyone started talking at once. I was almost deaf and seeing stars. I felt numb.

"Or what? Hello?"

To my left, Jermaine's hand was on my shoulder, a look of concern in his eyes as he spoke. I couldn't hear him; my mind was . . . elsewhere.

"I said, are you okay or what? Hello?" Jermaine repeated.

I leaned over with my hands on my knees, trembling. I felt like I might throw up. Other kids gathered in closer and gradually I heard people talking to me.

"Nice work, buddy."

"Way to go."

"You're in trouble now."

"Bro, what was that?" the Asian boy said, whose name I remembered was Kevin. He brought his hand up for a high five that I didn't reciprocate. "Bro, that was awesome! You stood up to Bruno! I can't believe it, I assumed you must know karate or something, though it didn't look like it."

Everyone laughed.

Jermaine's face was red; he was quiet. I felt sick. This Kevin kid seemed beyond excited. The crowd was talking amongst themselves. My ears had this ring in them and I saw black spots, though he hadn't hit me that hard.

"I didn't *do* anything. I almost got my butt kicked, and couldn't even hold my ground. What are you talking about?" I asked, finally addressing Kevin.

"Teavan . . . my man! But you did? There are, like, sixty kids here, some as big as him. And you were the only one man enough to stand up. And I can freely admit, I wasn't. Kudos to you. That was freakin' awesome," he said. "I mean, you didn't really do much, but at least you sorta held your ground. Usually, guys have a black eye and bleeding nose when they tangle with Bruno."

I shook my head. Had he witnessed what just happened? It was an embarrassment.

Looking past Jermaine, I tried to find the girl—Sybil—who saved me, but my heart skipped a beat when I noticed Rachel walking over. She smiled at me, Jermaine, and Kevin.

For a moment I almost forgot about Bruno.

"Are you guys okay?" she asked. "He's such a jerk."

"Umm, yeah, I'm okay," I answered, trying to smile.

Jermaine nodded. "Thanks to you and your cousin."

"Cousin?" I asked.

"Sybil," Jermaine answered. "The girl with the red hair, she's Rachel's cousin."

The two girls couldn't be more different. Rachel was stunning: dressed neatly, with her hair pulled back and every strand in place. Sybil, on the other hand, was the exact opposite. Her clothing was sloppy and uncoordinated at best, like she didn't care. I'd seen her every day for a week, and she never smiled. She seemed more like my sister, Suzanne, with an ever-present scowl.

"That guy is a real dolt. I think it was nice you tried to help out Jermaine," Rachel said, looking at me. "Don't judge the Iz by people like Bruno. Mostly everyone is really nice."

I heard the word *dolt*, and then the word *tried*. In her mind, I'd attempted, which means I didn't succeed.

"Well, your cousin was the real hero. I think she saved both our butts," I answered.

Rachel carefully reached up and pulled a leaf from my hair. "Lucky for you, Bruno had enough class to walk away," she added. "Anyway, I think that was very brave of you to stand up for someone you don't know, especially being the new guy. I wish more people would do that. Maybe Bruno would get the message." She smiled, running her hands through her hair.

Sybil came over and tapped Rachel's shoulder. "Let's go."

"Hey . . . Sybil? Thanks. That was super nice of you," I blubbered awkwardly.

"Yeah, thanks," added Jermaine.

She looked at us both with a cold stare. Not that friendly given the circumstances.

"Bruno is a total loser. He needs someone to call him out," she barked. She looked at me. "You almost did, but failed. And you, Jermaine, come on. What was that?"

We both looked down and kicked the dirt, embarrassed.

Rachel interrupted. "Sybil, Bruno is a bully, plain and simple. He lives to fight and embarrass people smaller than him. How can two nice guys stand up to that?"

Sybil gave Rachel a dirty look. "What's that supposed to mean? I'm not nice?" I had the feeling that wasn't what Rachel meant. "Whatever, let's go." She turned around and started walking away.

"Sorry guys . . . I hope you're okay. I gotta go," Rachel said as she ran after Sybil.

Kevin whistled quietly. "Wow, now, that was weird."

Jermaine agreed. "No kidding. An exciting first week here for you," he said, looking at me. "Now, Sybil may have saved your butt, but you saved mine," he held out my keys to me.

"Thanks," I said, taking them.

"Can I bike you home?"

"Sure," I answered, feeling a bit relieved at not having to cycle home alone. Bruno's comment of *See you soon* echoed in my ears.

Chapter 4

Jermaine seemed like a solid guy. As we biked to my place, he gave me the goods on Santa Isadora, or *the Iz* as the locals called it.

"So, what's the deal with you and Bruno?" I asked.

He shook his head. "Who knows with that guy. He's always had it out for me. We've been soccer rivals forever. And for a long time I ran circles around him, and he really hated it. His dad is uber-competitive and would always curse Bruno when I took the ball away or out-dribbled him. Maybe I pushed things too far, though I don't anymore. He's too crazy now. And tough. And he holds a grudge."

"No kidding," I said. "Do we have a school soccer team?"

"Yeah, we're decent. Kevin plays, too. You wanna join?"

I shook my head, and held out my leg. "No, thanks."

"Can I ask you something?" he asked, hesitantly.

"Sure."

"What's wrong with your leg?"

"Oh," I said, looking all serious. "I got stabbed by a gang member back in New York, right in the thigh."

"Dude! Are you serious?"

Doing my best to hold a straight face, I nodded, but then burst out laughing.

"What?" he asked.

"Nah, I'm just kidding. My legs—one is shorter than the other, ever since I was little. Just kinda grew weird. Makes it a bit hard to walk."

Jermaine shook his head and laughed. "Well, you never know. Could have been true; I don't know much about New York other than from movies."

At that moment, an animal jumped on the road up ahead. It was running toward us, down low along the gravel country road as we approached my driveway.

Jermaine yelped and spun his bike around with a look of pure terror. "Run!"

I calmly dismounted.

"Teavan, come on!" he yelled.

Smiling, I turned and knelt down, ready to be attacked by the oncoming four-legged beast.

Jermaine squinted and then returned the grin as Honey, my golden retriever, came bounding up and jumped on me, licking and wagging her tail.

"Jermaine, meet Honey. Honey, this is Jermaine," I said as he came over and knelt down to let her sniff him, then rubbed her back.

"She's beautiful," he said.

"Are you afraid of dogs?" I asked, surprised by his initial reaction.

He nodded. "No. I love dogs. I just saw something big on four legs running toward us, and my eyes aren't so good. I thought it was a wolf or a coyote."

"A wolf?" I asked. "Is it common for wolves to attack people on a Friday afternoon?"

"No, no. I've never even seen one," he said, as I let a nervous breath out. "Just that, you know, things happen is all."

"Happen?"

"Like country stuff, I guess. Wolves howling, coyotes chirping at night. Every once in a while a cow gets found slaughtered, or someone goes missing. Can be dangerous at night out there." He shrugged, kicking a stone into the ditch.

Wolves killing cows? I thought life in a small town would be dull, but at least safer than New York.

"Are you just messing with me now? Getting me back for the leg joke?" I asked.

He shook his head. "I wish. I don't even think it's normal, at least not in most towns anyway. We got family down outside of Santa Barbara, and they don't have any worries about wolves. I wouldn't let your dog roam around outside at night, either. She's a big dog, but no match for a wolf or a pack of coyotes."

The thought of coyotes attacking Honey sent an icy shiver down my spine. I had assumed she could always roam freely. Wasn't that the point of having two hundred acres?

"And here I thought Bruno and his thugs were going to be my biggest problem," I joked.

"Yeah, that's not good, either. That dude is unbalanced and getting worse since his brother died. Best to stay out of his way, and off his radar."

Too late, I thought. "He had a brother that died?"

Jermaine pursed his lips and nodded. "Yeah, about a year

ago. Was a couple years older. Just disappeared one night."

"He ran away?"

"Nah, I don't think so. Their family seemed pretty close. I mean, he was kind of a dick, but still. I think something got him, though most people said he ran away."

"Ugh, that sucks. No wonder Bruno is such a jerk. I'd be kinda messed up, too," I said, wondering how I'd cope if Suzanne just up and disappeared one night. We had our differences, but . . .

"Can I ask you another question? What kind of name is *Teavan?*" he asked.

"Oh," I chuckled. "My actual name is Steven. When I was born, my sister wasn't quite two-years-old and could not pronounce the letter 'S', so she always called me Teavan. I guess it just kinda stuck."

We had been walking our bikes and now approached the end of my grandpa's long driveway. Well, our driveway now, I guess.

"Do you want to come inside? Have a snack?" I asked.

"Nah, I gotta go. But thanks again for earlier. You have any plans tomorrow? Wanna hit a movie or bike the quarry in the afternoon?" he asked.

"The quarry?"

"Yeah, it's an abandoned granite quarry, a mile out of town. There are some decent jumps and drops there."

Trick biking wasn't really my thing. "How about the movie?"

He nodded and we exchanged numbers for texting.

The day had some serious ups and downs. New friend. New enemy.

It was an interesting end to the first week.

Dinner was better than usual that night—relatively. My dad seemed to make an effort and bought steaks for the three of us to celebrate our first week of school. Suzanne was still being hard on him about the move from New York and she didn't speak much.

"How was your first week, Suzanne? Do you like your school?" he asked as he set the slightly overcooked steaks on the table. Suzanne went to the other high school in town—Baker—because they had a *Design & Textiles* department that Redwood didn't. It was smaller and more trade-oriented. She had plans to become a fashion designer back in New York one day. However, I wasn't sure how good the classes could be here and just assumed she didn't want to go to the same school as me.

"*How was it?* How do you think?" she sneered. "It sucked, Dad, just like this town sucks. My high school is a joke."

My dad was trying to chew a piece of steak, unable to respond as he attempted to wash it down with red wine. Finally he said, "Oh, come on, it can't be that bad. Give it a chance. I'll bet there are some handsome young men on the football team that will catch your interest."

She rolled her eyes. "As if! I have, and will always have, zero interest in farm boys."

My dad winked. "We'll see about that when these *farm boys* come calling. You might like them; they might have actual manners and wear a belt in a small town."

I had no doubt the farm boys would come sniffing around.

Suzanne always seemed to have guys hanging off her, though luckily she wasn't boy crazy at all. Her wavy dark hair and apparently good looks always seemed to get glances she was unaware of. *Gross.* I was told we looked similar, though I was skinny, and the dark and curly mop of hair on my head never seemed to attract any of the girls' attention. Maybe a nice California suntan would help.

"Dad, there's, like, only thirty people in the junior class. Everyone is staring at me like I'm the new freak."

"Maybe it's 'cause you are," I mumbled, unable to resist.

She shot visual daggers at me. "Shut it, moron. We both know you *are* a freak. Did you find time between having zero friends and no life to join the programming club? Or just the loser's league at your school?"

I shrugged and gave an apologetic smile, not in the mood to start something.

"Suzanne, be respectful," Dad said.

She shook her head and her eyes narrowed. "He *disrespected* me first."

"We need to watch out for Honey," I volunteered, changing the subject. "A guy I met at school said they have wolf and coyote issues here."

My dad gulped more wine to wash down his steak, probably happy for the excuse to drink more. "Wolves? No, not in California. Maybe coyotes, but they won't bother Honey; she's too big."

At the mention of her name, Honey perked up, hoping for some morsels from the table. I snuck her a piece of steak.

"Well, that's what Jermaine said, and he's grown up here."

"Well, *Jermaine* probably has an overactive imagination and might not know the difference between a fox, wolf, or coyote."

"Dad, how would you even know? You never lived in California. Grandpa came west after you moved out. What makes you the expert on wildlife over someone that lives here?" I asked, suddenly mad that he always thought he was the authority on everything.

He smiled. "Okay, settle down. I'm just saying, from what I know, there haven't been wolves in California for a long time. But, *yes*, I could be mistaken."

"Could a fox kill a cow? What about a coyote?" I asked.

He thought about it. "Doubtful. Is that what he said?"

I nodded. "Yep. And people."

"*People?* Wolves have attacked the locals?"

"Well, no, but, he said some have gone missing over the years."

"Well, people go missing from every city in the country, that's not abnormal. That's just life," he said. "You have any idea how many people *per day* go missing from New York?"

I shook my head. "I have no idea."

"Well, neither do I, but it's a lot. I'll bet at least ten people a day go missing, so a couple people over a few years doesn't constitute a problem. I would even argue that is a positive statistic."

"Yeah, Dad, I know, I'm not stupid. I'm just saying . . . be careful."

"Well, maybe we should keep her inside at night until we are more familiar with things around here," he said, then looked at Suzanne. "Any thoughts?"

"Fine by me," she said. "Just another reason this place sucks. I think I'd rather deal with random muggers than whatever is out there." She motioned with her fork to the dark sky outside the kitchen window.

As if on cue, Honey whined softly under the table.

Chapter 5

The days in Santa Isadora were warm but dry, unlike the humid East Coast. It was refreshing to open the window at night and not rely on air conditioning to sleep. I wasn't quite used to the night sounds of crickets and owls yet; still oddly missing the honking of the insane cab drivers and sirens back home.

However, the nature sounds were much better background noise for reading, and I was a voracious reader. In that way I was kinda like my dad. We both loved books and got lost in the good ones.

After I checked some online threads, chat rooms, and crypto prices, I got ready for bed as I mentally calculated how much my small investment had changed. Who needed savings accounts when you understood digital scarcity?

On one of her rare good days, Suzanne had lent me her Hunger Games trilogy, and I was midway through the first one. The eerie night sounds of the Iz added to the atmosphere better than honking traffic as Katniss battled her way through the jungle.

I was lost in the story until I noticed Honey's head perk up, her ears swiveling around to catch whatever it was she heard. As usual, she was lying on my bed near my feet.

I listened.

It was quiet. Just the crickets and other night sounds I didn't recognize but which seemed normal.

Honey stood and jumped off the bed, walking over to the open window. She propped her paws up on the window sill to get a better look outside.

"What is it, girl?" I asked.

She looked back and tilted her head, whining softly.

I walked over and looked out, but could only see the reflection of the bedroom in the glass because of the bedside lamp. Honey was interested in something outside, probably a rabbit. She had taken to chasing rabbits since we arrived; I only hoped she never caught one.

I flicked the light off to get a better look. The yard was much easier to see now that the bedroom was dark, but I could see nothing unusual.

Except my bike.

I'd left it behind my dad's car. Doubtful he'd be leaving the house before me tomorrow morning . . . except it was Saturday. So he might.

Damn.

With my luck, he'd back right over it, and I'd be walking the two miles to school for the foreseeable future.

"Come on, girl." I nudged Honey off the window frame. "Wanna go for a quick walk?"

She bounced to my bedroom door at the mention of the

word *walk*.

As I slipped my bare feet into my dad's shoes, I opened the front door and Honey bounded outside. The air was so crisp and clean, and the insect sounds so loud. It wasn't something I'd gotten used to yet—it felt like I was camping. The stars here were infinitely brighter than the almost non-existent stars in New York. In the warmth of summer I meant to lie down here one night just to stargaze.

Despite its almost painting-like perfectness, it was a little bit creepy, too. Honey stood expectantly at the bottom of the porch steps, waiting for me. I considered going back inside to turn the porch light on but instead decided to quickly get the bike into the detached garage and be done.

The footfalls in the gravel from my shoes were loud in the silence. It would be difficult to sneak up on anyone here, which was probably a good thing. I glanced back toward the house as I leaned down to pick up my bike. I had a prickly sense someone was watching me from the dark.

"Hello?" I said.

Nothing.

I pushed the bike over to the open door of the garage and went inside, leaning it up against the workbench.

A faint noise outside the garage jolted me even more alert now, and Honey's stance went rigid after she ran back to the open door.

"What do you see, Honey?"

She looked at me, but then returned her gaze back outside. Her ears flattened to her head and she growled.

I put my hands on the workbench and felt around in the dark. I needed a stick or a weapon. Someone was out there, and Honey wouldn't growl if it was family.

My fingers instinctively curled around the handle of an old hammer. *Good enough.* Honey's tail was down and she was just standing there, but I couldn't see what she was looking at as I cautiously made my way over to the big door. From the faded light of the stars, I could make out the car and the house, and that was about it.

"What is it?" I asked, my heart pounding now, and wondering how the country could be scarier than a dark alley in New York.

Honey bared her teeth and barked aggressively. Something I'd never seen her do.

I leaned over to grab her collar, almost more afraid for her safety than mine. "Stay," I said, grasping her just in time as she was about to bolt.

"What's there?" I asked again, struggling to squint at the dark tree line behind the house.

Then I saw what she was fixated on.

Something sizeable was running near the trees, fast; something not human. There was an odd gait to its movement, almost like a bear, but it was too far away and too dark to make it out.

My lower lip was quivering as I struggled with the decision to either sprint to the house or stay put in the garage.

I didn't want to get cornered.

"Honey, run!"

Chapter 6

Holding her collar as best I could, I ran awkwardly back to the house. Honey kept trying to pull away to investigate whatever was lurking near the tree line, but I refused to let go.

I locked the door inside and finally released her. She was jumping around, still trying to look outside, and barking a little as I ushered her quickly back to my room, not wanting to wake anyone.

She immediately ran to my window and put her paws up to look in the yard. Her ears flattened again and a growl rumbled from deep inside.

I cupped my eyes with my hands and leaned against the glass of the upper pane for a better view.

My heart skipped a beat and I saw it.

A big dog sat on the edge of the gravel driveway near the trees, staring at the house. It was far enough away that I couldn't quite make it out. Maybe a husky? A German shepherd?

A wolf?

After unplugging my phone, I turned the flash off the

camera, held it up to the window, and took a few pictures. It was useless; it was too dark.

The dog or wolf started trotting off, and Honey jumped and let out a startling bark that scared the crap out of me.

"Shhhh!!"

But she kept barking, trying to jump through the window screen to get outside. The other dog loped lazily away without any apparent fear of my retriever.

My bedroom door burst open. "Would you shut her up??" Suzanne snapped, silhouetted by the light in the hallway.

"Suze! There's a dog or a wolf in our yard!" I said.

She walked over and looked outside. "Where?"

Cupping my hands against the window, I looked out, but it was gone. "Well, it *was* there, I swear. That's why she's losing her mind," I said, leaning down to comfort Honey as her barking finally stopped.

"Well, maybe don't let her out tonight."

"Too late, we just went out to put my bike away; that's when she saw it."

"Did it chase you?"

"No . . . but still. It was a little eerie."

Suzanne seemed unconcerned and turned on my bedside lamp, noting the book on the table. "How's the book?"

"Good, so far," I said. "You okay?"

She shrugged. "Meh. School sucks. This town sucks. And Dad thinks we should be excited about saving fifty cents on apples at the farmer's market. I can tell you this: I'm outta here after graduation next year."

Ugh. I hadn't even thought of her moving out. Difficult as she was, having her here was better than being alone. "Suze, you can't leave me here. That's only like a year away."

"I am *not* staying here. Hopefully, by then, Dad will change his mind, too. If not, I'm heading back to New York."

Living alone with Dad and his weirdness in the middle of nowhere seemed like about the worst thing that could happen—especially knowing Suzanne was back in New York. At least with her here we were both in the same boat and had a better chance of convincing him to move.

She walked over to the bedroom door. "Well, I'm off to bed."

"You think Mom will ever come back? Maybe she could save us from this place."

Suzanne's eyebrows furrowed. "Don't count on it. I gave up on her; it's been ten years. I'm still pissed at Dad for whatever he did to make her leave, but her abandoning us is unforgivable. I'd almost like her to show up and try to reconcile just so I could have the satisfaction of slamming the door on her face."

And with that, she closed my door, ending the discussion. She always got heated when I brought up our mom. She left Dad when I was around five, and we never heard from her again. She was mostly just a memory for me, but Suzanne had been eight and her memories were stronger.

Honey jumped back on the bed and walked in circles until she finally found the perfect place to curl up.

Lying back down, I picked up the book and tried to find the spot where I'd been interrupted.

Outside, something howled in the distance.

Chapter 7

On Saturday afternoon, Jermaine met me and I followed him to the Plaza Movie Theatre. It was the town's only cinema and looked like it needed some work. It wasn't quite like some of the high-tech theaters back home, but reminded me of the old ones that showed independent movies.

Jermaine and I decided to watch the latest *Star Wars* movie, though I'd already seen it. We grabbed drinks and some popcorn and sat down, mid-theater center. The seats were squeaky and well worn, with no built-in drink holders.

"You meet Mrs. Leclair yet?" he asked, popcorn in hand as we waited for the movie to start.

I shook my head. "No. Who's that?"

"Your neighbor in the big white house down the road. She's old; her husband died, but I don't think she has any kids. At least not here. She and her husband moved here years ago from, like, Transylvania or something. She's creepy; has an accent like Dracula."

I laughed. "Transylvania? That's not even a real place." Was it?

"It isn't?" he asked. "Well, I don't know, someplace in Europe. I heard that a lot of the weird things started happening when they moved to the Iz. The kids joke that she's a vampire."

"Are you serious? You don't actually believe that," I said with a laugh, wondering if any people in this out-of-the-way town had accents. In New York, it seemed like every other person was from somewhere else.

Jermaine shook his head. "Well, yes and no. I mean—I get it. It sounds stupid. But living here, weird things happen, and it just seems normal after a while. You'll see. Kids used to tease Old Man Leclair behind his back that he was a vampire and the cause of the dead livestock. Except he died a few years ago and nothing much changed, so maybe not. Maybe it's been her all along. And you live beside her!" he grinned.

As I was about to tell him about the dog in my yard the night before, something landed in my hair. Then something else. *Popcorn.*

Shoot. A drop of sweat formed on my forehead immediately.

"Don't look, but I think Bruno might be behind us," I whispered.

The color drained from Jermaine's face. "For real?"

Fishing a piece of popcorn from my hair, I showed it to him. With zero tact, Jermaine spun around to look, and then smiled. "Close, Teavan, close."

My anxiety lifted when I turned and spotted Rachel a few rows back with a big grin and popcorn in hand. She waved.

My fuzzy warmth drained when I saw Sybil next to her,

rolling her eyes and shaking her head just as the lights went out.

It was Jermaine who suggested they join us after the movie to get some ice cream. The Creamy was a block away and seemed like the local hangout, since there were no malls in town. The four of us got cones and sat down at one of the many picnic tables surrounding the old ice cream parlor.

"So, why did you move here?" Rachel asked, licking the ice cream from the side of her cone.

I explained the story of my grandfather, the house, and my dad.

"I remember seeing your grandpa at our church. He wasn't there every week, but attended pretty regularly. Will you guys be going?" she asked.

I shook my head. "Nope, I don't think so. We don't really do the church thing."

She smiled. "I see. Well, maybe you'd like if you tried. We can always use new people and volunteers. I'd be happy to take you."

Sybil broke in. "Rachel, don't be trying to recruit everyone into your church; not everyone is interested in being 'saved'. Just leave 'em be, not that I care either way."

"It's not *my* church; it's just church. And I was only letting him know he has options. Jermaine's mom goes, it's not weird."

The thought of going to church was not something I ever considered, beyond the occasional Christmas or Easter service. But going along with Rachel could be a good excuse to hang out.

A hand grabbed my shoulder from behind and I froze.

"You Hub's boy?" a gruff voice asked from behind. I turned to see a tanned, weathered man wearing dirty overalls and a yellow-and-green John Deere cap.

"Yes sir. Well, his grandson."

"I thought so."

He was quiet as we continued licking our cones, not quite sure what to say to him as he took his cap off and put it on the table, revealing a head of short, white hair.

"I counted your grandfather among my friends, though we didn't always see eye to eye. But he was a good man," he said, glancing at the others at the table.

I nodded, uncertain.

He stared across the road, squinting but looking at nothing in particular.

"This town is unique, and it has its secrets. Some of them are better left untold, or undiscovered. That is where we didn't always agree, Hub and me. You keep that in mind as you settle in," he said, putting his hat back on.

He leaned over and put his hands on the picnic table, looking back and forth among the four us. "Sometimes you need to ask yourself; just because I can, does it mean I should? Keep that in mind, will ya? Some things are better left alone."

And with that he tipped his hat and made his way down the road, not looking back.

As he widened the distance between us, Jermaine looked at me and smiled, vanilla ice cream around his dark lips. He broke into a laugh.

"And that, my new friend, is just another reason this town is weird," he said, finishing his cone.

"What was all that about?" I asked.

"Who knows? I don't know who he is, another old crackpot who's probably got an end-of-world bunker out of town. I've seen him around here and there, always reading the paper or something, watching people from under his hat. Probably gossiping with the old men playing shuffleboard in the afternoons."

Rachel leaned in and changed the subject. "Where's Kevin?"

Jermaine shrugged, then smiled. "Supposedly on a date."

"With who?"

He arched his eyebrow, then shook his head. "I dunno, some girl from Baker. I think he's actually just home helping his dad in the yard, you know how he is."

Rachel smiled. "Oh, Kevin, him and his ladies. How about you? Whatever happened between you and Alyssa?"

He shrugged, looking away. "I don't know. Things seemed to be going alright, then she just kinda lost interest, stopped texting. It got all weird."

"Did you have an argument or something?" Rachel asked.

Jermaine shook his head. "Not that I know of; it was like a light flipped, and she lost interest one day. It's not like we were serious or anything, but I thought things were good."

From the silence, Sybil actually spoke up. "It's because of her dad; he's a racist jerk."

"Huh?" Jermaine asked.

"Well, her dad and my dad are friends from work, and I get the feeling he's not fond of his daughter . . . you know," Sybil answered, looking sheepish for once.

Rachel's phone beeped and she checked it. "Shoot, I gotta

go, sorry guys. My mom has supper almost ready. You're welcome to join us," she said, looking at Sybil.

The girls got up to leave. "Enjoy your weekend, boys. And if either of you wants to join me tomorrow, the service is at eleven. Jermaine has my number." Rachel said with a smile.

Sybil nodded her goodbye as they left.

Jermaine looked lost in thought, staring off at the road.

"That's too bad," I said.

"About what?"

"That girl—Alyssa. If what Sybil said it is true. Stupid reason to not date someone."

He shrugged. "For such a so-called progressive state, sometimes it makes me wonder," he said almost to himself as he stood up. I got the feeling he didn't want to discuss it any further.

"You want her number?" Jermaine asked.

I played dumb. "Whose number?"

He rolled his eyes. "Yeah, I wonder who. I can see how you look at her. She's beautiful. I get it."

Was it that obvious?

"Well, I've been meaning to get some religion into my life," I joked. "Maybe I should get her number, just in case."

Jermaine texted me her contact info. "I wouldn't waste too much time on her; anything beyond friendship, anyway. She's, like, super involved in the church and all that. She doesn't date, and definitely nothing much before marriage, if you know what I mean," he said, winking.

I could feel my face turning red. "It's not like that at all."

He smiled. "Sure, sure. Call me tomorrow if you want to hang," he said, jumping on his bike. "I have a soccer game at two if you want to watch, or even join the team. We're always short players."

"Maybe. To watch, that is." I shook my leg to remind him. "I suck at sports, but I might watch." The truth was that I probably could play, but I was insanely uncoordinated—limp or not. It was always an easy excuse when I needed it.

The sky was filled with a bright red-and-orange glow as the sun dipped toward the western horizon on my ride home. Our place was about a quarter mile from the outskirts of town on a dirt road, and I found myself thinking back to the movie and ice cream. More specifically, to Rachel, I guess.

There was just something about her, this weird positive energy or aura around her. She was always smiling, and her eyes looked right *into* you when she spoke. Not just at you, like she was waiting for her turn to talk. She seemed to truly listen.

The girls back home never seemed to care about anything besides selfies and their looks. They'd smile and laugh together, but as soon as their best friend left the gathering they'd pounce on her behind her back, making fun of her clothing or something.

I didn't get the feeling that Rachel was like that.

Up ahead, at the end of our driveway, I could see the shape of Honey sitting there, waiting for me again.

Only as I got closer, I realized it wasn't her.

It was the dog—or wolf—from the night before. It had gray and white fur.

Where was Honey?

I stopped my bike, unsure of what to do, with about two hundred feet between us. My stomach felt queasy. Honey should be out here barking.

The animal bared its teeth and snarled, sending a shiver up my spine.

I couldn't get home; it stood between me and the house.

The wolf stood up, growling, and started loping toward me.

Chapter 8

Instinct kicked in.

I turned and biked left, toward the long and winding drive of our neighbor's house—the Leclair house. If Jermaine was right and the wolf was Mrs. Leclair somehow, then I was done for. She was herding me off the main road to the private confines of her heavily-treed acreage, to feast on me as she pleased.

Which of course was nonsense. But the imagination has a way of getting the best of you when your life is at stake.

I had nothing to lose, and broke into my fastest ride down her winding driveway. An old, white and weathered farmhouse came into view. It had a wrap-around porch on the front three sides, and a truck parked nearby. Behind me, the beast was easily gaining; I could hear heavy breathing as it ran, having already rounded the turn from the main road onto the drive. It wasn't sprinting, however. At least not nearly as fast as Honey could run, and she was almost eight.

My lungs weren't used to riding so fast, and they burned

with each breath. As I rounded the last bend, I could see someone on the front porch in a rocking chair with a book.

A slim woman with short brown hair.

"Help!" I screamed, coughing and pedaling as fast as I could.

She stood up calmly, with her eyes on me. She reached for something that looked like a broom.

I got closer to the front steps of the porch, another twenty feet to go, but I could hear the loping wolf not far behind.

The woman turned the object up, pointing it at me. It was a rifle.

It was weird. In those few seconds, so many thoughts crossed my mind, but the biggest was: *they won.*

They'd successfully herded me off the road and into their yard. I was caught between a gun-toting vampire and a blood-thirsty wolf.

My legs started to give out as I leapt off the bike. I wasn't going to make the porch. My weaker left foot caught a rock, and I was tumbling through the dirt faster than I could blink.

BANG!

The rifle's shot rang out as I covered my face, prepared for the animal's attack as well as her next bullet. As I curled up in defense, I thought for once my weak leg had saved me. Bought me about an extra second of time since I stumbled and she missed me.

The animal snarled and pawed at the dirt—maybe ten feet away. I peaked up through my arms; its teeth were bared with saliva dripping out. There was a look of hunger in its eyes as they bored into mine.

"You get!" the lady hollered. She was coming down the

wooden stairs of the porch. The animal shifted its gaze to her and started to back up, growling at her now.

She reloaded and cocked the rifle.

"Go!" she hollered again. "Or you get the next one between your beady little eyes!"

The animal turned and sauntered off, looking back occasionally. Still cowering in a defensive position, I looked around to the old woman. Her eyes and gun were trained on the animal—not on me. I exhaled with relief. The wolf's bushy tail disappeared into the trees at the far end of the lane.

"Are you okay, young man?" she asked with an accent.

My trembling nod turned into a shake. "I don't know . . . I think so."

I fought them as best I could, but tears welled up as my body relaxed from the complete and utter adrenaline rush. I felt like I'd been just inches from being mauled. Never in my life had anything so emotionally and physically intense happened.

"We'd better get you inside," she said, bending down with her hand on my back.

I didn't want her to see my tears—signs of weakness in a fifteen-year-old boy. With my head still down, I rubbed my eyes on my arm as best I could while standing up.

The woman held the gun in one arm, aimed toward the ground but still in the direction the animal had disappeared.

She wasn't that old, with short brown hair, and she appeared very sweet. Though she'd loaded the gun and attacked without hesitation when the wolf and I had come around the bend. She looked to be in her early fifties? Maybe she was Mrs. Leclair's daughter.

"Come in; let me get you something to drink. That wolf might be back, especially if he realizes this .22 is only good for shooting gophers." She grinned with a smile that reached up to her eyes.

The inside of her house was clean and tidy, with expensive-looking old furniture made with red velvets and ornate wooden legs. Around the windows were heavy burgundy drapes.

Very old lady-ish.

Despite her friendliness, I felt a little nervous as she closed the door and turned on a light. "Goodness, excuse the darkness in here," she said as she walked to the front windows and pulled the drapes open, letting the setting sunlight in.

Wallpaper covered the room. There were massive paintings bordered by heavy curled gold frames. *Definitely foreign*, I thought.

"I'm Geneviève," she said as she returned to the front entrance, holding out her hand. "Geneviève Leclair. Are you from next door?"

I nodded quickly and shook her hand, enjoying the almost melodic accent she had and her perfume.

"Hubert's grandson?"

I nodded again, surprised. She pronounced his name correctly, or at least how it was supposed to be said. Everyone just called him Hub, but Grandpa's name was French, pronounced 'Hue-bear'.

"And your name is . . . ?" she asked.

"Teavan," I blurted out, louder than I intended. "Do you live here?"

"Of course. Why do you ask?"

"Oh, no reason. My buddy said you were old, that's all."

Her face changed into a friendly pout. "Old? I'm afraid he was right."

I shook my head, not meaning it like that. "No, sorry. I meant like really old, more like a grandma. You don't look that old, more like my dad. My friend said you guys were old is all, so I was expecting different."

Geneviève smiled. "Ah, I see. Well, I'm not entirely sure how to take that. My late husband Luc was a little older than me, and your friend may have assumed we were the same age. Too much sun I guess! Why don't you sit down and I'll fix you a snack?"

Geneviève Leclair left the front room and disappeared into the next one. I did my best to brush off my jeans and sat on the floor against a chair, nervously surveying the room as I did. I didn't want to dirty her expensive-looking chair with my dusty clothes.

She came back in with two glasses of water and a tin of weird-looking store-bought cookies.

They tasted better than they looked. Not like traditional cookies, but they were good. Two small vanilla wafers with a layer of icing between them.

"Luc and I were very fond of Hubert," she said with a warm smile. "It was nice to move to such a remote town in America and have a bit of France next door."

I nodded, mowing down my third cookie. My French background was something my father never really celebrated or pushed on us. "Where are you from?"

"France as well, but a different region."

"Wow, what a coincidence."

She shook her head. "Well, no, not really. Luc and Hubert

49

knew each other many years ago, before we were married. They kept in touch over the years, since they had many similar interests. When Luc and I decided to move to America, Hubert suggested we come here.

"I must apologize to you and your family that I have not been by to greet you sooner. I heard you were in and welcomed the renewed activity next door. I've become a bit of a recluse," she said, smiling more to herself than me. "My Luc died, and then of course Hubert last fall. I haven't many other friends here, I'm afraid. Never really needed any."

I shrugged, not sure what to say. Maybe she had a pack of wolf friends somewhere. "That's okay. My dad isn't really that social, either. He's writing a book. Pretty much always either writing, reading, or researching. He probably hasn't even noticed, to be honest, Mrs. Leclair."

"Please," she interrupted. "Call me Geneviève. Otherwise it makes me feel old, and I hate formalities. Well, in any event, it is poor manners on my part. Though truth be told, I was surprised to see your family moving in instead of a For Sale sign going up. I thought that had always been Hubert's intention."

I shrugged again. "I don't know; we found out Grandpa died from a lawyer. He said the will wouldn't let us sell or something. Trust me, my sister and I fought Dad a lot over this move."

She raised an eyebrow, sipping her water. "That's odd."

"Odd? Well, I mean this town is nice and all, but we moved from New York. We grew up there and loved it. Neither of us wanted to leave. Not that this town is terrible or anything."

She smiled. "No, I understand that. I mean it's odd about his requirements in the will."

"Oh," I said, understanding. "Yeah, my dad wasn't happy. So, can I ask you something?"

She nodded.

"Please tell me that was a dog."

She shook her head. "I'm afraid not."

I knew my dad was wrong.

"Honestly, we don't get them very often; they're not generally a problem to humans. But . . . "

Leaning in, I waited. "But what?"

"Tell me, how old is your sister now? Suzanne, was it?" she asked.

"Yep. She's seventeen."

Geneviève leaned back on her red velvet sofa with sudden tiredness in her eyes. She took off her glasses and rubbed her face with both hands.

"Teavan, I'm feeling exhausted, and I need to do some thinking. It is important that I speak to you—both of you, tomorrow. There are things we should discuss."

She put her glasses back on, and she was looking me directly in the eye with an air of urgency.

"I'll drive you home, just to be safe. And I urge you to stay indoors tonight, and keep your dog inside too."

Honey!

I'd completely forgotten about her in the chaos of everything. A sudden dread crept up my back as I stood. "Sure, Mrs. Leclair . . . Geneviève. I forgot about my dog Honey— she's usually outside when I get home. We need to go; she could be hurt. Or worse."

I didn't want to think about the *or worse* as we stepped outside toward her pickup truck.

Scanning my driveway as we turned in, I expected to see Honey lying in a pool of blood, not moving. Anxious and frightened, I looked in every direction, calling her name out the window.

Nothing.

Mrs. Leclair stopped close to the house, and I ran out and bounded up the front steps and opened the door.

Honey was waiting and ran out, barking excitedly. For the second time that day, a wave of emotion rolled through me causing tears to well up. She licked me as I knelt and hugged her on the front step. Sometimes you don't realize how much you love something until the thought of losing it suddenly becomes all too real.

Mrs. Leclair was standing at the base of the steps. "Everything okay?"

"Yes. She was inside, I guess," I answered with a relieved sigh.

"Would you come by tomorrow? And bring your sister along?"

I nodded. "I'll see what I can do; she can be difficult."

"Let her know it is of the utmost importance," she said, heading back to the truck that was still running.

"Umm, Geneviève? Thanks again. For your help."

She cocked her head and smirked. "Any time, dear. That's what good neighbors are for. *N'est pas?*"

Chapter 9

Of course, over dinner that night my dad thought I was blowing the story out of proportion. That my life had not been in any real danger. But he did at least listen to me and took it somewhat seriously.

Suzanne just used it as an excuse for us to move away.

Jermaine texted me back that he was glad he didn't live so far from town and that I was screwed.

"Suze, I need you to come with me to the neighbor's tomorrow."

"Excuse me?" Suzanne responded as she and I cleaned the dishes; though mostly she was on her phone texting her old New York friends.

"Mrs. Leclair, the neighbor. She wants you and me to come by tomorrow. She has something important to say. She was friends with Grandpa and said she needed to talk to you, too."

"Why can't she just come here?"

I wasn't sure, but after what happened I wanted to give her the benefit of the doubt. Plus, I'd left my bike there. "Please, Suze? I don't want to go alone."

Frustrated, she shook her head. "Fine. There's nothing else to do."

Clouds rolled in that night: the moisture of rain in the air, the buzz of an electrical storm brewing as the winds picked up.

Honey never did like thunderstorms, but I did.

The smell and that blanket of humidity in the warm air brought me back home. It wasn't something I could put a finger on until I stood on the porch, watching the approaching lightning in the distance. It brought a distinct freshness to the night. A good soaking around these dry parts was something we needed.

Leaving the window open in my room was a tough choice; enjoy the sounds and smells of a storm, or risk the wolf coming back and freaking Honey out?

I hoped wolves hated storms and that it stayed in its den, so I left the window open to enjoy while I read. Sleep overtook me sooner than expected with the day's events taking their physical toll.

A sharp crack of thunder woke me hours later. The red glow of the clock on the nightstand blinked 12:00 over and over. The rain was coming down in waves, soaking the sill and floor through the open window. The soles of my feet got wet when I got up to close it.

The room felt crisp and refreshing as I crawled back into the cozy warmth of my covers. The comforting presence of Honey's stretched curled form was gone. "Honey"?

Only the sounds of occasional thunder and rain could be heard, along with the violent, howling winds. The big oak tree

54

in the yard was flailing back and forth, looking like it could lose a limb.

"Honey?"

Listening for the familiar sounds of her padded footsteps, I was alarmed when I heard banging on what sounded like the front door. I almost jumped out of bed.

Who could be here, in the middle of a storm, in the middle of the night?

An uneasy feeling slid over me as I made my way to the hall, electing to keep the lights off so I could see out the windows.

Answering the door to our apartment back home at two in the morning usually meant some drunken idiot was at the wrong door and couldn't get their key to work. But out here, there could be no mistake.

Maybe it was the outer screen door banging in the storm. The gusting winds would most likely rip it off its hinges if it weren't pulled tightly closed. As I reached out to unlock the bolt, an unmistakable knock came from the other side, sending my heart racing.

Someone was there.

I'm not proud to admit it, but I panicked a little. A bead of sweat trickled down my cheek. Lightning occasionally illuminated the room from the front windows.

Crap.

Maybe someone needed help. Maybe someone was being chased by a wolf. Maybe it was the wolf. Except a wolf couldn't knock on a door.

But a werewolf could.

I tried to laugh at myself to ease my own tension.

On either side of the big wooden door was a floor-to-ceiling privacy window, with white curtains covering each one. I tried to look through the somewhat transparent lace, but I couldn't see anything, just blackness outside.

If whoever was there saw my movement, I would have no choice but to open the door.

Chancing it, I ever-so-slightly moved the curtain aside to look out on the porch. I could see nothing until the next flash of lightning lit up the sky.

A wrinkled, elderly woman sat in an antique wooden wheelchair outside our front door. The winds blew her long, white hair in all directions, but she was looking down.

My head snapped back with my heart in my throat. Surely she needed help, but she almost looked scarier than some guy dressed in black. The image of her wheelchair and wild hair flying all about terrified me.

How did she get up the steps, alone, in a wheelchair?

I sprinted back down the hall, deciding to let my dad handle this. I ran into his room and sat on the edge of his bed, keeping the lights off.

"Dad?"

His covers were still up and tight on the bed. It hadn't been slept in.

Knock knock knock.

The old woman was knocking on the front door again. It sounded as loud as a sledgehammer in the still silence.

I ran across the hall but Suzanne was gone as well, her bed neatly made.

"Dad? Suze? Honey? Where is everyone?" I whispered in the hall.

Returning to my room, I looked out the window into the yard and saw Dad's car was gone. Had he taken Suzanne and Honey into town?

The outer screen door squeaked in this distance; the old woman was working the door handle as I crept back into the front room.

I was terrified, standing there staring at the door handle. The poor lady must need help, but my instincts kept me from opening it.

In a flash of lightning, her silhouette appeared smudged up against the privacy window—she was trying to look inside.

Tap tap tap on the glass pane.

My phone. I needed my phone. It was in my room.

Taking less and less care to be quiet, I ran to the bedroom. Frantically searching, I found it on the floor, unplugged and dead. Feeling around in the dark, I grabbed the charger and plugged it in. I sat trembling on the bed, waiting for my phone to turn on.

Lightning flashed.

In that split second, the old woman's figure was outside my bedroom window, which was impossibly high in the air. There was no porch beneath my window; it must have been six feet to the ground.

Tap tap tap on my window. There was no curtain now to hide behind in my room. She was staring right at me. In the darkness, her hair whirled around in the wind, but her features were hidden by the night.

I froze, shaking, unable to move.

She was seemingly floating outside my window in her chair.

Another flash of light, and this time her face lit up. It was gray, sallow, and wrinkled. But her eyes— they were wide open, looking right into mine. Her mouth was gaping in an insidious smile with crooked brown teeth.

Reaching forward with a gnarled hand, she banged on the glass until it shattered, and she began to laugh. A horrible, chilling, demonic laugh.

The rain was now blowing furiously into my room through the broken glass, and I sat frozen in fear, feeling the drops wet my face as she struggled to climb in the window.

I couldn't move.

Chapter 10

I blacked out, unable to see, but sensed her in my room. On me. *Licking me.*

Her putrid, warm tongue prodded my lips, nose, and face. Then she let out a soft whine. I jerked my eyes open in the dark. My arms were able to move again, and I grabbed at the intruding face to push it away.

Only it wasn't the woman anymore, it was the familiar face of Honey. She was standing on my bed, whining and licking me.

I tried to sit up, pushing her back, disoriented and trembling. The clock read 2:23 a.m. as I leaned over and turned on my reading light. Outside, the wind was blowing rain through the screen and I got up to close the window. Honey just sat there on my bed, looking at me with her head cocked sideways, as if waiting for me to say something.

My face was wet from her tongue, but the back of my neck and hair was, too, and the room suddenly felt so hot that I just lied on top of the covers to cool off.

The old woman. Her cackle. The way she looked at me.

Into me.

I was still shaking. It was pretty much the most terrifying dream I'd ever had. Even Honey's presence couldn't calm me down, and she always did. Jumping off the bed, I crept into the hall and looked in my dad's room, his ever-present light snore echoing off the walls.

Ditto for Suzanne, minus for the snoring.

Honey followed me into the front room, and I looked out the window, expecting to see *her*. However, everything appeared normal. I felt the lock on the front door and was surprised it wasn't engaged. Given the situation, this startled me; but since moving to the middle of nowhere we hadn't been as careful about locking up. It didn't seem like we needed to here. I locked it.

A drop of sweat slid down the side of my face as I strode back to my room. Gathering up the top blanket and pillow, I walked to Suzanne's door with Honey following, and I opened it as quietly as I could. Honey and I curled up on the floor together, and I hoped sleep wouldn't take me back to old woman. Suzanne would be upset when she saw me lying in her room, but dealing with her fury would be much more calming than being alone for the rest of the night.

The dream, the move, this town. Almost nothing was going right. I missed my simple life in New York. A killer wolf was stalking me; my neighbor was weird and had important news for me. And now this nightmare was stuck in my head, replaying itself over and over.

It was almost an hour before sleep finally came for me.

Suzanne was a deep sleeper. Honey and I were able to sneak out of the room just before eight on Sunday morning, and she didn't wake until almost ten.

It took her an hour to get ready, and we borrowed Dad's car for the short drive. Suzanne was happy not to walk and she didn't ask questions.

The day was warm and sunny. The clouds from the night's storm were gone.

A perfect California day.

Mrs. Leclair greeted us at the front door and suggested we go for a hike. There was a trail out behind her house that she liked to take in the mornings. She asked Suzanne about herself and how she liked Santa Isadora. It was pretty boring.

I was scanning the trees, half listening, and half watching for something to come out and charge us. I was far from over my fear of the wolf.

Clasping her hands together, Mrs. Leclair spoke a little louder, maybe to get my attention. "So, I wanted to discuss something with you both. Something of the utmost importance and something that will be difficult to digest. I'm afraid there aren't any alternatives. If there were, I would be inclined to seek them first . . ." she trailed off, looking down as she walked.

"Can you both promise to just listen, keep an open mind, and humor me?"

Suzanne looked at me, then nodded. "Sure, of course, Mrs. Leclair."

"Splendid," she said with a smile. "It has been my experience in this life that people see what they want to see, know what they want to know, and accept what their mind is capable of accepting. Believe me; I have seen a great many things that are unexplainable. And my late husband knew of even more. And we would know, we devoted much of our lives to it.

"Luc and I came here almost eleven years ago, to this small town from a not dissimilar-sized town in southern France. Our job there was complete, you see, and it was time to move on. Are either of you acquainted with the term *lycanthropy*?"

"Like-ah-who?" I asked.

She smiled. "Lycanthropy. The supposedly mythic ability to change into an animal, such as a wolf. A werewolf, to be precise."

Suzanne let out a snarky laugh. "Sure. Like Team Jacob, right?"

"Excuse me?" Mrs. Leclair asked in her velvety French accent.

Suzanne shook her head. "Nothing. Was a joke."

Mrs. Leclair continued. "Anyway—and please, hear me out—lycanthropy exists, for better or for worse. There are werewolves in this world. *Lycanthropes*. And there is one right here in Santa Isadora, and he seems to have taken to you, Teavan. I know it was him yesterday."

I was confused, shaking my head. "Wait. You think werewolves are real, and that there is one here that has it out for me?"

"More or less."

"And how do you know this?" I asked.

"It was our job, that's how. That's why we moved here and left France. They generally self-police themselves, through a Franco/Italian organization called the Gencara. In some regions of the world, factions have detached and no longer follow historic protocol. You see, tens of thousands of suspected werewolves were hanged in Europe in the last five centuries. Of course, most were likely innocent people, but nonetheless, it caused obvious distress and the need for secrecy.

"Secret divisions of the French Gendarmerie and the Italian Carabinieri joined forces in the early 1800s to form the Gencara, an organization meant to create and enforce rules and protocols to be followed wherever lycans moved around the globe. Keeping a low profile was paramount.

"However, like any group of people, there were dissenters to the rules, for their own reasons or because they simply didn't care. The Gencara's enforcement was generally enough to control this, until they truly spread across the globe over the last one hundred and fifty years. Policing the tight zone of Europe was one thing, but the world is another matter."

It was my turn to laugh, and I wondered how crazy this woman truly was. "So there are werewolf cops patrolling for lawbreakers. And let me guess, they go into special prisons with no full moon visible?"

Mrs. Leclair didn't crack a smile and a shadow crossed her features as she realized we weren't buying it. "I only wish this was a laughing matter, Teavan. Luc and I would have lived our life much differently had we been ignorant of all of this. And I wish I was, to be honest. The single, the *only* reason I'm telling you both is I think you have been targeted. It would never be my wish to open anyone's eyes to this world if it weren't necessary. Little good can come of it."

I threw a rock against the trunk of a tree about ten yards away, noticing her grim facial expression. Crazy or not, she believed it. "Okay, so who is it? And why has he targeted me? I don't know anyone here."

Mrs. Leclair looked at me, then to Suzanne. "I fear it will be both of you and your father."

Suzanne snorted. "Why me? What have I done?"

"It is nothing either of you has done, nor your father. It was your grandfather, Hubert. He was . . . like us. Doing the things that needed to be done. He died in the line of duty, so to speak."

Now I knew she was crazy. Grandpa died of a heart attack.

"Yeah, except Grandpa died of a heart attack," Suzanne said, voicing my thoughts out loud.

Mrs. Leclair looked confused. "No he didn't. The official story was that he was met by a mountain lion or pack of coyotes on a hike. Ask anyone in town."

"My dad told us that Grandpa died of a heart attack," I repeated.

"Well, maybe he said that to spare you the visuals. But I can assure you he didn't. And my Luc, well, he just went 'missing', but I know very well what happened. He's another unexplained Santa Isadora statistic."

We had circled around her property and her house was not far ahead. I looked over, continuing her game. "Okay, so why us?"

"I'm afraid Hubert didn't finish the job, and he upset the last remaining lycan in the target family. I suspect revenge on you is the best he can do to avenge his brother's death at your grandfather's hands," she said.

Suzanne smiled. "So what are we supposed to do, nail a cross to the front door? Get some holy water?"

Mrs. Leclair pursed her lips, looking at Suzanne with a stern and grave expression. "Kill him."

Chapter 11

Suzanne's eyes bulged. "What? You're saying we should find this wolf and kill it?"

The woman nodded. "Or in his human form. That might be easier."

Blood rushed to my head; I couldn't believe what she was suggesting. "You want us to kill some guy in town so that he won't get us first. Are you insane?"

Suzanne threw her hands up in the air. "No, Teavan, she's completely nuts. Or seriously deranged to suggest this. I have a better idea, Geneviève. We go to the sheriff, tell him about your story, and that you want us to commit murder."

"That would be a mistake, Suzanne," Mrs. Leclair said, motioning with her hand for Suzanne to relax. "I'm afraid Sheriff Vincent wouldn't approve of you killing his remaining son."

A shudder went through me as that sunk in. "Vincent? As in *Bruno Vincent?*"

She looked at me and nodded. "Yes. That Vincent family."

Now, I knew this was all the ridiculous ramblings of

someone maybe on the edge of dementia, but the mention of Bruno hit home. It made things a bit more personal. I explained to them about my run-in with him at school. "The weird thing was when Bruno realized who I am, he seemed very excited about it," I said.

"Hubert killed his older brother, Grayson. Despite numerous warnings, he'd been losing control of his needs and killing animals, and maybe even a missing girl. Luc and Hubert warned him a few years ago, as he had no mentor. His father does not have the curse and doesn't know about it. All their extended family remains in Louisiana, if there are any left that have the bloodlines, so the poor boy had no idea what was happening to him," she said as we approached the front of her house.

"Needless to say, he chose wrongly once he got the taste for blood. Unfortunately, the warnings meant nothing to him, and things began to escalate when a hiker disappeared. Luc aimed to have a final talk with the boy, explain the consequences of his actions. It wasn't something he liked to do; it was always best to guide the young ones in the right direction. But that night was the last time I saw my Luc. But I know what happened."

I interrupted. "You think Luc went to warn the guy and got himself killed?"

"Yes."

"So, how does Grandpa figure into this?"

Mrs. Leclair wiped a tear from one of her eyes. "Well, Hubert planned and watched, and avenged Luc's death early last year. He killed Grayson. But then, a few months later, he was found mauled on a hiking trail. I've suspected ever since that the younger brother, Bruno, also has the gene, but was just coming into his. I think he killed Hubert."

Suzanne rolled her eyes and shook her head with a smile. "Wow, well, you do know how to weave an interesting story! It has been entertaining, Geneviève, but I think we should be on our way," she said, then looked to me. "Let's go."

"Kids, there isn't much time. He won't give up, trust me," she said, trying to block our path.

"We'll take our chances," Suzanne chirped. "But one question: why us? Why haven't you done something about it? Isn't that why you are here?"

Mrs. Leclair's hands fidgeted. "I tried. I mean, I was always Luc's support. I am neither a killer nor a fighter. But I did appeal to the powers that be, in their world. I begged them to fix things, make it right, but they only intervene when they must. In their words, things were settled here, and they would not assist. They told me to move on."

Suzanne's eyebrow arched. "So, you want us to do what you couldn't. Is that it? Get revenge for you?"

"No! It's not like that; it is you that are in danger."

Suzanne had a good point, I thought, as she turned in disgust.

As we walked toward the car, Mrs. Leclair said, "What if I can show you proof?"

Suzanne stopped. "Of?"

"Well . . . it's in the basement," Mrs. Leclair said, motioning to the house and looking desperate.

"Ah, no thanks," Suzanne shook her head. "I think I've had just about enough; I'm going home. Teavan, are you coming?"

I felt torn, wanting a ride home but also wondered what she had to show us. I was a mix of curiosity and still a little fear of

Mrs. Leclair, but decided to take my chances. After all, it was the middle of a sunny Sunday afternoon; surely the wolf wouldn't be around if I biked home.

"See you at home in twenty minutes," I said to Suzanne.

"Suit yourself," she said, climbing into the car and turning the ignition.

I turned around. "Okay, what is it?"

Mrs. Leclair led me inside and opened the door to the basement, then flicked on the light, and we made our way down. There was a welcome coolness to the air. The room was mostly full of boxes and covered furniture. The floor was concrete. In a well-lit corner, there was a large workbench covered in tools.

Assorted rifles and a few handguns rested on wall-mounted gun racks. She led me over to the bench and pulled over a wooden box, like the kind at my grandpa's place that holds all his fancy old dining silverware. The inside was lined with blue velvet.

There were three shiny bullets inside, each neatly placed in small individual holders, but the rest of the slots were empty. Knowing nothing about guns, I thought they looked pretty new.

"These bullets were made here, by Luc. As you might guess, they are made of pure silver," she said, noting my curiosity.

Picking one up, I examined it. It looked like a new, perfect, silver-colored bullet. Though I didn't know what color real bullets even were. At the base of each bullet was a small engraved symbol with three arrows coming from one base, almost like a trident. For all I knew, these were store-bought.

"So Mr. Leclair made his own silver bullets, 'cause I guess you can't buy them, right?"

"Precisely." She nodded.

"What's this little trident symbol?"

Mrs. Leclair put her glasses on and examined the bullet I handed to her. "It is not a trident; it is the silver symbol in alchemy. So we will always know this is made of silver."

I nodded and put the bullet back in the case. Not knowing the difference in how bullets should look, it didn't mean much to me. Only that Mr. Leclair was a hunter, which gave me the creeps. Hopefully, she wasn't big on guns, since she was bordering on having dementia and all. Though for someone so pretty and classy, she seemed experienced with the .22 the day before.

At the far end of the room there was a large wall that looked newer than the rest of the basement, made of a different type of stone. There was a large, very solid looking wooden door in the center of the wall. The door was inlaid with black metal crisscrossing it.

"What's in there?" I pointed.

Mrs. Leclair looked a little uneasy and for once was at a loss for words. Then finally she said, "It was our cellar. Luc collected wine, but I sold off the majority of his collection after he disappeared. It was worth a small fortune, most we brought over from France when we moved. Some wine dating back to the 1970's."

"Cool," I said, walking over to the stairs. "Well, I guess thanks for the walk and the stories, Mrs. Leclair. But I gotta go, soccer game at two this afternoon."

"Come back, please, if you have any questions. I'm worried neither of you believes me."

"No, not really. But thanks anyway. And thanks for yesterday, too."

Chapter 12

Not wanting to sit around all afternoon thinking about Mrs. Leclair and my nightmare, I biked down to Redwood School to watch Jermaine's soccer game. Kevin was also playing, along with a bunch of guys from our grade. Jermaine was practicing before the game and gave me a quick hello wave as I sat down on the green outdoor bleachers.

"Hey!" I heard a girl's voice behind me.

I turned to see Rachel sitting with Sybil about six rows up and closer to the middle. I waved to her, my smile impossible to conceal. She patted the space beside her, motioning for me to come up.

I was torn between wanting to sit with Rachel but not wanting to deal with Sybil.

Dodging around seated families, I made my way up and sat down.

Rachel smiled, jokingly elbowing me. "I didn't see you at church this morning."

"Oh, yeah, right. I mean, I was going to join you, but my crazy neighbor had us over," I said.

"Mrs. Leclair?"

"That's her. Poor lady seems like she's fallen off the deep end."

Rachel shrugged. "I think she seems nice. Always cheerful and pleasant to everyone that I've seen. And she lost her husband not that long ago. I kinda feel sorry for her, all alone here. My mom thinks she'll probably move back to France, figures she has family there."

"Oh. Well, yeah, I mean she's super friendly and all, but seems a little crazy."

"Why's that?"

I laughed. "First off, she genuinely believes there are werewolves in Santa Isadora. *And,* that there are werewolves— or lycanthropes as she calls them—all over the world."

Neither of the girls spoke.

"Right?" I asked.

Rachel looked at me. "Most likely. There are lots of stories everywhere, but we have more than our fair share. I mean, if there can be divine perfection and good in this world, there must also be evil, don't you think?"

At that moment, the whistle blew, and the visiting team took to the field.

Baker High School.

Bruno and his buddies' team.

I shook my head, disbelieving. "Bruno plays? Like, how small is this town? Our school has a game and they have to play *his* team?"

"Teavan, there are only two high schools here. The other games are either away or from other towns in the county. It's not that unusual," Rachel said with a hint of annoyance.

"Yeah, sorry, it's just that in New York there are like a hundred different schools our teams used to play."

"Well, I guess this just isn't New York, is it?" Sybil snorted, finally chiming in.

"Sorry, I didn't mean, like, it's better or anything; just you know, given what happened on Friday and all . . . I just didn't think it would be Bruno's team," I said.

The game started and we stopped talking. It quickly became evident that Bruno was the best player on either team: faster and with better dribbling skills than anyone else. He also didn't seem to be even liked by his own team; he never passed, just tried to be a hero on every play. But he did score the first two goals, so maybe his teammates didn't mind.

Redwood kicked the ball out near the bleachers, and Baker got a throw in. Bruno looked up and saw me, and his face turned red as a scowl set in. He pointed to me. "Hey, *Gimp!* Why don't you get down here and play, help these losers out?"

Everyone was quiet, even his players.

Sybil held up her middle finger and mouthed something to him which he ignored.

He continued. "Maybe you could play goalie, *Gimp*, seeing as how you probably can't run or kick a ball!" he yelled, then laughed at his own joke as his other player threw the ball in and the game continued.

Gimp. I'd been called worse, so I was used to it, but it hurt. Especially in front of such a large crowd. Especially in front of Rachel.

She looked over and touched my knee. "Don't pay attention to that Neanderthal."

I could feel that my face was red, and everyone around us

was looking at the *gimp*. I hated that guy.

The game continued, and things got back to normal, with Redwood trailing 3-1. Jermaine scored the only goal so far. He was actually really good.

It was midway through the second half as I was telling the girls about a funny childhood story that I faintly heard *Gimp* again. As I turned my head, I instinctively ducked as the soccer ball whooshed over where my face had been just seconds before, hitting the bleachers and bouncing up and over.

"Are you okay?" Rachel asked, her face red with concern. "That was close. Good reflexes!"

Bruno snickered on the field, then winked at me. He'd been the kicker.

The match went on, but my easy-going mood was gone.

The only highlights was sitting next to Rachel and the cool afternoon breeze that caused her to sit close enough to me that our legs touched. That part I kinda liked.

Kevin and Jermaine came over after the game as we climbed down to the field. Kevin whistled. "Man, that dude has a helluva kick! Are you okay?"

"Yeah, I'm fine," I said.

"I mean, he targeted you from that far away and nearly got you squarely in the head! If he wasn't such a jerk, he could be a star player, if nothing else. And you shoulda seen your face just as you turned. Teavan, it was priceless!"

His exuberance at my expense was getting old, quickly. "Yeah, I get it, Kevin. I'm a loser; I'm the joke."

"No, man, that's not what I meant. I don't mean no disrespect, it was just epic is all," he added, though no one else laughed.

Jermaine patted me on the back. "Good thing you ducked."

"Yeah, as I said, it's fine."

I hoped that this public display of personal embarrassment meant that we were now even, in Bruno's eyes. It was a crappy afternoon but would be worth it if it was.

Chapter 13

Sunday nights were always a bit depressing; the end of the weekend and the dreaded alarm to be set for Monday morning. A whole week of school ahead.

Honey was up on my bed while I read. My phone buzzed on the table.

It was a text from Rachel. My stomach fluttered.

How are you doing? Still shook up from that near fatal soccer ball kick? I just wanted to check in, make sure you would be in class tomorrow! Sweet dreams

My heart raced, and I read the text a few times. I can't explain it, but the simple message gave me butterflies. Was I supposed to respond?

Why did she have such an effect on me? None of the girls back home did; they all felt kinda like sisters to me. At least *most* of them did, anyway. Plus, I was never really part of the in-crowd, so mostly I was a bit of a loner. Being crappy at sports and walking with a limp didn't exactly lend itself to popularity with the girls, or at least not girls as pretty as Rachel.

I typed and deleted a message multiple times.

All good, just finishing some homework. You have a good sleep too.

After hitting SEND, I had second thoughts. Should it be more personal? Would she think I didn't like getting her text? At the same time, I didn't want to seem too eager, since guys don't in books and movies.

As usual, I was probably overthinking things.

Though it took three tries to get back into reading, I eventually did, but with a smile on my face.

Monday morning came too fast. One of the so-called cool kids, Joel, sat a few rows behind me as people slowly shuffled drearily into class.

"Hey, Teavan. Nice work with Bruno on Friday. I heard you almost took one to the head yesterday; did your girlfriend save you again?"

Turning around, I said, "Huh?"

Joel was a big kid on the football team. Dark, short hair and pock-marked skin. "Sybil, I mean. Wasn't she there beside you to stop the ball? Or were you too busy crooning over Rachel?" he said with a laugh, getting the guys around him to join in.

Everyone was staring and laughing at me and I turned red. Biting at his taunts was the last thing I needed to do, so I turned around without comment.

"Maybe you should get Sybil to sit beside you today, keep you safe?" he asked.

At that moment, I heard someone cough-whisper to Joel,

"Shhh."

Everyone turned to the back of the room where Sybil stood, red-faced, apparently listening. Joel quieted up, pretending to look at his phone.

She walked over to his desk, scowling. "What's that Joel? You want to sit with me today?"

He looked up, feigning surprise. "Errr, no?"

"Joel, do you study stupidity or does it just come naturally?"

He leaned back. "Excuse me?"

"Sorry Joel, did I say that too fast for you? Were you born on the highway or something?" she asked, looking down on him with a smirk.

"Highway? I don't know."

"Oh, I was just wondering, 'cause you know, that's where most accidents happen. I only ask because along with everyone else, I've noticed your sister is almost ten years older than you and all," she spat.

Joel shook his head; he wasn't quite getting it. But he was turning red at all the snickering directed at him.

"Wait, is that supposed to be an insult?" he asked, confused.

"Joel, Joel, Joel . . . " she said, shaking her head then looking at everyone. "I was very much hoping to have a battle of wits, but I guess it's wrong to attack someone who is completely unarmed."

Now even Joel's friends were busting a gut, and his face was beet red. He started to stand up when the teacher came in. "Now, settle down everyone," she said, trying to hush the crowd's laughter.

Sybil took her seat near the back, giving him a fake smile. She was witty, quick, and ruthless. I made a mental note to never cross her.

Joel didn't say much to me the rest of the day, his hostility now silently directed toward Sybil. I was glad I never actually said anything and that the focus came off me.

The week was quiet, uneventful, and thankfully packed with texting between Rachel and me. Jermaine, Rachel, Kevin, Sybil, and I sat together for lunch every day now. Sybil rarely said much other than rolling her eyes at what I could guess were what she deemed stupid adolescent comments from Jermaine, Kevin, and me. I always got a kick out of Kevin's constant need for attention from girls that he never actually received.

I noticed a pretty blonde girl staring at Jermaine from a few tables over and nudged him. "That girl keeps checking you out," I said.

He looked up and saw her, but she quickly looked away.

"Is that Alyssa?" I asked.

Rachel nodded silently from across the table, but Jermaine didn't say anything. "Why don't you ask her to join us?" I asked.

Jermaine shrugged. "I've reached out enough; I'm done. If she's that influenced by her dad then I don't want anything to do with her either way."

Kevin smiled, trying to change the mood. "How about Ava?"

"Ava Murphy?" Rachel asked.

"Yeah," Kevin said, winking.

"What, because she's half black you think I should go for

her? Maybe we're a better match?" Jermaine snapped.

"No, bro, not that at all." Kevin grimaced. "I just thought, you know, she's pretty hot and all, and she's always watching our soccer games. Maybe she's into you."

"Ava's not my type and she's outta my league, anyway," Jermaine answered.

This time Rachel spoke, smiling at Jermaine. "No, you mean you are out of her league."

Chapter 14

Sybil was absent on Thursday, and Rachel was more boisterous than usual over lunch. As we walked back to class, she asked if I would walk her home after school since Sybil was out. Of course, I agreed immediately.

"So, did you have a girlfriend back home?" she asked as I walked my bike and she strode beside me.

I could feel the beginnings of my face turning red. Her first question ran so personal. "Me? Ah . . . no. Not really. How about you?" I asked, reversing the question from me. "Do you have many boyfriends?"

"Many?"

"Sorry, no, I don't mean it like that. I meant, like, have you had many boyfriends?"

"So you think I'm easy?"

Now I knew I was really turning red. *Ugh.*

"No! This is coming out wrong. I meant . . . "

Rachel smiled and then laughed deeply, poking me with her finger. "Just teasing you."

I shook my head and sighed. My words never seemed to

come out quite right in her presence, especially when she was staring at me. Her gaze was always sincere, like she had no other thoughts on her mind and she was genuinely listening rather than just waiting for her turn to talk. It was a nice change from so many kids my age, but in some ways it was also harder to deal with. Insincerity was easier to brush off without thought or comment.

"Oh, phew, yeah, I don't know what I'm saying," I mumbled.

"I think I know. The answer is no, I don't, and haven't had any. My folks aren't too keen on me dating, as you can imagine. Except for maybe a few boys at our church, but most of them are kinda *blah,* to be honest," she answered.

Without thinking, I blurted out, "But if a guy went to your church, they would approve?"

Now it was her turn to blush as she turned away. "Maybe."

We walked a bit longer in silence, finally turning up toward her house and then stopping at the end of her front walk.

"You never answered my question, 'not really' isn't an answer. Did you leave a girlfriend back in New York who you miss?" she asked.

"No, nothing serious; I dated a couple girls, but nothing to write home about," I answered, maybe stretching the truth a bit. The truth was that the only communication I had from New York was my two buddies I grew up with, but even we weren't that close.

She seemed pleased with the answer—maybe even relieved?

"Are you going to the party on Saturday?" she asked.

I shook my head. "No. Whose party?"

"The Anderson twins, Chloe and Christy. They're

sophomores," she said.

"Oh, I see. Nah, I don't think so, I wasn't even invited."

She cocked her head with a smile. "It's a small town, I'm sure you can go. You can join Sybil and me if you'd like."

I just nodded quickly, suppressing a smile.

She turned as she walked to her front step. "I can't stay out late, but it might be fun to swing by for a couple of hours. See you tomorrow in class?" And with that, she gave me a wink, a small wave, and skipped up to her door.

Friday flew by and Saturday night came quickly. Jermaine, Kevin, and I locked our bikes up at The Creamy, where we were to meet up with Rachel and Sybil. We decided to walk to the party from there. We thought showing up on bikes might not be that cool.

Sybil rolled her eyes. "I'm pretty sure it won't make much of a difference either way for you three."

Rachel smiled and pretended to elbow Sybil. "Oh, come on, you grouch, be nice."

"I might not be with you guys all night," Kevin announced as we walked. "There are a couple of females there that might be worth my time, if you know what I mean."

Sybil coughed. "You're walking someone's dogs?"

Everyone laughed except for Kevin. "Ah, no. But, Jermaine, if you don't mind I might try to wheel up Ava tonight if she's there."

"Mind? No, I could care less. But good luck."

Kevin held his chin high with a smile. "It's not about luck, my friend. It's about charm, and the uncanny attraction the ladies have for me."

The Andersons' house was a large, rectangular white home on Walker Road. The lawn was perfect; all the shrubs and trees were nicely trimmed. They looked rich.

Cars dotted both sides of the street, and the inside was jammed with people.

Jermaine looked a little nervous. "You guys sure you want to hit up this kind of party?"

Kevin winked. "Think of the ladies, Jermaine."

Rachel piped up, but ignored Kevin's comment. "We need to at least say hi. Chloe and I played baseball together for years, and she asked me to come. She knew I wouldn't come alone. It's fine."

The music was cranked up as we made our way in through the front door. It was loud, crowded . . . and seemed pretty cool. I'd never been to a real house party before. One of the first things I noticed was that we looked like the youngest and smallest. It seemed like it was all seniors, the guys were so tall; I felt like a little kid.

"Let me find Chloe or Christy; you guys can go to the kitchen," Rachel said, pointing to the busy back kitchen area.

People were drinking from red Solo cups, and playing games on the dining room table. There were plastic bowls of chips on the kitchen island counter, and everyone congregated around them, chatting over the music. The four of us found a quiet back corner where we could stand.

A beefy, blond guy who was probably well over six feet tall in a letterman jacket spied me and came over. "Hey, are you Suzanne's brother?"

I gulped nervously and nodded. "Yep."

He smiled. "I thought so, you kinda look like her. She's

cool."

"Ah, thanks, I guess," I said.

He handed me his cup. "I'm Jason. You want a beer? There's a whole keg."

Reluctantly, I took the cup. It was almost full, and I eyed it suspiciously.

"Relax kid, it's just beer. A friend of Suzanne's is a friend of mine."

I'd never drank much beer before, besides the odd sip from one of my dad's on a hot afternoon. Jason turned to grab himself another one, and Kevin tapped me on the shoulder.

"Bro! Jason Kemper gave you a drink, that's huge! Can I have a sip?"

"Sure," I said, handing him the cup. Kevin took a big gulp; his eyes watered as the carbonation hit him and he burped.

"Excuse me."

Sybil confidently grabbed her own and then sipped it while looking at her phone. Jermaine, Kevin, and I shared the one Jason had given me, waiting for Rachel to come back. She eventually returned, and I quickly gave Kevin the last sip as she approached, not wanting Rachel to see me with it.

"So? You guys meeting some people?" she asked, sipping a can of Coke.

We all shrugged, but then Jermaine said, "Teavan knows Jason Kemper."

I shook my head quickly. "No, I don't. Who is he?"

"He's a football star at Baker. How do you know him?" Rachel asked.

"He recognized me; I think he must know my sister from their school."

Rachel smiled. "She's pretty."

"Huh?" I said.

"Your sister, she's very pretty. Why didn't you tell us? Her features are so delicate and defined, and I love her curly hair! Chloe just introduced us in the dining room."

Was my sister here? At the same party I was? She wouldn't be happy with me.

Kevin winked. "Agreed. She's hot."

"Kevin, I don't want to hear that about my sister," I said, rolling my eyes. "Rachel, did you tell her I was here?"

She nodded.

Ugh.

"Is that okay? You might need to get used to it; social circles are a little smaller here, they cross grades sometimes," Rachel explained, then turned to Kevin. "And Kevin, Ava is here, too. She's in the other room as well. I told her you were looking for her."

Kevin's face turned red and he bit his lip. "Huh? You did?"

"Well, you said you wanted to meet up with her. She's in there," she said, pointing to the other room.

"Ah, thanks," Kevin mumbled nervously, thrusting his hands in his pockets. His overly confident tone seemed to disappear pretty quickly.

Rachel turned to Jermaine and me and winked with a grin.

I could feel someone staring at me from across the room; it was giving me a weird tingling feeling. Not the good kind. I spotted Jed McGregor, Bruno's buddy.

The blood drained from my face. Bruno was probably here, too.

A concerned look spread across Rachel. "You okay?"

86

I shook my head. "No. I think Bruno might be here. His buddy is over there; don't look, though."

"Seriously?" Rachel asked, but she didn't look. "Don't worry about it. It's a big party, and your sister has some football guys that seem to be fawning over her. Maybe having her here will end up being a blessing."

"That'd be a first," I said, scanning the crowd for Bruno. I could feel the hair on the back of my neck prickling when I heard his familiar voice.

"Well, well, look who's here." Bruno smirked as he circled us. "If it isn't the newest kid in town and his two bodyguards, Churchmouse and Orphan Annie."

Chapter 15

Sybil slid her phone into her back pocket, and her posture went rigid. Jed and Mike came up beside Bruno. We all stood in the back corner of the kitchen, unnoticed by the crowd.

"H-hey, Bruno," stammered Jermaine. "Good game last Sunday, you had some great shots."

Bruno paid him no attention and glared at me.

I remained silent, scared to say anything. I didn't want to antagonize him. Rachel grabbed my hand and looked at Sybil. "Come on, you guys, let's go. They can have the kitchen."

Bruno put his hand in our way. "I don't think so." Then he looked at me. "Wait, so first Sybil has to defend you, and now even Churchmouse is taking care of you? You really are a joke, aren't you? Aren't the men supposed to take care of the girls? Or is this how it works on the East Coast?"

Sybil rolled her eyes. "No, Bruno, it's just not 1950 anymore."

He ignored her. My blood pressure was rising, and my face was getting hot. "Bruno, what's your problem with me? What have I *done* to you?"

His fake smile turned angry, with his lips pursed. "We have a score to settle."

"Over what?"

Bruno looked around, pretending to be thinking, then looked directly at me. "Family history."

My head was reeling; had Mrs. Leclair been right about some feud between Grandpa and Bruno's family?

"Come on, Laurent, let's go outside and settle this like men," he said, his face twisting and turning red with hatred. "I don't want to break anything here, just you."

Now my pulse was really pounding, but I dared not move.

A girl came busting into the circle with a drink in hand. It was Suzanne.

"Teavan! What are *you* doing here?" she asked merrily.

Evidently she didn't notice the tension or the standoff. I shrugged. "Errr, nothing, Suze. Just hanging out."

Bruno snarled at her from behind. "Beat it, wench," and he pulled on her shirt to remove her roughly from the circle. Suzanne spilled her drink.

"Hey!" she yelled out, spinning around. "You spilled my drink!"

Bruno pointed out of the circle, looking at her. "Leave. *Now.*"

Suzanne looked surprised and finally clued into the situation. "Teavan, who is this guy?"

I was literally shaking with anger. I watched Bruno and my sister, unsure of what to do, knowing that if I stepped in things would quickly escalate. At the same time, I wanted to crack him for even talking to my sister in that way. My clenched fists were sweating.

"Suzanne, are you okay?" said a deep voice from behind.

It was Jason Kemper.

Suzanne looked back and forth. "No, not really. This jerk just pushed me and spilled my drink."

Now Jason's face went red and he set his cup down. "Bruno, please tell me this isn't true," he said, walking up to Bruno until they were just a foot apart. Jason must have had six inches and forty pounds on him.

Bruno looked up, unwavering. "I don't have an issue with her, just that kid."

Jason looked over to me as Bruno pointed.

"Well," Jason said. "That *kid* is Suzanne's brother, so he's off-limits. Now leave."

They stared each other down, Jason breathing heavily through his nose with his mouth in a scowl.

Bruno smirked, looking up. "Or what?"

Jason laughed, stepping back. "Bruno. Are you kidding me? Everyone has given you some leeway over the last year, because of Grayson and all. But you've pressed your luck too far." He reached over to grab Bruno's shirt but wasn't quick enough. Or maybe it was the few beers he'd had, but Bruno swatted his hand to the side and hurled both palms into Jason's chest, sending him stumbling back onto the kitchen table. Drinks, chips, cups, and everything else crashed to the ground.

"No, Jason. You mean you've pressed your luck too far," Bruno snarled, then smirked as Jason tried to get up.

Even Jed and Mike stood back, looking surprised and a little scared at the quickness and ferocity of Bruno's actions. The music turned off, and guys came running over in matching letterman jackets. An offensive lineman-sized guy helped Jason off the ground. "What happened?"

Jason shook his head, pointing at Bruno. "Vincent. He's gone too far; I'm done giving him a free pass."

Everyone looked at Bruno, who just stood there with a scowl on his face. "I don't need a free pass, Kemper."

A pretty blond girl came running in between them. "Outside!" she yelled, pointing to the front door. "Take it outside!"

Jason stared down Bruno, but nobody moved. "Okay Bruno, you heard Chloe. Outside."

Bruno smiled. "Fine by me."

Everyone started talking and crowding to the front door as Bruno turned around, looking at me. "You and I, we're not done, Laurent."

I gulped; just glad his immediate focus was off me. And to be honest, at that moment I was looking forward to seeing him get a beating.

Chapter 16

They squared off on the front lawn, a senior against a freshman. "Don't worry Bruno, I'll be gentle," Jason said, his fists up.

Bruno smirked. "I won't." And with that, he kicked Jason's leg hard, causing the big man to lean forward grabbing at his shin in pain. Bruno used the opportunity to punch him square in the nose, sending Jason reeling back, blood instantly dripping from both nostrils.

Jason wiped his nose, looking at the blood on the back of his hand with surprise. His face contorted in rage, his meaty fists balled up, and he lunged at the smaller Bruno. He ran headfirst into him, picking Bruno up onto his shoulder and running him backward into a parked car, slamming him onto the hood as Bruno's head smashed against the windshield—hard. The glass cracked.

Bruno looked dazed and cross-eyed as he rolled off the other side onto the pavement. The crowd of onlookers went wild with taunts and jeers. Jason stood ready. "Get up!"

Surprisingly, Bruno stood from behind the car, rubbing the

back of his head. He turned his neck awkwardly, and I heard a crack; then he rolled his head around, stretching it. "That all you got, Kemper?"

The crowd cheered. I couldn't comprehend how a kid my age could get up so quickly from such a nasty throw down.

Jason shook his head. "You just don't learn, do you?" With that, he walked around the car into the middle of the road. The streetlights shone down on him and Bruno, sending their boxing-stance shadows across the road. Jason looked more guarded this time.

The crowd whooped as the boys closed in on each other. Jason jabbed, hitting Bruno squarely in the face, the thud of his fist connecting to Bruno's cheek.

He followed with a right hook, then an uppercut. The horrible cracking sound of Bruno's lower jaw hitting the upper jaw rang out as his legs looked shaky. Jason finished him with one last punch to the side of his head, sending Bruno to the pavement again.

"Now stay down Vincent!" he called out amidst everyone cheering.

Bruno looked up, his mouth bleeding. There was hatred in his eyes as he crawled to his hands and knees, spitting out blood on the pavement.

"Vincent, I'm warning you, *stay down*."

Bruno's face contorted into a blood-lined smile as he looked up at Jason, who then shook his head in disgust. "Fine, you asked for it."

Jason ran in and brought his foot up directly into Bruno's stomach, lifting him off the road and sending him tumbling away. The thud sounded as if a rib might have snapped.

Bruno was lying on his back, panting, as Jason put his hands up in victory. The guys in matching jackets all patted his back, congratulating him.

"Damn kid wouldn't give up," one of them said.

"Kemper!" Everyone turned around as Bruno stood again, spitting a mouthful of blood onto the street. "I haven't cried uncle yet." He laughed with a look of madness. Bruno rolled his neck again and cracked his knuckles. There was a collective gasp that he could even stand, let alone want to keep going.

The distant sound of sirens could be heard over the murmuring of the crowd, and everyone stopped to listen. Someone yelled out, "Cops!"

Bruno stood staring, blood dripping from his mouth. "I ain't done, Kemper."

Jason looked around uneasily. "Well, I am. I'm not getting into trouble over this." He turned to his buddies, "Come on, let's go."

Bruno did end up running off, once everyone saw that Jason left first. Before he turned to go, he looked at me and mouthed, *You're next*.

I shuddered as our little gang jumped into the car with Suzanne and took off.

"Was that the guy Mrs. Leclair was talking about? I think he goes to my school," Suzanne asked as we drove off.

"Yep. That's him," I said.

Sybil, Jermaine, Rachel, and Kevin were crowded into the back seat of Dad's car. Suzanne asked for directions to where each of them lived so she could drop them off. Nobody wanted to bike or walk home.

Suzanne shook her head. "That kid . . . there is something wrong with him."

Kevin leaned forward. "Yeah, and he's getting worse."

She looked at me. "Did you tell them what Mrs. Leclair said?"

"Not really." I proceeded to tell them the whole story as Suzanne drove around aimlessly so I could finish.

It was Jermaine who spoke first. "Well, if someone is cursed in this town, I wouldn't be surprised in the least if it was Bruno. That dude is not right in the head."

I laughed, then said, "Well, sure, except believing in werewolves is about as right as believing in faeries. Just because he's nuts doesn't mean he's a werewolf. It just means he's a bully, and his wires have gotten crossed in the head."

Everyone stared at me.

"Right?" I asked. They just shrugged.

Rachel spoke up. "Like I said at the soccer game, we have more than our fair share of weird things here. If we have powers of supreme good, which I know to be true, then unfortunately the opposite is also true, Teavan."

The thought sent a shiver down my spine. They all were quiet. My friends back in New York would have laughed at such a story.

"So the opposite of supreme good is evil, which is a werewolf?" I asked. "Or is it just Bruno that is evil?"

"I don't know, but I'm just saying there could be something to the story," Rachel answered.

We dropped everyone off, stopped at The Creamy to put my bike in the trunk, and drove home. Honey was safely inside the house, and my dad was on his computer. Suzanne asked that I keep my distance from Bruno. It wasn't something I needed to be told.

I closed my window and drew the blinds before crawling into bed.

Sleep didn't come easily, but at least I got a nice goodnight text from Rachel. A text from her always seemed to make me feel better.

"A movie?" I asked Rachel on Monday, replying to her question.

"Yeah, you know, like at the theater? Like you and me?" Rachel joked.

"Sure." I fumbled after she suggested during lunch we go to a movie Tuesday night. There were only two playing: the latest *Avengers* and some new thriller. I had a feeling she wasn't an *Avengers* kind of girl.

"A thriller?" I asked.

Rachel grinned. "Perfect. Pick me up at six thirty? You can meet my parents."

My delight turned to mild dread at the thought of meeting anyone's parents, but I feigned a smile. "Sounds good."

Tuesday night rolled around, and Suzanne dropped me a few houses down from Rachel's. She wanted the car that night and Dad said she had to drive me and pick me up to have it. A small price.

Rachel's house was compact but very well kept, with not a weed to be seen. A jovial looking man answered the door. "You must be Teavan?"

I nodded, sticking out my hand. "Yes. Nice to meet you, Mr. Denning."

"Nice to meet you, too," he shook my hand firmly then stood aside, waving me in. "Come in, come in. Please."

Mr. Denning sat me down in the front room and riddled me with questions about New York, my father, and how we liked living in the Iz. He was less scary than I had pictured him— which had been like a TV minister who would quiz me on my beliefs—though he did ask me which church we went to. I explained we hadn't attended much since we moved, and he looked disappointed.

"I see . . . " he said.

Good thing I didn't mention that we never went.

Rachel came into the front room; she looked beautiful as usual. Or almost more beautiful if that was possible, smiling radiantly. "Hey, you! I see you met my dad?"

I nodded. "Yes."

Following behind Rachel was Sybil. She looked at me and just gave me the *hello* nod.

"Hey," I said, trying to hide my disappointment at her joining us.

Rachel noticed my surprise. "Do you mind if Sybil comes?"

"Oh, of course not. The more, the merrier," I lied.

We made our way to the front door. Mr. Denning looked at me. "Have them home by nine thirty, please, Teavan."

"Yes sir," I said as we stepped outside.

With his index and middle finger, he pointed to his eyes, then to me. Like we were in a movie.

I'm watching you, I imagined him saying.

Chapter 17

Rachel positioned herself in the middle of our little threesome as we made our way down the sidewalks toward the Plaza Movie Theatre. She was good at keeping the conversation going, since Sybil was often quiet and I was shy.

"No *Avengers*?" Rachel asked as we stood in line, looking up at the NOW PLAYING signs.

I shrugged. "I didn't see you as the *Avengers*-type."

Rachel smiled, play-punching me on the shoulder. "See? That's one of the things I like about you, Teavan Laurent. You think about things. Most guys would just see what they wanted to see, but you actually give it some thought and care."

My face warmed at the compliment.

Sybil rolled her eyes behind Rachel. "Well, I would have liked to see it."

Rachel spun around. "Well, we can see it instead? I don't mind if you both want to go to *Avengers*."

Knowing Rachel didn't want to see it, I said, "Next week? Maybe the two of, or I mean, the three of us can go next week?"

Sybil said, "Sure," as she paid for her ticket. I offered to pay for Rachel's, but she already had her money out and insisted.

We got some popcorn and soda and sat down. Rachel, as usual, positioned herself in the middle. Sybil excused herself to use the restroom before the trailers started.

Rachel bumped me with her shoulders, pretending she'd done it by accident when I looked over. "Is it okay that I invited Sybil?"

"Sure, why not?"

"Well, I know she can be grumpy sometimes, but my dad thought it would be a good idea. If it makes you feel any better, she didn't really want to come."

I wasn't sure how that made me feel. "No, I mean, I don't mind at all that she hangs out with us."

"Are you sure?"

"Yep," I lied again.

"Wonderful! Cause I love hanging out with both of you!" She giggled, throwing a piece of popcorn at me.

Sybil returned and the movie started shortly after. It was very intense. There were aliens on earth, and the main family had to escape Boston and hide in the country, though the aliens eventually found them.

It turned out to be an excellent choice. Within ten minutes of the movie beginning, Rachel slipped her left hand into my right, and our hands interlocked in the dark. Halfway into the film, she was leaning up against me, jumping at the scary moments and holding my hand tight. Her hair smelled like lavender, and her light perfume mixed in with it was making me dizzy. I was half thinking of her and half watching the movie.

It was marvelous.

When the lights came on, we tried to secretly untangle our sweaty hands, but I saw Sybil glance over and roll her eyes. I got the feeling she didn't want me stealing her best friend's focus.

When we got back to Rachel's house, I agreed to walk Sybil home after, since she only lived a few blocks further. I awkwardly hugged Rachel and said good night, then she and Sybil hugged.

"See you both tomorrow," she said as she bound up her steps, her dad coming to the front door.

"'Night, Rachel," I called after her.

Sybil and I walked in silence as I texted Suzanne the address to pick me up.

Sybil spoke. "So, what are you doing exactly?"

"What do you mean?" I asked.

"Like, why are you wasting your time with Rachel?"

I kept walking, not sure what she was getting at. "I don't know. I kinda like hanging out with her, I guess?"

"You know you won't get what you want, right?"

"Which is?" I asked, suddenly feeling defensive.

Sybil shook her head in frustration. "What every guy our age wants. That's what. I'm just warning you: it's a waste of time. You're not totally ugly, and being from out of town gives you enough edge that you could probably get a girlfriend."

Was she saying what I thought she was saying? "Ah, Sybil, that's not my intention."

"Sure."

"No, really. I'm, like, not usually into girls. I mean, I *am* into girls, but I've never dated anyone or even gone on a date before, even if it was with three people. I'm not like that, if that's what you mean. I'm surprised you think that."

She didn't speak at first, but kept up her pace. "Well, if you hurt her, I'll hurt you. Just know that, okay?"

"Umm, okay," I mumbled, not knowing how to respond. "Can I ask you a question?"

Sybil shrugged. "Sure."

"Why don't you like me?"

She looked a little surprised at the question. "Like you? I don't *dislike* you. I just don't trust guys, especially the ones interested in Rachel."

"You don't think she can take care of herself," I said.

She shook her head. "No, that's not it. Rachel isn't streetwise; she's too trusting. She always sees the good in people and chooses to ignore the bad. It will only get her hurt. Maybe I am the yin to her yang. She needs a dose of reality sometimes."

I arched my eyebrow. "Or maybe you could do with a little of her positivity? Have you stopped to think maybe being like her isn't all that bad?"

"So, what, so I can have some adolescent boys fawning all over me? No thanks."

"No, so maybe you have some real friends and enjoy life a little, that's all. It seems sad to see the negative everywhere and have such a dreary outlook on people and life."

She continued walking, head down. "Well, it works for me."

We arrived at her house, and she made her way up to the front door, not even thanking me for walking her home. "Remember what I said, Teavan."

"Sure thing," I mumbled, too quietly for her to hear. Then a bit louder, I called out sarcastically, "Thanks for such a great evening, Sybil!"

She gave me a dirty look as she closed the door.

Good night to you, too.

Dad was sitting at the kitchen table, working on his laptop when Suzanne and I got home. Honey came bounding to the front door to greet us.

"How are the world travelers?" he asked.

We both entered the kitchen, scrounging for leftovers in the fridge.

"That good, huh," he answered himself.

"Fine, Dad. I saw a movie, it was pretty cool," I said, feeling bad that neither of us had answered him.

"I see," he said. "So, this weekend, I signed up for a writing conference in San Francisco. I'll be leaving first thing Friday morning, and I'm driving."

Suzanne spun around. "What? You're taking the car?"

My dad laughed. "I thought that would get your attention. Yes, I'm taking the car. It's only a few hours from here, and I know some people going. It's a good West Coast networking opportunity."

Suzanne groaned. One of the things she loved about him writing was that he didn't need the car much, and it was generally at her disposal.

"When are you back?" she asked.

"Sunday night, probably late."

Suzanne frowned, but then perked up. "Okay."

"Will you two be all right here alone?"

"Sure," she answered.

"No parties, Suzanne."

"Of course not." She smiled.

I wasn't sure if she was serious or not. She left the room with a mischievous grin on her face.

As I lay in bed later, going over the night, a smile spread across my face as I remembered the warm softness of Rachel's hand and the smell of her hair as she cuddled me during the movie. Even with Sybil there, things went better than I hoped or expected.

Sybil's comments upset me, though. I knew she didn't like me, but why would she think I was some lecherous freshman looking to score with her cousin? Was that the vibe I gave off?

The last thoughts I remember before falling asleep were of the weekend coming up and dad going out of town. I only hoped Suzanne was not planning on having a big party; that was the last thing I needed.

Chapter 18

"You can have Friday; I get Saturday."

That's all Suzanne offered me about the weekend.

"And on Saturday, you either need to be in your room or somewhere else. Got it?" she ordered the next night, away from Dad's listening ears.

"I guess." I shrugged. Despite our differences, we had unspoken rules about keeping certain things from Dad. Keeping each other's backs.

Jermaine was excited by the news. He was going to sleep over Friday, and I invited Kevin as well.

"You gonna invite your girlfriend?" Kevin asked, smirking.

"She's not my girlfriend. But yeah, I thought I'd ask to hang out. Maybe we can watch a movie or play cards. Maybe barbecue some burgers?"

"Sounds good," Kevin answered as we walked to English class Thursday morning. The *To Kill a Mockingbird* paper was due next Wednesday, and I hadn't even started reading the book yet. The rest of the weekend was gonna be slow. "You mind if I invite a couple of ladies?"

Jermaine burst out laughing. "Like who? Your little sister and her friends?"

Kevin played it cool, ignoring the jab. "No, I'm juggling a couple girls from Baker, had a double date planned on Friday. I don't want to cancel, figured they could just come, too."

"Sure, you invite all the ladies you want, as long as they don't walk on four legs and aren't in elementary school," I joked.

Kevin shook his head. "You two of little faith . . . if you only knew," he grinned.

Jermaine biked over straight after school on Friday; the other three were coming at six. Big surprise: Kevin was coming solo; apparently his ladies had canceled.

I'd never really looked around the property before, so Jermaine and I grabbed some old baseball bats from the garage (just in case of any trouble) and set out to investigate the as yet unexplored land behind the house.

There were scattered groups of trees here and there, surrounded by long, dry grasses and shrubs. It looked to me like good grazing land for cattle. But then again, I knew nothing about farming.

Some of the big, old oak trees looked perfect to build a tree fort in, or just to climb. That was something I hadn't done much of growing up in a congested city. I was embarrassed to admit it, so I kept it to myself, thinking I'd be back another time to try my hand at climbing. When was too old to climb trees?

Maybe you never were.

Further in, we stumbled upon a run-down cabin surrounded by more thick-trunked oak trees. There was an old-fashioned water well that had a circular wall of old weathered river stones about three feet high around it. There was a small, peaked wooden roof where the now-missing bucket would have been lowered from using a pulley.

"Look, Jermaine," I pointed it out.

We ran over and looked into the well.

"Hello!" I yelled down, expecting to hear my echo. There was a slight echo, but not much. It was dark inside and stunk of decaying leaves. I couldn't see the bottom, and there was no longer a rope attached to the pulley.

Jermaine dropped a stone. It was silent for a second, then we heard a soft *kerplunk* as it hit the dark water far below.

"I guess there's still water," he pointed out.

"Let's check the cabin," I said.

The structure looked old and decrepit. It was small, square, and made of warped, graying wooden boards in dire need of paint. There was a sagging and tilted front porch with steps leading up to it. There were a few windows on the sides of the building. One of them missing—its broken glass and frame lay in the tall grass beneath the empty sill.

Dead leaves surrounded the cabin and some odd-shaped iron tools, possibly from farming a hundred years ago. They were rusted and covered in weeds now. It didn't look like this place had been lived in for a long time.

"I wonder if your grandpa came back here?" Jermaine asked as he carefully stepped up and tried the front door. It was locked from the inside, with a small keyhole bolt lock that was old but looked newer than the rest of it.

"Hello!?" I called out as we knocked.

Jermaine started to kick the door.

"What are you doing? Don't break it!" I cried.

He stopped and looked at me. "Why not? You own this place, and it's just some dusty old shed. How else are we going to get in? Do you have a key?"

I shook my head.

He had a point. I followed his lead and kicked as well—like the police do in the movies when breaking down someone's front door. After a few swift tries, the wood splintered in a cloud of dust, and the door swung open with a creak.

We could make out some timeworn furniture in the room as we waited for our eyes to adjust to the dark.

A few tables. Shelves crammed full of books. More old, wrought iron-type farm implements in one corner, and chairs stacked against another wall.

In the middle of the room was a slightly less ancient looking table, but still something my dad might even object to using. And he wasn't picky when it came to furniture.

The table was round and had three matching chairs surrounding it. Some tattered wooden boxes sat on top, about the size of shoeboxes. I blew the dust off one, but the sound of my blowing caused slight movement in the corner.

We could hear some squeaking sounds.

"Jermaine? What is it? R-raccoons?" I stammered, backing away, trying to see in the dark. There were bookshelves in that corner, but I didn't see any movement along the floor.

The squeaking continued.

I readied myself for a raccoon to leap out and attack. Or worse.

Nothing moved.

"Teavan!" Jermaine cried as he stumbled back into one of

the chairs, knocking it over and creating a ruckus.

For a split second as my eyes adjusted, it appeared, impossibly, as if there were hundreds of mice crawling on the walls and ceiling. The sudden sound of the chair tumbling seemed to spur them into action, and the room immediately filled with flying mice. I backed up, toppled over the fallen chair, and sprawled out onto the dirty wooden floor as the rodents came awkwardly flying right over and out the front door.

Only I realized they weren't mice.

They were bats. Hundreds of them.

Jermaine dropped to the floor alongside me; we shielded our eyes and heads with our arms. We stayed curled up in that position until it was quiet again.

Carefully, I peeked out from between my arms, scanning for movement in the air or on the walls. Everything was still.

"I think they're gone," I whispered, standing up. "I've never seen a real bat before, well, besides at the zoo. Do you think they're vampire bats?"

He shook his head. "Nah, I don't think vampire bats are even real. They're just brown bats; you see them lots at night. Good for eating bugs. But I have heard they can carry rabies. They scared the crap out of me."

Me, too.

I inspected the books on the shelves. The spines were cracked and faded; I could not easily make the titles out. Many of the books didn't even look like they were written in English, and some might have been in Japanese or Chinese. I pulled one off the shelf and blew the dust off it.

Le Chasseur et Sa Proie.

I didn't know what it said, but the book looked pretty dull, and was almost falling apart. No pictures.

Maladies du Sang was another one.

Lupus ad Prædandum.

Mutazioni del Sangue.

They might have been French, probably my grandfather's college books he carted from France. I realized that we never really celebrated our French heritage; it wasn't something my dad talked about very often. But Grandpa had a lot of French pictures and books around the house. It kinda made me want to explore it a little.

On the table, I lifted the lid of one of the wooden boxes. It was full of odds and ends: pennies, paperclips, broken pencils. There was a small, brown leather pouch tied closed. Loosening the tie, I opened it and shook out the contents into my hand. A few irregularly shaped metal tokens—coins? They were so old and tarnished I couldn't read the inscriptions. One caught my eye that was a little bigger than the rest, a little less than two inches in diameter. A leather strap threaded through a small hole in it creating what I assumed was a necklace. It was highly detailed, small circles around the circumference almost like a clock, then tiny symbols of varying sizes within. One looked like a moon, another one almost like a trident. In the very center there was a circular brush stroke of a dog—or a wolf. There were no words inscribed and the other symbols meant nothing to me. Holding this token, or medallion, almost gave me a light buzz, like when you put your tongue on a nine-volt battery. Except I liked it.

There was also a piece of dark metal shaped into the letter C, a little bigger than a silver dollar that also had a small hole in it but no strap.

Jermaine examined the coins. "These look ancient; they might be worth something. You should keep 'em." He then squinted at the C-shaped object. "What was your grandma's name?"

I closed my eyes; my memories of her were foggy, but then I smiled. "Camille."

He grinned and stuffed the C and the coins back into the pouch and handed it to me. "Let's get out of here and keep exploring. This place is dusty."

I slid the bag into my pocket and decided to return one afternoon to take a closer look at the cabin. We closed the door as best we could and continued our hike through the patches of trees to the northernmost fence. It led west, back toward Mrs. Leclair's land.

"What's that?" Jermaine asked, pointing up ahead.

We marched toward where the barbed wire fence was down. The wooden fence post was broken, snapped off at the base.

I tried to lift the broken post, but it was heavy with all the barbed wire nailed to it. "I guess I should tell my dad to fix this. Though it's not like we have any cows to keep in."

Jermaine tried to pick it up, too, with equal success. "Or maybe it's more about what you want to keep out."

I forced a laugh.

He continued. "Don't you think it's weird your fence is down? Like, it's not old, this wood is still good. Not like it's rotting."

I inspected the round post more closely—it was snapped off right at the base where it went into the ground. The wood inside the break was fresh and clean, unlike the weathered outside surface of the post, but it didn't look like it was sawed. Kinda gave me a chill. What could have broken such a thick piece of wood?

Jermaine smiled and tried to do a scary impersonation. "Maybe . . . maybe it was . . . the werewolf of Santa Isadora!"

We both started laughing, although I was more nervous about the fence than I let on. My phone buzzed; it was a text from Kevin. He was at my place. I showed it to Jermaine, and we raced back to the house.

Chapter 19

The girls arrived on their bikes just after six, and Rachel had an apple crisp that she and her mom made. I was in charge of the burgers. Or, at least, cooking the frozen patties we had.

Things were different with Sybil. She was just as cold to me. But at least now it was like we'd talked, gotten things off our chests. She was honest with me, and I was half honest with her. That little chat seemed to make things slightly better.

We ate the overcooked burgers, had some apple crisp, and decided to forgo a movie and instead play a card game they all liked called Salad.

It was one of the best nights I'd had in a long time, finally feeling like I had new friends and a sense of belonging. The lingering glances and occasional touches to my shoulder from Rachel didn't hurt, either.

Our little group of five misfits was odd, but we worked well together, except for Sybil, of course. But even she seemed to soften a bit as her competitive side emerged and she got the best score of the night.

As nine thirty rolled around, Sybil checked her phone and

announced she and Rachel had to go.

Rachel frowned, "We have to be home before ten."

We gathered the cards and stood up from the table. Jermaine kept twitching his head, looking at me funny. "So, *we gonna escort the girls home?*"

"Huh?"

Jermaine shook his head at me. "The bikes. It's dark. Should we *escort* the ladies home??"

Oh, now I got it. "Yes. Yes, of course."

Sybil looked back as she put her shoes on. "We're fine. We don't need your help."

As I walked over to find my shoes, Honey was jumping around me. "Nah, it's good. The guys are staying over, and it's not like we have to be home or anything. We'll drop you two off and be back before ten."

Rachel smiled and winked. "Our knights in shining armor."

Sybil rolled her eyes.

As the five of us on our bikes approached the center of town, we stopped, and Jermaine suggested he and Kevin would drop Sybil off, and that I could see Rachel home. Then we'd meet back in ten minutes at the town center.

Sybil tried to protest, but Rachel cut in. "Great idea, Jermaine."

Rachel and I drove down the center of the road, slowly weaving back and forth, chatting about nothing in particular until we arrived at her place. I got off my bike, deciding I'd walk her to the front door. I was sweating a lot more than the cool evening suggested I should be.

This was my chance. Jermaine handed me a layup. Would she recoil if I tried to kiss her?

The lights were off as we neared the front door. I kept thinking her dad was probably watching us in the dark. This wasn't going to work.

"Why are all the lights off? Parents go to bed?" I asked.

Rachel shook her head. "No, they're out. They're at a fundraiser."

My heart started beating too fast again, palms instantly sweaty.

"Oh, do you want me to come in and wait until they get back?"

Rachel laughed. "Very subtle, Teavan, very subtle! But I'm not that kind of girl, you know."

Ugh! That wasn't what I meant at all.

I could feel the heat in my face. "No, no! I don't mean it like that. I meant so you wouldn't have to sit alone and all."

She winked at me. "I know, I just like making you blush, and it's not hard to do."

Phew.

"Oh, okay then." I stood there awkwardly, hands in my pocket. "Well, thanks again for coming, and please thank your mom for that apple crisp. Tonight, it was . . . it was a lot of fun," I said, and I meant it.

"I agree," she answered, opening the front door as I made my way toward the porch steps. "You know, Teavan, you can't come in, but if you wanted to, you could give me a tiny kiss goodnight?"

My blood pressure instantly rocketed up again. I *hated* that the blood vessels in my face could so easily give away my emotions.

Despite the immediate dry mouth, I shyly walked over to

the open door where she held it. I leaned in to kiss her perfect, olive-skinned cheek. At the last second, she turned so our lips met.

I closed my eyes instinctively and held my lips against hers, never wanting that union to end. It was like an incredible current of electricity flowed back and forth between us, and I could smell the freshness of her hair and light perfume again. It was a moment I would have drawn out forever had she not slowly pulled back.

"Bike safely, Teavan," she said with a wink, and her own cheeks flushed.

My first real kiss, and with Rachel Denning.

Not just some random girl at spin the bottle.

With a skip I hopped down the steps to her sidewalk in one leap and strode happily to my bike, breathing in the fresh night air; the sounds of crickets all around.

It was the best night I could remember in a long time.

Chapter 20

Well, up until that point it had been the best night ever. But then things went downhill faster than I would have thought possible.

As I meandered the streets on my bike toward the town center I wondered if I should tell the boys about the kiss. Or keep it between Rachel and me.

I was grinning from ear to ear; totally oblivious to my surroundings, when out of nowhere I got knocked off my bike from behind. I tumbled and fell as my front tire turned and crashed in the middle of the street.

My palms were scraped and bleeding from the pavement. I sat up, shook my head, and looked around. The night was quiet, and there was nothing nearby.

I knew my tire caught something, but I could swear I'd been pushed from behind, though I hadn't been paying attention.

"Hello?" I called out. "Anyone there?"

Crickets.

I stood and pulled my bike up, warily keeping an eye on the

dark shadows between the houses for any movement. There was rustling nearby, and I was hit from behind and knocked to the ground again before I could spin around.

Rolling over, I looked up to see Bruno Vincent standing under the streetlight with a fiendish, shadowed expression on his face.

He stood straight with his arms crossed as I came to my senses.

"Look who's out dropping his favorite girl off, how gentlemanly of you. Is that a New York thing?" he asked, circling me on the pavement.

I shook my head, wanting to buy some time to get my phone out. Maybe try to run. He could tell what I was thinking. "Don't bother, *Gimp*. You'll never outrun me."

That stung.

I stood up, noticing that my elbow was bleeding as well.

"M-my dad," I stuttered. "He's just over there, waiting for me."

Bruno shook his head. "Don't lie. I know he's out of town, and I saw Rachel's parents were at the community center. She's all alone. Why didn't you go inside? Do you think I should head over there after, maybe pay her a visit?"

He had been watching us. My fear turned to fury, my blood pressure skyrocketed, and my face went red from anger this time. "Don't say that," I warned him.

"Or what? Let's see. Sybil isn't here, and Jason Kemper isn't here. Who's going to defend you this time?"

I hoped Kevin and Jermaine would come riding to the rescue, but thought better of it. They were probably hunkered down at the park bench, hoping I was getting invited inside to hang with Rachel longer.

I lashed out. "Just what is your issue? I don't get it. I don't even know you. Why do you have it out for me? What *family history?*"

He smiled, slowly walking circles around me.

"So, you seriously don't know?" he asked suspiciously.

"No, Bruno. I *seriously* don't know."

He nodded as if he was thinking, if that were possible for such an ape. "Well, kid, I owe your family some . . . retribution as they say. Payback. You see, your grandpa killed my brother. And he tried to kill me."

I shook my head in disbelief. "No. That's not true. My grandpa wouldn't hurt a fly."

"Yeah, well, he did. He killed my brother in cold blood, and I saw it. Shot him. He came after me, but I escaped."

"But . . . but, why would he want to kill your brother?"

Bruno smiled. "Oh, who knows? He thought he knew everything, that guy. Said we had bad blood—tainted blood. That we were animals, and if we couldn't be trained we needed to be stopped."

"Animals?" I felt a shiver at the thought, my brain flashing back to the conversation with Mrs. Leclair. Almost not wanting him to answer it.

"Well, he called us a *lycanthropic mutation*. But I like to think of us as just plain old werewolves," he said with a wolfish grin.

My eyes were seeing stars; I fell to one knee, nearly losing consciousness. "Is this some kind of weird joke you have with Mrs. Leclair?"

His head twitched and tilted. "Mrs. Leclair? Why, what did she say to you?"

Rubbing my face, trying to see if I was dreaming, I said, "Well, she said *that*. She said that you and your brother were werewolves, and that my grandpa was involved in policing them. I wondered if it was some town joke."

"Oh, so you did know," he sneered.

"Yeah, but I thought she was nuts."

"Well, she is nuts. But she's right. Those two self-righteous pricks thought they could police everyone; they thought they could act as judge, jury, and executioner. Do you think it's right, Teavan, that when they thought my brother was bad they just had a right to kill him? He was only seventeen."

Thinking about that, I shook my head. It did seem wrong, no matter how bad someone might appear. They should have let the police deal with it.

"I guess not. They should have involved the cops," I answered. "But I don't know what he did."

"Well, yeah, I guess it gets a little gray since my dad is the sheriff and all. But either way, he made the decision that my brother—part of *my family*—had no right to live, and that his word was the law." With these last words, Bruno's voice cracked; he wiped his eye with his arm.

Standing again, I was breathing heavily, not sure where this was leading. "So, what can I do then to help make things right?" It seemed like our honest discussion was making some progress toward a resolution.

Bruno began to laugh. "What can *you* do? Well nothin'. It's more about what can I do. Hub Laurent took my brother away from me; he was my blood, my *best* friend. My dad, he's a hard man, but my mom is still busted up about it. She's always crying, looking at his school pictures. So unless you can bring him back to life, there's nothing you can do. Only what I can do."

"And what's that?"

"Make things equal. See that your family suffers as much as mine has," he said, eyeing me up. "I'm guessing, then, if this is all new to you, then you don't have the gift. Or the *curse*, as your grandpa would say."

Surprised, I asked, "Huh? Me? The curse of what?"

"Bein' a werewolf. Just like your grandfather was."

Chapter 21

"What? That's a joke."

"Believe it. I saw Hub change. Why do you think he felt he needed to police the 'tainted ones'?"

I shook my head. "I don't know. What about Mr. Leclair? Was he one?"

"No. But he was in the know. Those two were thick as thieves, runnin' round acting as executioners when they felt like it," he seethed. His fists were clenched and his was jawline tight; his body was quivering, sweat on his forehead glinted in the light. "Your grandpa was old, but he was strong, believe me. I tried to fight fair; I wanted to enjoy putting him down in our lupine form, but I couldn't do it. When we took out Mr. Leclair, he had a pistol with two silver bullets left. Your poor grandpa, he was crying like a baby when I held the gun to his head. He was on his knees, begging for his life."

"What?" I spun around. "You killed him?"

Bruno looked surprised. "Well, of course. That was the least I could do. He got off easy since I had to use a bullet," he said with a laugh. "I mean, I did change and enjoyed mauling him up after, but unfortunately the bullet is what did it."

Seeing only red through my teary eyes, I thought of that woman who once lifted a car off her child using the super strength of adrenaline. I could feel it coursing through my body, feeling like I could pick up a car. Like I could beat Bruno with ease.

I charged, my fists swinging. They connected to his shoulder and we wrestled to the ground, except he quickly got the upper hand and sat on my chest with my arms pinned down. "Now, that ain't no way to fight, kid. Is that what people do in the big city? Just start swinging when the other guy ain't lookin'?"

Struggling to get free, I twisted with everything I had, but his grip was like an iron clamp. And he was so heavy. The energy drained from my rigid body. He was smiling, leaning over me, our faces about twelve inches apart. He sniffled and horked a big gob of spit, then opened his mouth and let it drip, the thick mucus slowly stringing down and then dropping between my eyes.

I screamed out, "Get off!!"

Bruno jumped off as quick as a cat, stood back, and let me get up. "Okay kid, I can fight fair, unlike you. Now let's face off squarely, like men this time."

"I'm not going to fight you," I hissed at him, wiping the spit off my face.

Bruno was shaking, the muscles in his arms and neck corded and tense in the glow of the streetlight. Despite the brisk evening air, his shirt gleamed with sweat and his breathing was getting heavier. His eyes bored into mine, though they weren't quite focused. They turned black, the shaking got worse, and he gripped his chest in pain and howled. "No!!"

As I stood and watched, Bruno Vincent was changing. His arms were getting longer, and with each deep breath his chest expanded and didn't contract until his shirt began to rip at the seams. His face twisted and he snarled as he grabbed at it and fell to his knees, groaning.

I should have run, but I couldn't stop looking.

His body stopped shaking, and his breathing became more regular while his chest and arms slowly shrank back to normal. I was stunned, my eyes wide in terror as he finally looked back up, trying to catch his breath.

"You're lucky, kid, that was close," he said, then coughed. "Sometimes when I get upset, it just creeps up on me, and I can't control it, especially if the moon is near full. Once I've changed, I don't have much sense anymore."

I shook my head, back and forth, stuttering, "Th-that's impossible . . . this can't be true, this is just another bad dream."

Bruno fixed his shirt, looking at the stitching that had torn then up to me. "Unfortunately for you, it isn't just a fairytale. The boogeyman is real."

Something jarred my memory. "It was you, wasn't it?"

"Huh?"

"It was you, that day on the road—you chased me to the neighbor's."

Bruno smiled. "Yes. You realize I could have caught you, right?"

I shrugged, thinking back to the chase.

"I just wanted to scare you. Make life a little less relaxed for you," he said.

"Please, Bruno, I need to go," I pleaded, my lip quivering as I realized the extent of the situation. "I had nothing to do with whatever my grandfather did; we weren't even close, ask anyone."

"Well, you should hope you do have your grandpa's curse, 'cause otherwise your gimp leg will be the least of your problems. And when I'm done with you, I'm going to Rachel's to pay her a visit," he said, then winked at me.

Images of this monster creeping outside Rachel's door filled my head: her answering the door with a smile, thinking it was me, as he attacked her. Rage flooded me, and I flung myself at him once again, punching as hard as I could, deciding if I had to I would gouge his eyes out.

There was no honor here, only life and death.

Except Bruno was too strong. He was inhumanly strong for his size, and he kept laughing to induce more anger in me, blocking my punches and my hands as they reached for his eyes. He wrenched my right arm up behind my back. I screamed as red-hot pain flooded through my arm and into my shoulder. Then he pushed up even harder, and I heard and felt an internal *snap* as my arm broke.

It was unbearable, and I fell to the ground, limp. My right arm dangled, throbbing. My eyes were full of not only tears of anger, but tears of pain now.

"Whoops!" He laughed, then kicked me from a kneeling position to the ground. "That was for my mom."

I rolled over, trying to alleviate the agony, trying to get my arm at an angle to soften the pain. "Bruno . . . my arm. It's broken, I need a doctor," I cried and gnashed my teeth.

"My brother didn't get a doctor. And neither do you."

He leaned over and grabbed my collar with his left hand, then punched my face with his other. The warm, coppery taste of blood filled my mouth, and I did the best I could to curl up into a ball. My whole body was hurting, in more pain than I thought possible.

Only it wasn't over yet.

Bruno grabbed my left arm and dragged me off the street and over the sidewalk, into the darkness between two houses. He dropped me there, like a ragdoll. Faintly, I could see him grab my bike from the road, carry it over, and throw it farther into the darkness.

"You want some more?" he asked.

Shaking my head, I held up my good hand in defense. "Please, please, Bruno . . . no!"

He smiled. "Okay then, *Teavan*, let's shake on it." He reached out, pretending to shake my outstretched hand, only he grabbed it lightning fast and twisted it with a quick jerk.

More searing-hot pain spidered through my other shoulder, and I heard similar internal crunching sounds again as my left arm fell limply to the ground.

Bruno leaned over, holding my face roughly between his fingers and keeping me sitting up. "Don't worry, kid. I won't kill you. I want to enjoy this process, so that's all you get for now. I was kinda hoping it might spur something in you, but I guess not."

He let go, and my vision failed as my face dropped into the grass in the most unbelievable agony imaginable.

The last thing I heard before I blacked out was, "Oh, and Teavan, don't worry about Rachel. I'll say hi for you."

Chapter 22

I jolted awake from my spasming injuries. I tried to sit up in the dim shadows of the nearby homes, but both my arms were useless. Rolling left or right caused excruciating pain; I gave up and lay on my back, unable to catch my breath.

Something was wrong. Very wrong.

My stomach twisted in agony, like I had the worst stomach cramps imaginable. My whole body tightened, going rigid, and I could feel something like a black mass spreading from my stomach. Its tentacles reaching outward and filling up my body cavity like acidic syrup, burning towards each limb. My jaw was clenched so tight I couldn't scream, and I struggled to breathe through my teeth as my body convulsed.

I tried to concentrate on getting up, overcoming the pain, and warning Rachel. It gave me strength until another wave of burning rolled outward toward my extremities, and I prayed to be knocked out.

Only I remained conscious.

The mass was expanding, but it needed more room; it was pushing in every direction. My chest distended, my lungs couldn't get any air, and my ribs started to crack outward.

Please please please let me die.

My arms and legs felt like they were being ripped apart as the ligaments tore and broke, the bones stretching and cracking. The imagined black tentacles moved up into my neck, doing its damage, and into my lower jaw as it thrust forward and disconnected from my upper jaw.

It was finally too much, and my body gave out.

* * *

Minutes—or hours later—I awoke.

Everything was different.

The evening sounds were incredibly loud, like my ear buds were connected to microphones placed in each garden and tree in the area.

And the smells.

As I lay sideways in the grass and took in a deep breath, I could swear it had been freshly watered then cut just minutes ago. It was overwhelming.

Hunger. My stomach burned, but not with pain now, but with *need.* Ravenous hunger throttled me awake, and I opened my eyes, blades of grass an inch away as I lay on my side.

Things were not right, but I was feeling better. *Much* better.

The most delicious scent possible waffled past me. It was like the moment the lid was removed from a freshly cooked roast beef; when the humid aromas escaped the pan's enclosure and flooded your senses.

I needed to eat it. *Now.*

I jumped to my feet, and my legs instinctively carried me at lightning speed through the yards and bushes of the street. The scent of roast became more pungent with each step.

Only it was like I was being carried along for the ride; fast, and low to the ground. Willing myself to slow, I looked down and stumbled.

Two giant gray paws stood in the grass.

They moved as I willed them to.

Before I could register the shock, I was running again. My quarry was not far, and my body craved the nourishment it would provide. There was no choice, it was instinctual.

The roast turned out to be a brown rabbit, which I caught off guard and quickly took down under the umbrella of a pine tree. I tore at the fur and meat as it kicked and pulsed in my jaw, nothing had ever tasted so good. All other thoughts vanished to the back of my mind.

More. I needed more. Meat was all I could think of.

Time passed. Time that I do not recall. I was sleeping peacefully when the next thing I knew the sound of aggressive growling woke me, jostling my eyes open. I instinctively curled and prepared to be attacked.

My stomach churned, and I felt sick.

The floor under me was cold cement, and it was dark. The silhouette of a snarling, four-legged creature was visible in the large doorway.

Sitting up, I noticed I was sweating, though the room was chilly.

And I had no clothes.

What the—?

I pulled my knees up tight, and the animal slowed its growl, sniffing and coming closer. Panicking at the thought that it was the wolf, I felt around in the dark for something to use as a weapon; I felt so open and defenseless in this room, sitting naked on the cement.

My hand wrapped around the metal base of a spade, and I carefully dragged it over and held it up—ready.

Chapter 23

The animal inched closer, then started to whine.

"Honey?" I whispered, recognizing her sounds.

She came over tentatively, sniffing; and then as she realized it was me, she jumped and started to lick my face, neck, and chest. No doubt she loved the salty sweat on my skin.

Everything was a blur, but ever so slowly it came back to me: Bruno. The beating. The pain. Then eating, then . . . here?

Rachel.

Standing up and looking around in the dark, I realized I was in our garage. I grabbed a dirty rag hanging off the workbench and did my best to wrap it around my waist, then walked barefoot to the big open door.

It was still dark out, but there was a faint glow on the eastern horizon; it was nearing dawn. Where were my clothes? How did I get here?

I walked, awkwardly and in some pain, to the house. My whole body was sore, my arms included, but they seemed fine other than a dull ache. It felt as if I'd had a first-time workout with a military instructor for six hours the day before.

Honey ran beside me, jumping around and whining.

"It's okay, girl." I patted her.

The lights in the house were on.

Suzanne was sitting on the front room couch, looking distraught, staring down at her phone. Why was she still up?

Honey and I walked up the steps and opened the front door.

Suzanne shrieked when she saw me, and ran over and gave me the biggest, deepest hug ever. I held my rag with one hand and sorta tried to hug her with the other arm.

Grabbing my shoulders, she pushed me back at arm's length and stared at me.

"Where were you? What happened, Teavan? Where are your clothes?" she asked.

I wasn't entirely sure myself. "I don't know. I was . . . in the garage, sleeping on the floor."

"And how did you get there? When?"

Racking my brain, I tried to remember.

"Bruno. Rachel!" I cried out, still foggy. "Is she okay?"

A dark look crept over Suzanne's face. "What do you know?"

I shook my head. "Nothing. I saw Bruno, and he beat me up, real bad. Said he was going to her house after. That he was going to hurt her."

Suzanne stood back, both her hands pushing the hair off her face. "Rachel is in the hospital. I thought you were hurt, too. Kevin and Jermaine couldn't find you, so they went to her house. They found her on the front lawn—bleeding, torn up, and unconscious. I . . . I thought you were dead. They found your bike and clothes scattered a few blocks away. And your shirt was ripped and bloody."

Suzanne's eyes welled up as she told me this, tears escaping from each eye, and she sat on the ottoman. For the first time since I could remember, she broke down in sobs of sadness, not anger. I walked over to her, even though I wanted to get some clothes on, and rubbed her back.

"I'm fine, Suze. Really. I'm sorry I didn't call, my phone is missing. I'm . . . honestly, I don't know what happened."

She shook her head. "Your phone—it's broken and still in the pocket of your mangled jeans."

"How is Rachel now?"

"Not good. She's at the hospital, in surgery. The police are looking for you. We'd better call."

Though I felt anxious at the thought, I nodded. "Okay."

She kept looking at me, shaking her head. "Did you do meth or something tonight?"

"What?" The worst I'd ever done was drink a third of a beer, and that was only a week ago. "No, of course not."

She looked wary, almost nervous. "I just don't understand why you undressed after you dropped her off, left your bike, and walked home. And why were your clothes bloody? Did you fall off your bike?" She stepped back again, holding her phone. "And you are filthy. And you ... smell bad. Anyway, I need to call the sheriff; I promised I would."

As Suzanne made the call, I went to the bathroom and looked at myself in the mirror. There were no cuts, bruises, or . . . anything. My body was sore, but considering what Bruno did, I seemed fine. My usually skinny, pale chest even looked a bit muscular. Raising my arms and making circles, I was amazed they weren't broken. Nothing made sense.

I had a quick shower. The water ran light brown from the dirt in my hair and skin. I put on some jeans and a clean shirt, and brushed my teeth—they felt so gross. In the family room, Suzanne told me the sheriff was on his way over.

"And what's with your jeans?" she asked, looking down.

I looked down, seeing no stains. "What?"

"They look too short, especially your right leg." My right leg was the shorter leg, and I always had it hemmed an inch more than the left.

"I dunno," I said, then realized something. "But Suze, the sheriff is Bruno's dad! What do I say?"

"Teavan, tell him the truth. This is serious."

His beating was all I could think of. And then . . . the vision of something happening to him, *changing*, also came back. His chest. His arms. Mrs. Leclair's warnings.

"Suze, there's more to this . . . "

At that moment, red-and-blue lights flashed outside, and she walked to the front window to look out. "He's here."

Sheriff Vincent was a lot nicer than I'd imagined. He was nothing like Bruno. He came in with a smile but looked exhausted. He took his hat off and sat down. He questioned me about the whole night, up until I left Rachel's place.

"And then you ran into Bruno?"

"Well, yeah, you could say that. But it was more like he ran into me," I corrected.

Sheriff Vincent sighed. "He informed me you two had your differences."

Differences? That was putting it mildly. I explained the beating he gave me, leaving out the real or imagined part of him transforming.

He looked at his notepad. "So you're saying he attacked you, broke both your arms and beat your face repeatedly with his fists, kicked your ribs, and then dragged you off in the dark. Is that correct?"

I nodded. "Yes, sir. Then he said he was going after Rachel."

He stared at me. "Teavan, would you mind lifting your shirt please?"

I stood and pulled my shirt up, trying to look down at my belly button.

"Well, that's very odd. You don't have a scratch on you, and yet this all happened just seven hours ago. And then you undressed, left your phone, and ran home. Please try to see this from my point of view, son. Have you been taking any illicit substances?"

"No! I've never done any drugs, I swear."

He nodded. "Nothing seems to fit here. Can you see how your story doesn't add up?"

Looking around, I had to admit even I couldn't answer as to what had happened. I could have sworn my arms were broken. And my face should have been covered in bruises. And . . .

"Listen, Mr. and Mrs. Denning are with Rachel now at the hospital. We will know more when we speak to her. If my son had anything to do with this, I can assure you there will be no leniency. At this point, we—myself included—believe she was attacked by a dog, possibly a pit bull. She might have heard noises outside, maybe something was getting into the garbage and she startled it."

Suzanne leaned forward, trying to cut me off as I began to complain. "Thank you, Sheriff. Please let us know how she is if you hear any updates."

He put his hat back on and walked over to the front door. "This has been an awfully long night; I am exhausted. I see no evidence of any foul play on your part—yet—but maybe some poor decisions have been made that I *hope* you will not make in the future."

Nodding, Suzanne replied, "Thank you, Sheriff."

"Night," he said, walking out and letting the screen door shut behind him.

Suzanne glowered at me in frustration. "You sound like you *are* on drugs. I'm going to bed, and you should as well. I sent Jermaine and Kevin texts that you are okay; they both went home when we couldn't find you. We'll finish this in the morning."

Reluctantly, I nodded and headed toward my room, Honey wagging her tail behind me. My body ached and I was dead tired.

Sleep came quickly; my dreams were strange, fast-paced, and almost feral.

Chapter 24

Suzanne just stared at me when I shuffled into the kitchen at almost two in the afternoon on Saturday. My sleep was much-needed; I never moved until I woke and looked at the clock.

"I've called off the party, and you ruined my night last night. You owe me *big time*, you know," she growled, sipping a coffee.

As best I could, I finished the story from the night before. About the change in Bruno, and then . . . the weird memories I had. And the rabbit. Did that even happen?

"That sounds like dreams. Drug-induced dreams."

While recounting the events, I managed to eat three bananas and four bowls of cereal. By the fourth bowl, even Suzanne commented. *"Four?"*

"I'm starving." I shrugged. "Listen, Suze, I'm begging you, come to Mrs. Leclair's. I need to talk to her. And I need to get my bike, wherever it is, and my clothes. I don't think she's crazy after all."

Suzanne pursed her lips, staring at me, but also hearing the honest desperation in my voice. "Fine, I'll go. Thanks to you, my plans are canceled, anyway. And your bike is out front; the sheriff dropped it off last night. He has your clothing as well, but he's keeping it for now."

"Why?"

"I'm not sure . . . maybe they're testing the blood to see if it matches Rachel's. I mean, I wouldn't blame them," she said.

They think I did it?

We got dressed, and Suzanne kept giving me weird looks as we got ready to go.

"What?" I asked.

"You're walking funny," she said.

"Gee, thanks, I hadn't noticed," I said, feeling the general soreness in my legs.

She shook her head. "No, not that. Like, you're walking differently, taller maybe. And those jeans are too short."

My shirt felt tighter, too. The oversized breakfast was taking its toll.

Mrs. Leclair was sitting out on the porch as we pulled up and laid our bikes in the grass.

"I was wondering if you would be by. I heard there was some trouble last night," she said, standing up from the rocking chair as we approached her steps.

"Can we talk?" I asked.

"Of course," she answered.

We sat outside, and I recounted the night's events, mostly about Bruno and Rachel.

She listened intently. "And you think you saw him . . . transform?"

I nodded. "Yeah. Something happened, something *not natural*. But then it was like he was fighting to not change, and it reversed."

"And he hurt you badly?" Her eyebrow arched up.

"Yeah, but . . . then things got fuzzy. I just, ah, woke up back at home in the garage. My wounds were gone," I answered quietly.

"Any strange dreams about how you got home? Memories?" she asked.

"Sorta . . ."

Reluctantly, I told her about the memories of the searing-hot pain, running outside, and the rabbit, and then Suzanne added that I'd shed my clothes and ran home naked. I flushed, looking down in embarrassment at that part.

Mrs. Leclair was quiet, just rocking back and forth. She looked out in the distance, seemingly lost in thought. Finally she said, "This has become much more complicated, I'm afraid. I hoped it wouldn't come to this."

We waited for her to continue.

She looked at us both and cocked her head as if coming to a decision. "You see, there were two groups of lycanthropes for many years, maybe thousands of years. We *think* they originated in Italy, though nobody knows how or why; though there are lots of legends, of course. Over the years they migrated up into France, and the French and Italian factions self-governed, so to speak, keeping themselves in check, especially after they became hunted. Slowly, things got sorted out, and the legend of the werewolf remained just that—a legend.

"However, a little over two hundred years ago, another

faction broke off. There was a young girl; her name was Sabine Martin. She was the youngest daughter of a prominent lycan family in France. However, at the age of seventeen, Sabine fell in love with a human boy and got pregnant. Pregnancy before marriage at the time was bad enough, especially for an illustrious family. Mixing blood with a non-lycanthrope was unfathomable.

"She decided to run away, electing to keep the baby and leave France. She secretly booked passage to England and snuck out of the country. She lived there for a few years, then eventually made her way to America. Lower Louisiana, to be precise. She married a Frenchman in New Orleans, and they had more children together. They were able to live in peace and yet still keep up their French heritage to an extent. And continue the diluted lycan bloodlines.

"That is where the Vincent family originates, at some point, anyway. A bit of a mutt lycanthrope you might say, of mixed and weaker blood, according to the French. Unlike your grandfather, Hubert, who was of pure French lycan blood," she said, looking at us both expectantly.

"And?" I asked.

Suzanne leaned forward, understanding something that I had missed. "Wait. You're not saying . . . ?"

Mrs. Leclair nodded. "I am saying that, Suzanne. Your grandfather was also one. A stronger, more pure lycan; but he was getting old. He was determined to snuff out the rule breakers so the rest could live in peace. He hoped the bloodlines would adulterate and that the genetic mutation would eventually dissolve itself out of existence."

Bruno's comments came to me. He hadn't been lying. "So, it's true?"

"Yes, Teavan."

"Are you sure?" I asked.

She stood up. "Come, both of you, please. I want to show you something."

Following her into the house, we made our way into the basement, and she led us to the wine cellar. The massive door must have been three inches thick. As she pulled it open, its iron hinges creaked.

She flicked on the light inside, illuminating a small, stone room about ten feet by ten feet. No furniture, just empty.

"Yeah? The wine cellar?" I asked.

"No, I'm sorry. I lied about that, Teavan. This was a secure room you grandfather helped build. On some full moons, when he knew he couldn't resist, he would come here before dark. We would lock him in there until morning. The walls and door were too strong for him to break through. It was his idea."

The weight of what she was telling me was sinking in. "If Grandpa was a werewolf . . . what about my dad? What about me?"

Chapter 25

"As far as Hubert knew, your father doesn't know anything about it."

"But, is he . . . ?" I asked.

"No, it often skips generations or vanishes completely," she answered.

"What if you get bitten by a werewolf? Do you become one, too?" I asked.

She smiled and shook her head. "No, that's just a silly legend. It's a recessive gene. You either have it or you don't. The saliva from a lycan will only give you a nasty infection if the bite doesn't kill you."

Then another realization swept over me as the term *skips a generation* replayed itself. "Wait. Am . . . I?"

Mrs. Leclair stood there with her eyes narrowed and a look of sadness in them. "Maybe. It does sound like it; all the signs are there, I'm afraid. For everyone, it reveals itself at different times during adolescence, sometimes even as late as twenty years old. Usually, it just manifests one night on a full moon. Traditionally, the parents would know to be on the watch for it. And if it does manifest, the lycan was brought into the inner circle. But as lycans have spread geographically further apart, the gene has weakened or vanished. It came as no surprise to Hubert that your father showed no symptoms. It was his plan, so it was more of a relief."

"Was there a full moon yesterday?" I asked.

"No, though it's not far off. Your gene seems to have manifested out of necessity, a sort of self-preservation. Your body went through great physical and emotional stress, and it needed to heal. It was your time," she said.

Flashbacks of the paws, the running, the smells, the sounds. *The eating*. It felt like a dream, but I knew she was right. My stomach churned uncomfortably.

"Did it somehow . . . heal my arms? My bruises?"

She nodded. "A lycanthrope can heal from *almost* anything—remarkably quickly—and your body did just that. Bones break, mend, and re-grow stronger. Bigger. Your muscle would also have grown. Sometimes even diseases disappear, like diabetes and other such afflictions the youth can suffer from. In some ways, it can be a blessing. But in most, I'm afraid it's a curse."

Mrs. Leclair sighed. "Even in his human form, Bruno will be growing stronger and faster, with heightened senses. You will, too. But similar to Bruno, you will be slower in your abilities than your grandfather because of your mother's non-lycan genes."

Suzanne looked at me up and down. "Teavan, you *are* different now. You stand taller; you seem bigger."

I thought back to the mirror in the bathroom, and my jeans and shirt being too small.

"The transformation requires a lot of energy; you will find yourself hungry after changing to or from your lycan state. And on a full moon, you will likely have no control. This will need to be watched, Teavan. You could hurt someone very badly, if not worse."

Quietly, I thought over all that she said. All that it implied. It was kind of exciting in some ways, and extremely scary in others. I tried to will myself awake, end this strange dream. It couldn't be real.

"If I'm a werewolf, as were my grandfather, Bruno, and his dead brother. Then how many are there? Is this town full of them?"

She shook her head. "Heavens no, thank the stars. It's just you and him. He's after you because of who you are. This is no accident."

"So, Bruno," I said. "He started to change, and it wasn't a full moon?"

"He was upset, excited. It can happen when you want it to, once you have control. Most still have trouble stopping it on full moons, though it gets easier with age or more direct bloodlines. The responsible ones always have a safe room they have access to," she said.

Suzanne sat down on the basement steps and thrust her hands in her hair. "This is crazy. Totally crazy."

Mrs. Leclair strode over with a severe look in her eye. "Teavan, was it you last night? Were you the one that attacked the Denning girl?"

I could feel the blood rushing to my head. "Me? No! I would remember that. I *wouldn't* do that. It was Bruno, he said he was going there. He did it, I swear."

"And yet . . ." Suzanne interrupted.

"Yet what?" I snapped, looking at her.

She shrugged, avoiding eye contact. "And yet you saw her last, don't remember anything, may have changed into a wolf, and had blood all over you. That's what."

Her accusation stung. "You think it was me, don't you?"

"I don't think you would ever do something like that on purpose. Consciously, I mean."

Heat spread into my face and neck. "But why—?"

"Settle down," Mrs. Leclair said, holding her hand between us. "Was the blood on your clothes? Or just on your body?"

"Both," Suzanne answered.

Mrs. Leclair smiled. "If you had attacked her in your canine form, there wouldn't be any blood on your discarded clothes now would there? You would have changed first."

It was my turn to grin, and I spun around back to Suzanne. "Exactly!"

She shrugged. "Maybe; that does make sense. Trust me, I hope so, this isn't something I'm hoping to be right on."

"Well, I believe you, Teavan," Mrs. Leclair said. "But this all goes back to what we discussed last time. Bruno needs to be stopped, and I can't do it."

Suzanne was thinking, and she spoke up. "What if we just film him, you know, and show the police?"

"His father is the police here," she answered.

"Well, another police department. Any town, I don't know," Suzanne suggested.

"If you happen to show the wrong people, Suzanne, bad things happen. As you can imagine, a great many people have far more invested in this never coming to light, than for you to prove something about a local bully. Even if you could get it on film, these things tend to get sorted out . . . internally," Mrs. Leclair warned.

"We have suspected presidents, some of the best athletes, CEOs. You name it, they have often been either full lycanthropes or partial ones. They're faster, more alert, and have heightened senses. Why do you think some of the world's best winemakers are in France and Italy? Or chefs? The superior smell and taste genes go a long way. These people tend to excel; the last thing they want is for anything like this to ever come to light.

"I'm afraid," Mrs. Leclair continued, as she picked up a box on the table in the back corner where her husband had melted silver, "there is only one viable solution. Trust me, I've been thinking about and testing this for thirty years. He's bad, and he'll get worse. More brazen."

This time her suggestion didn't seem so crazy.

"And he has it out for you, maybe all three of you. You heard what he did to that poor Denning girl, and she has nothing to do with this. And like your father, his father is not in the inner circle; it's not like we can appeal to him for help. Bruno is coming for you. You'd best strike first."

Chapter 26

We left Mrs. Leclair's and agreed to be in touch later in the week. There was a full moon on Thursday, and she pleaded for me to spend the night locked up in her basement for it. Suzanne let out a nervous laugh as we left and said we would think about it.

Someone was sitting on the front porch as we pulled up to my house.

Sybil.

"Hey," I called, leaning my bike against the side of the garage.

She came over with her fists clenched at her sides, face twisted.

"Why aren't you calling or texting me back?" she snapped.

I was confused at her hostility; she was on my list to call after our visit with Mrs. Leclair. Honey was barking excitedly from inside the house, wanting to be let out.

"My phone—it's busted."

"Yeah, right. Or you just don't want to talk about last night. About what you did."

I held my hands up. "Wait. First, how is Rachel? Suzanne called the hospital, but they won't tell us anything since we aren't family."

Sybil shook her head. "Well, she's not dead, if that's what you're asking. Eighteen stitches, a few broken bones, and she's unresponsive. So we don't yet know what happened to her. Or *who*."

She was red-faced and glaring, completely ignoring Suzanne who stood silently next to me.

"Sybil, can you chill for a minute? You are next on my list to call, but my phone is toast, and you can't even begin to believe what I've been through over the last twenty hours. Please, come inside and listen for a minute?" I pleaded.

She laughed. "What *you* have been through? Rachel is in the hospital, and you think you have been through a lot? Are you kidding me?"

Suzanne stood forward. "I understand your anger, but just hear him out. Please?"

Sybil looked back and forth between Suzanne and me.

"Fine."

We went inside and sat down. Honey was jumping excitedly and licking everyone. Suzanne and I explained the whole story.

Everything.

Sybil remained quiet the entire time, but it felt like she was just waiting until the end of the story so she could pounce and take me by the throat.

But instead she shook her head. "No clothing at all?"

"Nada," Suzanne answered.

"I mean, I knew you were weird, but this takes the cake.

But I didn't see you doing any drugs last night," she said with a laugh, eyeing me warily.

Sybil stood. "Teavan, stand up."

As I got up, she stepped uncomfortably close, looking me in the eye, her warm breath in my face. "That's odd. You are taller, now that you mention it."

I pointed to my hiked up jeans. "See? It's true."

"Well, that doesn't mean anything; you are a terrible dresser to begin with," she said.

Suzanne let out a laugh as she filled our waters.

"Gee, thanks," I answered, turning red again.

Sybil sat down at the corner of the table, and lifted her right arm on top. "Come on," she said, wiggling her hand.

"You want to arm wrestle me?" I asked, looking at her.

She nodded. "Show me, Mr. Werewolf."

"Well, if that part about me is even true, I'm, like, not transformed right now."

"But the old lady said that Bruno was stronger even when normal, right?" she asked.

Sybil had a point.

My right arm met hers from across the table, and we clasped our hands together.

"Yuck," she said, shaking her head. "You are all sweaty."

Shrugging, I said, "Sorry, it's hot in here."

She shook her head. "Not really, but whatever. Ready? Go!"

Immediately she thrust with everything she seemed to have, almost wanting to break my arm. Taking out her frustrations. Her face grimaced, her teeth clenched, and her freckles almost disappeared into the redness.

Had I not known Sybil better, I would have thought she was playing a trick on me. Pretending to try as hard as she could, but actually exerting nothing.

Except she was.

She looked me in the eye, and growled through her clenched teeth. "Finish it!"

Slowly and with more ease than I thought possible, I lowered her arm until the back of her hand touched the table top.

She jumped up from her chair, stretching out her arm and fingers, shaking her head in disbelief. "That's impossible. You . . . you are a weakling? How . . . ?"

Suzanne took her place immediately. "Let me try."

She was a little stronger than Sybil, but not much. I was victorious even sooner this time, not wanting to drag it out. Suzanne also got up and stretched her arm. "Damn. That is weird."

The ease with which I beat them both reiterated the fear inside that this was all true. But at the same time, I kinda felt giddy at this newfound strength. I kept that part quiet.

"So, now what? So you are a lot stronger than you look. Can you somehow prove more?" Sybil asked.

Shrugging, I said, "I don't know how it works. When I changed . . . it just kinda happened. Out of necessity, said Mrs. Leclair. But she said on Thursday a full moon is coming, and I need to barricade myself in her basement safe room."

"And what about Bruno?" Sybil asked.

"Bruno? I don't know; I'm not calling him to join me."

Sybil shook her head angrily. "No, you idiot. I mean, will he also change on Thursday?"

Suzanne spoke, "According to Mrs. Leclair he should; seems like he's way too young to control it."

Sybil stood and started pacing, seeming to formulate a plan. "Well, maybe someone stays with you at the Leclair place to keep an eye on you and see if anything even happens. And someone else goes to the Vincent home, with their phone, for pictures and video. I volunteer."

Staring at the floor, I thought about Mrs. Leclair and her warnings about bringing this information public. But the alternative was impossible, too. This was the only way.

"You can't go alone, Sybil," I said, looking up. "You need help. And what if he . . . turns on you? Sees you? How will you even know where to find him?"

"I think I know where he'll be. The Vincents have a guest cottage near their house, like a treehouse without the tree. Bruno and Grayson spent their summers sleeping in it. I imagine he still does. He'll be in there."

"And what if you need help?" I asked.

Sybil looked at Suzanne. "You should stay with Teavan at Mrs. Leclair's. It's gonna have to be Tweedledee and Tweedledum."

They had been my first and only thought, too. I didn't want any more people a part of this, but at the same time, we needed help. "Okay. Let's meet them tomorrow and tell them everything. We will have to work out how we all get out for the night, like some kind of mass sleepover at each other's houses."

"But where? Where do we actually sleep?" Suzanne asked.

It was quiet as we considered each alternative; explaining to our parents that we were sleeping at other kids' houses. And somewhere we could arrive—late. There was only one option.

"Mrs. Leclair's," I said.

At that moment, there was howling in the far distance outside. Honey jumped up from under the table and ran to the front window, putting her paws up on the sill and looking around as the hair on her neck bristled.

"You better call your dad for a ride home, Sybil. It's getting dark," I said.

Sybil went to the front window and looked out at the darkness falling to the horizon. There was another howl, and Honey's ears went down, flat to her head, and she growled.

"Maybe just this once," she said with a quiver in her voice, sliding her phone out from her back pocket.

* * *

Both Suzanne and I called the hospital again on Sunday, but they wouldn't give us any updates on how Rachel was doing. It was killing me.

As we waited for the guys to come over, I closed the door to my bedroom and decided to do something I had never done.

I got down on my knees and leaned against my bed with my hands together, and closed my eyes.

Dear God. I don't know how to do this, as you probably know. But I am praying for someone. Rachel. She's hurt, real bad, and I pray to you to help her recover. I promise if she does, I'll be a better guy. A better person. Just let her be okay. Please.

Amen.

Remaining there for a few minutes, I repeated my awkward

prayer a couple of times, not knowing if I was doing it right. Or if there was anyone even listening. But Rachel believed and she needed this. I decided to pray every day until she woke up.

When Kevin and Jermaine arrived, we told them what happened. They weren't nearly as skeptical as I would have been had I not witnessed things firsthand.

"I told you, man, weird things happen here," Jermaine said.

Sybil had been with Rachel all morning at the hospital—no change. When she got to my place, we all walked over to Mrs. Leclair's place to get her advice for Thursday, to show the guys the safe room, and to ask if everyone could stay over.

Mrs. Leclair lifted a hand to her face and shook her head. "Oh dear. Why have you gone and spread this? It was only for your ears; it was just you two implicated in this. Few outsiders know. You three are now at risk just knowing."

"I'll take my chances," Sybil answered.

I shrugged. "I'm sorry, Mrs. Leclair. We decided we can't kill him, that we *need* proof instead. And I can't be the one to get it, since on Thursday . . . you know. And it was Sybil's cousin that was hurt, so she *is* in on it."

Mrs. Leclair put her hands on her hips, surveying each of our faces as we stood outside on her porch. "What will you do? Simply waltz up to his house, get a video of him changing, then walk away? You think he won't see you? Smell you? You'll never make it out; this is much too dangerous."

We told her about the guest house and how he would probably be in there. It seemed to take forever for me to change, so they would only need a minute or two of video and be long gone before he was done transforming.

Mrs. Leclair sat down carefully on her rocking chair,

steadying herself as she did. "It goes faster with time, I'm afraid. The more often you change, the quicker it happens. You won't have twenty minutes."

"Okay, fine, we take, like, thirty seconds of video, run back to our bikes, and arrive here before he even knows what happened," Sybil suggested.

"And what if the transformation is faster?" Mrs. Leclair asked, looking up.

Everyone was quiet; someone's feet shuffled nervously.

"I will allow you to stay here on one condition: if he comes close, you shoot him and end this. There are still three silver bullets left downstairs. Do any of you know how to use a pistol?" she asked.

Sybil nodded. "I do, and it's a deal. *If* he attacks us, I will warn him, and if that doesn't work, I will take care of him."

A mixture of worry and relief crossed Mrs. Leclair's face. "Yes, but what I'm afraid of is you trying to warn him. There might not be time. Don't hesitate, child. Just do it."

Chapter 27

Sleep was difficult those next few nights, and I continued my nightly prayers for Rachel. I dreamt of her each night, hopeful each morning she would wake up.

Dressing for school was frustrating, to say the least. My shirts were tight, and my jeans were worse—shorts were the only option. I had to wear flip flops until I could convince my dad for money to buy new shoes, even though it was against school rules.

There was an excitement among the group of us. Sybil was quiet, but that was normal. There was no update on Rachel, and Sybil checked her phone constantly during class. Given the situation, the teachers let it slide. Despite my protests of innocence, Sybil said the family still didn't want me to visit Rachel. How could they think I was capable of hurting her? She was all I thought of lately. Well, her and my *situation*.

Even more whispers seemed to surround me those next few days than when I'd first started school here. I heard the words *Rachel*, *drugs*, *New York*, *bad kid*, and other things like that. They whispered so quietly I shouldn't have heard anything—but I did.

And the smells.

Just talking to people, I could almost taste what they had for dinner the night before. I could detect fish sauce and rice vinegar around Kevin. Jermaine's was more straightforward—burgers.

The cafeteria was at first difficult to sit in, the smells in there were overwhelming. Especially the East Indian foods that were warmed up. Where once I thought Indian food all smelled the same, I could now discern layers of different spice scents all comingled together. I wanted so badly to walk around and sample everything, but I stuck to my sandwiches that now seemed like such a bore. I wanted steak or chicken. Or lamb.

"Hello? Teavan?" Kevin waved his hand in front of me; I was lost in thought about food as we finished our lunch.

"Huh? What?" I shook out of it.

He laughed. "Bro, you are zoned out. I asked how you feel? Jermaine was just saying how you walk differently. Bigger strides, like you're more confident today. Do you feel more confident?"

I hadn't heard anything they were talking about, but as I considered his comment, I did feel different. Not necessarily confident, but like I just didn't care as much? More goal-focused, like on getting to class quickly rather than trying to stay on the periphery of people's sight.

"Maybe?" I answered.

Kevin checked his phone. "We gotta go, boys. Gym starts in seven minutes."

Traditionally, gym class was a favorite of most guys my age. To skip lectures, if nothing else. For me, it was anything but enjoyable. Hobbling, tripping, and limping my way as best I could was the norm.

This day was different.

"Mr. Laurent. Is there a reason why you are wearing *flip-flops* to my Phys Ed class?" Mr. Bigley asked as we lined up in the gym after changing.

"Sir, my shoes. They don't fit; this is all I have," I answered as everyone laughed and stared at my feet.

He rolled his eyes. "Fine; you are excused from participating. You don't need to wear sandals in the future to be excused."

The class filed outside for a warm-up run and then a lacrosse scrimmage. I caught up to the teacher and tapped his shoulder. "Mr. Bigley? Can I still play today? My sandals are fine."

He raised an eyebrow. "Wait. This time you *want* to play?"

Shrugging, I held up my foot and answered, "I'm feeling better today."

"Suit yourself," he answered. "Just don't roll your ankle: those aren't proper gym shoes."

Even with flip-flops on, after a slow and awkward start, I was able to figure my stride and catch up to the leaders as we completed two laps around the outdoor field to warm up. I'd never jogged that fast or that smoothly in my life. Even with expensive prosthetic shoes.

And I could have gone faster. I smiled to myself, holding to a non-official third place at the finish.

Lacrosse went even better.

Trying moderately hard, but not my hardest, I was probably the best player in terms of raw physical skill on the field. Everyone noticed, and lots of people commented to me, especially from my team.

Joel got more and more physical as the game went on, frustrated by my newfound speed and skill. My flashy goals against his team probably hadn't helped the situation as I taunted him for failing to stop me from shooting.

Every time I got near him—if the teacher wasn't close—he cross-checked me. I was caught off-guard the first time and stumbled, but came to expect it after that.

With a minute left in the scrimmage and the score tied, Simon threw me the ball as I neared the opposing team's goalie, preparing to shoot. As I wound up, it was as if everything shifted to slow motion.

As I looked to the upper left corner of the net, the goalie unconsciously moved there to stop the shot. But then his focus shifted behind me with a slight look of alarm. The hair on my neck stood, and I instinctively braced my legs and bent forward, holding my lacrosse stick in hand with the ball firmly in its netting.

From behind, a body slammed into me. It was Joel, and he clearly hadn't expected me to bend over at the last second. His aimed cross-check at my shoulders missed, and his momentum carried him over my back and sent him sprawling to the ground.

The goalie looked down at Joel in surprise as I stood up straight and whipped the ball into the lower right corner of the goal.

There was no chance he could have saved it.

My team cheered from behind and the tie was broken.

Looking at Joel, who was staring up at me, I winked and said, "Nice try."

He glowered at me, wiping the dirt from his bloody elbow.

I probably should have been more humble about the game, but it was the first time I'd ever been the hero in *any* sporting event.

My smile was impossible to contain as Mr. Bigley blew his whistle and my team patted me on the back with lots of "Great shot" comments as we headed inside.

As we shuffled to the changing room, I wished Rachel had been there to see me, but then felt guilty for being so shallow as she lay unconscious in a hospital bed.

Wednesday came with no improvement in Rachel. Her body was healing, but she was still in a coma-like state and unresponsive. The doctors seemed very hopeful, however.

As Thursday night loomed closer, our group's anxiety hit new highs. Each of us had arranged to sleep at another's house, hoping none of our parents would question the others. At our age and on a Thursday, we weren't too concerned.

As I emptied books from my backpack into my locker after school Wednesday, a shadow appeared at my feet; someone was behind me. A sick feeling crept over me.

"Hey, *Gimp*."

I turned around. Mike Thompson was standing there with a fake smile on his pimply face. Though we now were almost the same height after my little growth spurt, he still probably had twenty pounds on me.

"Screw off," I said, turning back to my locker.

"I got a message for you, Gimp. Bruno is out front, wants a

friendly chat," he said.

Kids started to gather around, a semi-circle forming. I could almost hear the smile in his voice.

Pretending to be interested in my locker contents, I ignored him.

The instinct to move alerted me just a split-second too late as he shoved me against the open locker frame. My head hit the side of it with a thud.

"I'm talking to you, boy!" he snarled from behind.

Within an instant, rage and an adrenaline rush swept over me. Before he could say anything else, I spun around and grabbed his shirt at the chest with both hands, catching him completely off guard. I violently pushed him backward to the opposite wall of lockers, and his body and head slammed into the metal doors with a clang that echoed in the corridor.

Mike's face turned from astonishment and surprise to anguish as the crash reverberated through his body and up into his skull. He tried to slump down, but I held him hard against the bent lockers, not allowing him to fall.

"Call me *gimp*, one more time!" I screamed in his face, spittle flying from my mouth.

His eyes were rolling around involuntarily, but he raised his arms, trying to pull free of my grip. As his weak hands yanked at my wrists, I turned and flung him across the tiled floor.

He stumbled, fell, and then rolled before coming to a stop ten feet away.

My rage was only beginning. He tried to curl up as I stomped toward him.

"Yeah? Where's the tough guy, now?" I yelled, my fists up, hoping for him to stand and hit me.

A hand grabbed my shoulder. Just as I spun around to crank whoever it was, I detected the unique smell of Sybil's shampoo and stopped my fist instinctively just inches from her wincing face.

She opened her eyes cautiously and glared at my retreating fist. "Teavan, stop!" she hissed. "You need to leave. Come on," she ordered me as I tried to control my urge to turn around and finish Mike.

Just as she grabbed my bag from the floor, everyone scattered. Mrs. Pringle, our geography teacher, stepped into the hall.

"What is going on out here?" she asked, looking around, then seeing Mike on the ground. "What happened?"

Sybil tried to pull me away, but I resisted, and pointed down at Mike. "That guy is from Baker, here causing trouble. I think he must have tripped."

The teacher looked around, confused, but nobody said anything, including Mike, who tried to stand, rubbing the back of his head. "I was just leaving," he grumbled and avoided eye contact.

Mrs. Pringle walked him to the front of the school, and we all followed. Everyone was talking and whispering, while Sybil pleaded with me to go the other way. Jermaine and Kevin were quiet. Across the street, Bruno and Jed sat on the grass beside the parked Jeep, safely off school property. Mike hobbled over to them.

Mrs. Pringle shouted across the road, "You kids go home, or I'll call your principal and get him involved. You have no business here unless you have a game. Now go."

Bruno raised his hands in mock defeat. "We're going, we're going. We don't want no trouble." Then he looked at me with a smirk.

"I wondered, Laurent, when I heard I supposedly beat you up but you had no bruises. I guess everyone was right: you must be on drugs!" he shouted. Everyone looked at me for a response.

But Mrs. Pringle raised her mobile phone, holding it out like she was about to make a call.

Bruno and the guys jumped in the Jeep. "All good, teacher. We were just leaving. I got the information I needed."

Chapter 28

"You think it was a test?" Sybil asked Jermaine as we walked our bikes toward her house after. We thought it best we see her home safely.

Jermaine bit his lower lip. "I dunno. It was just weird, you know? Like, why would Thompson come to the school and egg Teavan on to start something? It's like Bruno sent him in to see. And, I mean, if he *did* bruise you up on Saturday, now he's seen that you're not only fine, you're even better."

That rattled me. Did they still not believe me? "Bruise me up? Jermaine, he *broke my arms*. It wasn't a bruise. I didn't imagine it."

Jermaine looked sheepish. "I hear ya man. Just saying. It's just weird and all."

Everyone was silent for a few moments, then Sybil spoke. "Well, he knows now. You could have put Mike in the hospital, and he's bigger than you. And you have no injuries. So if there was any wonder about—your *condition*—then it's settled."

I guessed she was referring to the potential genes I may or

may not have inherited.

Kevin shook his head. "If we know about him changing tomorrow, then he'll suspect you will too."

"And what does that mean?" Jermaine asked.

Kevin's fingers massaged his imaginary chin stubble. "I don't know, Bro, but it can't be good."

The tension and fear about Thursday night hung heavy on all of us as we quietly made our way home.

Happily—for me—my dad bought me some new shoes at McNally's after dinner that evening. So that was a plus.

And Honey, she acted strangely all night, whimpering and giving me odd looks. Like she was unsure of me; or maybe it was just that she sensed my anxiety.

Before bed that night and after my prayer for Rachel, I read for almost an hour; but then I laid awake until well after midnight, unable to fall asleep.

Just before I finally drifted off, I heard howling in the distance.

It was like a warning.

It was three in the morning when I woke, the normally peaceful figure of Honey on my bed missing. Moonlight streamed in through the old curtains flanking the window. Clicking noises came from the hall—or from the kitchen. I figured my dad must be up making a snack, so I wandered over. The kitchen lights were off, and his door was closed as I walked by his room. As was Suzanne's.

"Honey?" I whispered in the dark.

There was no response, just some light tapping on the front

door.

At once, I knew who it was this time. It was *her*.

Except I also realized I was in a dream, and I willed myself to wake.

It didn't work.

She pounded now on the front door. Even though I knew it was just a dream, I was afraid.

Knock knock knock.

The old hag was tapping louder, laughing; then she started banging at the door with her open hand. She tried the door handle, but the deadbolt was locked.

Until I heard the familiar *click* as the bolt disengaged.

At this small victory, she began to squeal with joy, sending icy shafts of fear into my chest as I stepped into the kitchen. Peaking around the corner, I could see the front door opening with a creak, and she awkwardly wheeled herself over the threshold and into the entrance of our house.

Her unpleasant voice cracked, wispy and airy. "Teavan?"

Back in the dark kitchen, I felt along the counter for the wooden knife block and grabbed the biggest handle. The heavy blade would not slide out. None of them would.

Her chair squeaked from the front room as she wheeled farther into the house, sounding closer to the kitchen.

Sprinting toward the back door, I jumped down the three steps at the back entry and turned toward the basement, another ten steps down. None of the light switches worked, and it was even darker as I descended into windowless stairwell.

The basement was unfinished, and there was a door near the bottom step to close it off. The old woman was laughing away upstairs, looking for me, calling my name. I opened and slipped through the door into the main area of the basement, then closed it as quietly as possible, hoping she would give up. From up above, I could hear her chair on the linoleum of the kitchen floor, bumping into the table.

"Get up here!" she cackled at the back landing. "I have something for you. You know you can't escape it. Hee hee!"

Leaning against the door to hold it shut, I surveyed the gloomy cellar for an escape, knowing there was no way out. I closed my eyes and willed it to be over. To wake up.

I prayed for her to go; to leave me alone. *I should have gone to church with Rachel.*

"Teavan . . . don't make me come down there," she said with a hiss, her voice sounding more angry and masculine now.

My eyes were getting used to the dark and they were fixed on a stack of boxes, while my head involuntarily just kept shaking back and forth with a *no* motion.

There was racket upstairs. The wall shook, and the old woman let out a yelp as her wheelchair fell down the three stairs to the back door landing. Seconds later, there was more clatter as she and her chair toppled down the longer set of stairs into the basement. She was crying out as she plunged, but then it was silent after she hit the bottom and her wheelchair smashed against the closed door.

My heart—beating faster than I thought possible—was the only audible sound. My breathing was labored; my eyes were closed.

The doorknob turned and rattled. *She wasn't dead.*

Coughing and spitting, she groaned through the closed door. "*Ouvre la porte.*"

She was *right there*. Just on the other side of the flimsy interior door. There was no way out. It was more of a storage room, much smaller than the upstairs footprint.

Impossibly, she began to push the door open. I was sliding along the cement, unable to stop it with all my body weight.

The old woman began to laugh again at her triumph, and I could faintly see her boney hand reach around the door feeling for me. My body wouldn't move; it was in a state of shock. I couldn't will it to roll, stand, or run. Pushing, I tried to slam the door closed on her arm but couldn't.

Through the dark space, her shape came crawling around the door's edge, wheezing. Her long, white, wet hair dragged along the dusty floor. I wondered if it was possible to die of fright, or for a fifteen-year-old to have a heart attack. Either would have been preferable at that moment as her hand grabbed my unresponsive leg.

"There you are! You've been a bad boy, making me wait outside and then come down here." She coughed up a gleaming liquid on the floor. With her free hand, she wiped her mouth, then smiled, revealing decaying brown and crooked teeth.

"You can only get away for so long, boy. In the end, our destiny is what it is. You can delay, but not escape," she cackled, dragging herself onto me. Her breath was horrid: searing and rotten as her face came to mine. Paralyzed, I could only move my eyes now.

"*Ne discute pas, c'est le seul moyen . . .* " she whispered as her long, wet tongue slithered from inside her filthy maw onto my face. It pushed its way into my defenseless open mouth, and I fought futilely to bite and push it out. I was unable to breathe and started to choke and heave as her tongue went down my throat, filling up my insides with something that burned.

Before my eyes closed, I noticed a necklace hanging down below her chin. The pendant was small, but its shape jarred a memory. Before I could place it, I began to lose consciousness, barely able to make out her shrieks of delight.

Her sounds slowly faded into the distance, and things went dark.

And then it was over.

Once again, I woke in a cold sweat from the nightmare, back in my bed. Only this time Honey was nowhere to be seen.

Chapter 29

With Thursday morning came an overwhelming dread of the events ahead. I turned over and pushed my face into the pillow, and wished more than anything that I could fast forward my life precisely twenty-four hours. I had no desire to plow through this day.

I was so tired; my sleep had been restless, short, and troubled.

"Knock, knock," I heard a voice say from the door. Suzanne was standing there with a half smile. "Dad said I could have his car today. I figured maybe I should drive you?"

I squinted at her with one eye, nodding my head. "Good idea."

"Hurry up; you slept in," she said as she gently closed my door.

If only I could crawl under the covers, skip school, then skip the country.

The update from Sybil was that Rachel was unchanged. Her

parents still wouldn't let me near her hospital room, even though Sybil assured them I was not on drugs. They elected to wait until they spoke to Rachel first.

The gang was quiet all day and through lunch, everyone lost in thought. I wasn't sure they were taking this seriously, but their quietness led me to believe they might be. Or maybe they were just nervous about going to Bruno's to take pictures, regardless of whether or not he was a werewolf. I didn't blame them.

For me, I was scared. Scared that this was real, that he really was a werewolf. What if one of them got hurt? And I was distressed at the thought of a full moon bringing on a transformation in me—again. It had been the most painful experience of my life. I figured I should take a few ibuprofens before letting Mrs. Leclair and Suzanne lock me up for the night.

Should I bring a sleeping bag?

Since my phone was gone, Suzanne had everyone's numbers in hers. The group of them had agreed to recharge phones after school and meet with Mrs. Leclair for the "sleepover" at seven o'clock.

Sybil was going to video record, Kevin would take pictures, and Jermaine would keep watch. Mrs. Leclair figured transformation would happen after eleven, since it used to for my grandfather. Sybil, Jermaine, and Kevin would bike over to the Vincent house at nine to wait, prepare, and observe.

"Will you guys be able to hear me through this?" I asked Mrs. Leclair as she opened the big door to her safe room. I had a book, a pillow, and a sleeping bag with me.

"We can sort of hear you, Teavan. Are you really going to

bring that sleeping gear in there?" she asked.

"Well," I mumbled, "I had to make the sleepover look real to my dad, so I might as well use it."

"Suit yourself," she answered. "I hope it wasn't expensive."

The implication made me shiver, and we were quiet as we headed back upstairs. Mrs. Leclair showed Sybil how to load the pistol and where the safety was.

The clock on the wall showed eight thirty. The gang was quiet, and Suzanne was on her phone. Mrs. Leclair was puttering in the kitchen, preparing some snacks for them to bring.

"Remember," she said to Sybil. "As soon as you have *anything* on video, just leave. Be quick about it. And if he comes after you . . . don't hesitate."

Sybil sighed. "I know."

As they got ready to leave, I stood. "You guys?"

The three of them looked back as they put their shoes on.

"I, uh," I mumbled. "I just wanted to thank you for everything. Thank you for helping me, for believing me. I know this all sounds crazy, but I'm really lucky to have friends like you here."

Kevin joke-punched me on the shoulder. "Anytime, bro. We may not be a big city, but small-town peeps have big hearts."

Jermaine flashed me a smile with his perfect white teeth against his dark lips. "You owe us big time for this, you know that, right?"

Sybil was last. "This isn't just for you. This is for Rachel," she said as she put on her sweater. "We'll see you guys in a few hours."

"Be careful!" Mrs. Leclair shouted as she dried her hands with a tea towel. They got on their bikes and quietly rode off. Mrs. Leclair closed the door and sat back down at the kitchen table.

She looked at Suzanne and me. "So? Thoughts? Concerns?"

Concerns? I put my head face down on the table and rubbed my head. "Well, how many hours do you have?"

Mrs. Leclair laughed. "Yes, I suppose you probably have a great many questions and concerns, don't you. Well, we have some time before you should go downstairs."

We were both quiet, thinking.

"Suzanne, why didn't you go with them? To . . . help?" she asked.

Suzanne raised her eyebrows. "Well, they're not really *my* friends. But if this is all legit, I think I should be here with my brother." She looked at me and winked. It was weird how this whole bad situation had actually brought out the best in her. She'd finally put her angry guard down and seemed to care a little.

"I see," said Mrs. Leclair.

"What else can you tell us about Grandpa?" I asked.

Mrs. Leclair leaned back. "Hubert and Camille came to America before your father was born. Both had the lycan gene but were committed to its eventual extinction and keeping others in line, as Luc and I were. They moved from France to give their future child—your father—a better life; a life shielded from their kind. The less exposure, the less chance the mutation had to resurrect itself. Lycanthropes generally form a tight-knit community and bonds, inexplicably drawn together. And as more congregate, the likelihood of continued mutation increases. So if they're further from their kind . . . well, you get the picture.

"Camille and Hubert were very much in control when in their wolf forms, but the need for a safe room remained. It was like charging a battery on a slow charger. It could stay on for many moons, but eventually that energy had to be released—they needed to transform all the way. Neither of them wanted to be on the loose if they could help it. Eating a deer seemed harmless at the time, but the next morning it tended to revolt them in their human forms."

"What do you mean, *all the way*?" I asked.

Mrs. Leclair left the room momentarily and returned with a sizeable binder full of papers. The leather binding was faded and weathered, and the corners of some pages stuck out. "You can look through here if you like. This is a scrapbook Luc and Hubert put together years ago, though much of it is in French, Latin, and Italian."

She set the scrapbook on the table and I anxiously opened it, flipping pages of mostly foreign text, clippings, and pencil-style sketches of people being attacked by werewolves.

Mrs. Leclair got up to grab the teapot and filled her cup again as I scanned for entries in English. She sat down and flipped to a marked page for me. It was handwritten, and I read it out loud:

"Lukánthrōpos split from the werwulf species circa 1150 a.d., with the latter unable to attain humanoid wolf incarnation, limited to canid form. Unlike the werwulf, the lukánthrōpos was not bound by lunar cycles, though it was strongly influenced, and once experienced could at-will change to its humanoid wolf form, or to the full canid figure. This humanoid wolf possessed superior cognitive abilities to its further-transformed canid cousin, thus representing an intellectual evolution of the species."

"I don't get it," said Suzanne.

"Me neither."

Mrs. Leclair scratched the back of her head. "It means the modern lycan can either run on all fours like a wolf or change less to a two-legged half-human, half-wolf state that retains more of the person's thoughts."

"So which one is all the way?" I asked.

"On all fours, *canid* . . . it's more primal," she answered.

I flipped closer to the beginning, looking for English, and found some more entries:

Lycaon, in Greek mythology, a legendary king of Arcadia. Traditionally, he was an impious and cruel king who tried to trick Zeus, the king of the gods, into eating human flesh. The god was not deceived and in wrath devastated the earth with Deucalian's flood, according to Ovid's Metamorphoses, Book I. Lycaon himself was turned into a wolf.

The story of Lycaon was apparently told in order to explain an extraordinary ceremony, the Lycaea, held in honour of Zeus Lycaeus at Mount Lycaeus. According to Plato (Republic, Book VIII), this ceremony was believed to involve human sacrifice and lycanthropy (assuming the form of a wolf). The Greek traveler Pausanias implied that the rite was still practiced in the 2nd century AD. Lycanthropy comes from the Greek lykoi, "wolf" and anthropos, "man".

"The story goes back two thousand years?" I asked.

"So it seems," Mrs. Leclair answered.

Another clipping read:

The lycans were believed to have moved north over the centuries, eventually settling in France, Germany, and Italy. In France, they were known as loup garous; the word loup means "wolf" whilst garoul means a "man who can turn into a wolf" – a werewolf in English, werwulf in German.

A pack of loup garou went astray in 1764 and began to openly hunt and kill villagers in the Gévaudan region of southern France. Before they could be internally controlled, they mauled over eighty French citizens. Hunters were summoned by the locals and government; everyone was under suspicion for years. This prompted another wave of migration, but this time west. As the loup garous moved further from Europe in the last few centuries, they settled in Eastern French Canada and Cajun Louisiana and became known as rougarou.

"Was that the Sabine girl you mentioned, that moved to America?" I asked, pointing to the clipping.

"We think so. She left France so many years ago and became the genetic matriarch for the *rougarou* faction for two reasons. One, she was pregnant with a human's genes. However, she also left because of this incident. There was widespread suspicion of their in that particular time in history where they were hunted so fiercely; everyone was suspect. The Gévaudan killings set them back hundreds of years, reigniting the fears and energy of the French people. Understandably, it was difficult for them for decades."

"So, Bruno is a rougarou? What's the difference?" interrupted Suzanne.

Mrs. Leclair pursed her lips. "I suppose he is. It's really just the name they give it in the bayou, but by definition, they are more of a mutt than a pureblood French *loup garou*. His ancestors come from half lycan and half human, so, in theory—weaker. Your grandfather and father have pure blood, but you are only half because of your mother. It is interesting it never manifested in your father, but has in you. Maybe because of necessity at the right time in life."

"Wow," I said, trying to picture it. "That's crazy. So the French lycans are more pure? Stronger than their western counterparts? Does that mean I'm stronger than Bruno? I have better blood?"

She shrugged. "Possibly. His genes are more watered down than yours, but at best you are only fifty percent pure. Who knows how much inbreeding that child has in his family. You have better blood, but he has more experience.

"Anyway, all of this led to the need for extreme secrecy, rules, and protocol. Rebels were dispensed with, no questions or exceptions. There was no room for error, too much at stake for all. And now, well, imagine if it was made public. Someone would undoubtedly find a genetic marker, and for the public's so-called safety, testing would be mandatory. That is why it is still so secret, spoken of only in folklore."

The thought of mandatory testing and putting Bruno in jail, or a zoo, brought a smile to my face. But at the same time . . . it meant they would come for me, too.

"Is there any way to stop it? To—cure it?" I asked.

She shook her head. "No."

This was something I would be stuck with forever. And possibly my children. How could I ever live a normal life? Live in a big city? Put my future family at risk? The weight of it all hit me on a whole different level now.

Suzanne held up her hand. "Mrs. Leclair. I know it's not related, but, do you know anything about our mother? Did her leaving or disappearance have anything to do with all this?"

Her question took me by surprise. She rarely talked about Mom. She'd been gone for so many years now, and it always dredged up anger or sadness in Suzanne.

Mrs. Leclair tilted her head quizzically. "Your mother, was it—Allison? No, not that I know of. But I know very little. Hubert seldom spoke of her, other than his overall disapproval of your father's choice in marrying her. From what I understand, your father and Allison met, fell in love, and got married rather quickly—against the family's advice. I gathered she and Hubert never got along very well. He said she was 'flighty and irresponsible'. Sorry, those are his words, not mine. And then when she up and left, he said 'I told you so' to your father, and that just drove the wedge further in their relationship. Which was already shaky at best. I don't know much beyond that, I'm afraid."

Suzanne's phone beeped. "They are at Bruno's. He is in the summer cabin watching something on his phone. His parents are in the house. All quiet so far, according to Jermaine's text."

Mrs. Leclair looked up at the clock, then to me. "It might be best if you head downstairs soon. It's almost time, dear."

Reluctantly, I made my way to the basement, placing the sleeping bag and pillow in the middle of the safe-room floor. Suzanne and Mrs. Leclair stood in the doorway, smiling awkwardly.

"Any further advice?" I asked, trembling a little.

Mrs. Leclair came over with a knowing smile and gave me a motherly hug, holding me tight. Her warmth and perfume felt good. As I pulled away, she held tighter, almost knowing that I needed it more than I knew.

"I will have a big breakfast ready for you in the morning; you will be starving," she said, finally letting me go. "But remember this: You will be okay. It will become less painful and quicker each time you change. Just let it happen, don't fight it; this room is safe. Your grandfather always said he practiced a form of mindfulness when in his altered state. Instead of letting the wolf instincts and needs utterly take over, he would do his best to hold on, hold the line that bound his morals and humanity to his thoughts. He was quite adept at retaining his thoughts and consciousness when he walked on all fours, though much better on two legs, of course. Keep this at the forefront of your mind; let go physically but not mentally. Keep a grip on who you are. Seek the light."

I nodded but didn't really understand. "I'll try."

Suzanne stood there, shuffling her feet and looking at her phone. "See you in the morning?"

"Let's hope," I answered. It felt like we should have hugged, too, but neither of us was very touchy-feely. Maybe it was growing up without a mom. I was tempted to initiate . . . but didn't.

Mrs. Leclair closed the big door, and I could hear the latching process on the other side as she bound it in place.

The room was so quiet. A small light was built into the ceiling, flush with the stone and with what looked like an inch of plexiglass covering the bulb.

I laid out the sleeping bag and pillow and lay on top, pulling out my book. Before even getting it open, I realized there was no way to concentrate on reading right now.

The feeling of complete loneliness crept over me. I longed to be on the sofa, listening to my dad babbling about his latest story but still feeling the warmth and security of him beside me as we mindlessly streamed some show. Instead, I was sitting alone in this dimly-lit cellar, locked inside a cage and waiting for the pain to come.

Chapter 30

The wait was over an hour.

Then a small cramp started in the pit of my stomach. It grew into a solid pain that expanded. Pacing around the room, I tried to suppress it, terrified of it overtaking me again despite Mrs. Leclair's warnings to let it be. Easier said than done. Like knowing you need to throw up but trying your hardest to keep it down so as not to suffer through it.

The black throb spread, despite my mental protests, and I bent over in agony. My teeth clenched and my eyes closed to weather the waves of internal acidic cramps. My hand— the skin was bubbling, rippling; coarse, brown hair sprouted from my fingers as the nails turned an opaque gray color and grew longer. Involuntarily, I yelped, then doubled over again onto the floor, flopping about as each limb grew, cracked, and reformed itself. Though this was much worse, it reminded me of having the flu: debilitating cramps, fever, and sweating, but feeling utterly alone in your state. Like nobody could help you; it was something you just had to go through.

Writhing about on the cement floor, I could feel it coming

for me—the blackness, the pangs of hunger. The spasms slowly began to wither. An apparition of the old woman in her wheelchair stood out in the darkness when my eyes were closed.

I shook the vision off and opened my eyes, springing up to my feet. Everything was different; I was taller. Holding my hands out, I saw the hairy claws that were not human or canine, and I clasped them into fists with a roar.

Bruno. It was coming back to me now. I wanted *him.* And he wanted me; we were drawn toward each other. I loped to the door, growled, and pounded on it, yelling to be let out as it shook in its frame.

"Let me out!" I screamed as I battered the wood with my fists.

Jermaine, Kevin, and Sybil. They were in danger; they couldn't be near Bruno while he was in this state.

"Open it now!" I howled again, kicking at the door. *I could be there in minutes. Save them.*

The power I had brought a smirk to my face as I flexed my arms and hind legs, feeling like I could easily leap up onto the roof of a house.

Hunger stung me deep inside.

I needed food. Meat.

Another change was coming—the next wave. It felt good. It felt natural.

But somewhere deep within, a voice told me to control it, to *stay.* Shaking my head, I walked around the room, trying to think, to remain thinking. *Remember Suzanne*, I thought.

"Suze?" I called out. I wasn't convinced my voice was working; it didn't sound right.

It was quiet.

Hunger pangs struck again, then anger at how much it hurt. Why was there no food here?

I ran to the door and slammed it with my shoulder. It shook but held.

Another wave of spasms began. That familiar blackness was coming from the core of my being, making its way outward, and I fell to the ground and let it have its way for round two.

Pain flooded my body once more, and I could hear the internal cracks and crunches of bones shifting as my body thrashed on the floor.

Finally, it stopped. My eyes opened as I leapt to my feet, but on all fours this time. The smell of another was here, *in this room*. Running around frantically, I sniffed the corners and found it all over. Concealed, but there. The smell of another, similar to me. Belonging to me. Or rather, I belonged to it.

The smell's source was close, like it was floating up near me, but I couldn't quite grasp it. Then it hit me.

Grandpa.

He had been here. The scent was old, but I knew it to be him. These thoughts brought peace to my muddled mind, closer to the light, and away from the calling darkness as I continued sniffing every inch of the room, my four feet effortlessly trotting around. The full wolf form had taken over.

Suzanne? I could smell her. She was close, but not in here. She was near the door, right on the other side, her presence overwhelming. Her fear—it was radiating through the door. What was happening to her? Why was she afraid? I growled in anger, but couldn't form the words *let me out*.

Darkness called again, primal needs and hungers pulling at

me. Like treading water in a whirlpool when you know that peace is just letting go and ceasing the struggle.

A voice inside said not to let go; but it was more natural to give in. I finally did.

And to be honest, it felt *so* good.

Chapter 31

There was knocking in the distance. Far away.

It was persistent. And either it was getting louder or I was getting closer to the source. Doing my best to focus on the sound, I followed it in my darkness, and eventually opened my eyes. I was lying on the floor of the safe room, and someone was knocking on the door, calling out my name.

I grabbed my ripped up shorts and put them on as best I could for modesty. "Hello?"

My body was sweating, and my need for food overwhelming. I called out again, "Suze? Mrs. Leclair?" Scraps of sleeping bag and pillow were strewn all over the room, white fluff everywhere. The book was intact, thankfully.

Latches were clanking behind the door, and then it slowly opened up. Mrs. Leclair's head peeked around the door until our eyes met. She smiled. "Good morning."

"Err, hi," I said, momentarily confused, my mind zeroing in on the smell of bacon, eggs, and chocolate croissants wafting through the open door. "Do you have food?"

She came in farther, and waved me out the door and

upstairs. The most delicious scents were flooding my senses, and I realized I was beyond shaky-hungry. There were so many questions about last night, but food was my most immediate concern.

Suzanne stood at the top of the stairs and eyed me as I skipped up. She was quiet then looked away.

"Hey," I said, reaching the top step. "How . . . how did it go last night? Where are the other three?"

Her lips pursed, then she whispered, "They're sleeping in the living room."

Brushing past Suzanne, I sat down at the kitchen table, feeling relieved, and happier to see a big breakfast prepared than I'd ever been before. "May I?" I asked, looking at Mrs. Leclair who was just reaching the top of the stairs.

She nodded. "Of course, dear."

Grabbing the tongs, I heaped what seemed like a pound of greasy bacon onto my plate, then stuffed a wad of it in my mouth as I pushed a pile of eggs beside the bacon. Croissants, fruit, and about a gallon of water as well. My body craved the water like I was a parched desert.

Suzanne sat opposite, watching as I ate with a strange, almost nervous look in her eye.

"What?" I asked through a mouthful of egg.

She shrugged, and checked her phone unnecessarily.

Mrs. Leclair shuffled about, putting more eggs on the skillet. The clock on the wall read seven fifteen in the morning.

"So? What happened?" I finally had enough air to ask; the food satiated my hunger.

"What do you remember?" Suzanne asked.

I recounted the pain of the change. Then being scared for

Jermaine, Kevin, and Sybil. Wanting to be let out, but nobody would listen. Then me changing again—further. Smelling things . . . smelling Grandpa. Smelling Suzanne. Then things went fuzzy.

Suzanne was quiet and listening intently. Mrs. Leclair turned around. "When you did the second change, were you able to hold on? Hold on to being you, once on all fours?"

I couldn't be sure. "I don't know; maybe not. I remember trying to, running around, the room was rich in scents. But then it was hard to keep control, to keep *present*. I think I let go or gave in pretty quickly at that point."

Mrs. Leclair coughed lightly into the arm of her dress. "I see. Well, it takes practice, but it is good you had the presence of mind to remember to at least try."

I grinned involuntarily. "Grandpa . . . I could smell him. I *knew* it was him. It was so clear! Such a strange thing, his scent brought me back so quickly to memories of him."

Mrs. Leclair smiled. "I'm glad, dear, for your sake. That room has been sanitized—with bleach. I guess it doesn't totally get erased."

Suzanne was still quiet. I leaned over and grabbed her cool hand in my warm palm, not something I normally did. "You okay?"

She nodded. "Yeah. It was, just a little more than I expected. Everything. I feel a little uneasy, I guess."

"Everything?" I asked.

She grimaced and looked away, unable to meet my eye. "You, your change. It was . . . scary. Not natural. You sounded like a caged grizzly trying to escape. I was afraid the door would come off. Then the other three came back, and . . . they had a similar story. It was a lot to digest in one night."

"Really?"

Suzanne pulled out her phone and showed it to me. I pressed the PLAY button on the screen, and a video started. In Mrs. Leclair's basement, the phone faced the stairs but then swung around and focused on the heavy door of the safe room. The door kept shaking in its hinges, the whole wall almost trembling. A guttural but muffled roar came from the other side. The sound of Suzanne's cries could be heard as the phone dropped to the floor and the video stopped.

I flicked sideways in her camera roll but there were no more videos. "Was that . . . me?"

They both nodded. Suzanne put her head down. "It was so scary. It . . . it wasn't you. There was this anger, this raw animal fierceness. I was tempted to open the door, thinking it couldn't be you, that you were in danger from whatever was inside," she looked up, tears welling.

"But deep down, I knew it was you. I couldn't listen anymore, and I ran upstairs and sat outside. Even from out there, I could hear the distant growls. It was horrible," she said, tears streaming down her face.

I reached out to grab her hand again, but she pulled back and put them under the table.

"I'm sorry, Suze."

Peripheral movement caught my eye. Sybil was standing at the doorway to the living room. Her hair was all wild and disheveled. Behind her, Jermaine and Kevin peeked around, looking uncomfortable as they made their way into the kitchen.

"Good morning, Wolfie," Sybil said with a chuckle as she slapped my back.

I smiled, happy to have the mood lifted a little. "Hey guys. How did it go on your end?"

Kevin sat down beside Suzanne at the round kitchen table, and Jermaine sat next to me. Kevin reached out for some orange juice. "Not good, bro. Not good. That guy is full on werewolf. Unstoppable."

Deep down, I already knew it. "Everything okay though?" I asked.

Jermaine picked at some bacon on his plate. "Well, define 'okay'."

"Like, did you guys get the video?"

They all nodded.

"Can I see it?"

They shook their heads.

Sybil clasped her hands in front of her, elbows on the table. "So, we got there. His parents were in the house, and Bruno was out in that guest house-cabin thing. We snuck up and saw him in the window. He was doing something on his phone. It was quiet for a while. We were almost ready to give up, quit the wild goose chase. Then Bruno . . . he arched his back, like he was in pain all of a sudden. He let out a moaning cry, then jumped up on a chair between spasms and put his phone in the rafters for some reason.

"After it seemed to subside, he opened the door to the cabin, but went back to the center of the room." Sybil shook her head, then mimicked throwing up. "There are multiple images I never want to remember about last night, and the next is one of them. Bruno stripped naked and threw his clothes in the corner. I had my phone ready, and even though that was not something I'd ever want on video, I started to record anyway. After that, things got very ugly."

Jermaine had a grave look on his face as he nodded in agreement.

"Bruno fell to the floor," she continued. "And he started to change. Hair sprouting everywhere, legs bending at unnatural angles, feet expanding. His skull . . . it reshaped itself, so his jaw was sticking out. It was the scariest thing I've ever seen. A hundred times worse than any horror movie." For the first time since I'd known her, Sybil actually looked shaken. Her ivory skin got even whiter at the memory.

"I . . . I was still holding the phone up, and Jermaine remembered to get his phone for some still photos. We thought one or two with his, and my video, and then we'd run. Only when Jermaine took a picture, the auto-flash was on and reflected brightly in the window. The Bruno-wolf thing's head snapped up and looked out. He growled something guttural, but he was still twisting on the floor."

Sybil looked at Jermaine, her eyes squinted in anger.

Jermaine shrugged knowingly. "I said I was sorry."

"What happened?" I asked, eager to hear the next part.

"Well, Twinkle Toes here spun around in fear of being spotted and knocked the phone out of my hands. It flew into the dark and *both* of these guys ran like a couple of gazelles and left me by myself. The phone was missing—I couldn't see it anywhere in the dark—and Bruno was howling by then. So I gave up looking and ran after them," Sybil said.

Kevin held his hands up. "Teavan. You *gotta* understand," he said, looking at me. "He was *coming* for us, like, for real. We had to go. Shit was *going down*."

I had no doubt he would have come for them with no

mercy or control.

"We ran," Sybil continued. "And *they* shrieked so loud I knew Bruno would have no trouble tracking us. But it turned out to be a good thing, I guess. Bruno came out maybe thirty seconds later, and we could hear him running . . . *fast*. He was barking and growling, and we ran past the main house toward the road where our bikes were stashed. So much for him taking twenty minutes to transform. It was closer to two minutes. Maybe one."

They all shuddered at the memory and shifted in their seats.

"Anyway, Sheriff Vincent must have heard all the screaming and ran outside. He came out with a gun and fired off a few shots, but we didn't know if it was at us or at Bruno," Sybil said. "We just kept running. He hollered for us to stop, that it was safe now. When we looked back the Bruno-wolf had changed direction and gone the opposite way after the gun shots. We didn't take the chance and were on our bikes and gone in seconds. We saw the sheriff's squad car a few minutes later driving up and down the roads, but we stayed well hidden until he was gone. Then we high-tailed it back here."

Mrs. Leclair was shaking her head in disapproval, though it seemed she'd already heard the story from the look on her face.

"What about the gun? The silver bullets?" I asked.

Sybil shook her head. "Still in my backpack. It all happened so fast . . ."

"What about the picture, can I see it?" I asked.

Jermaine shook his head. "It's just a bright light in a window."

"And the video?"

"On my phone," Sybil said with a grunt. "Somewhere near his cabin."

This time it was my turn to grimace as I took in a deep breath, thinking of the implications. He'd seen them, and Sybil's phone was there for either Bruno or his dad to find. Neither was good.

We had no video. No pictures. And now Bruno knew that they knew. He'd be forced to clean up loose ends.

And quickly.

Chapter 32

It was next to impossible to concentrate in class that day. Of course, going to school seemed like the dumbest idea of all time, but we'd promised our parents that a Thursday sleepover would not affect Friday classes.

I sat there, oblivious to what the teacher was telling us about the constitution, and went over the previous evening's events in my mind. What we had to do. What outcomes were possible.

Glancing around, I noticed people whispering about whatever the latest gossip was, something that I wasn't in the know about. The secrets being passed around about who liked who seemed so ridiculously trivial. *Who freakin' cares.*

Later that morning, Sybil was heading outside for break instead of toward the lunch room. I reached out to her shoulder. "Where you going?"

She jumped a little at my touch. "To see Rachel."

"Can I come?"

She bit on her cheek. "It's probably best if you don't. She's not awake, anyway."

"Please? Just let me tag along. She's in this because of me," I pleaded.

Sybil shrugged. "Suit yourself. But her parents won't let you see her."

The community medical center wasn't far, so we walked. The sky was cloudy, and the air was breezy and cool. I broke the silence. "So were you born here? In the Iz?"

She shook her head. "No. I was born down in L.A., but I moved here when I was seven."

"To be closer to your family?"

"Sort of. My mom . . . she died. She had cancer. And my dad, well, he hadn't been around that much up to the point when my mom got sick, so he didn't really know what to do with me. My mom's sister and the rest of the family lived here. My dad thought if we moved, at least I would be close to family, and maybe he'd have some help raising me."

I felt kinda bad and didn't know what to say. "Oh, sorry to hear that."

She continued, "So, my aunt and the family spent a lot of time with me, and I was over there a lot. Rachel and I got real close, like sisters, I guess. And her mom became like a mom to me."

"That sucks about your mom," I said, looking down at the sidewalk as we strolled along.

"Yeah, that's my heartbreaking story. Now the person I'm closest with is in a coma-like state," she said.

Walking slowly as we approached the medical center, I kicked a pebble off the sidewalk onto the street. "I'm not sure what's worse, having your mom die or having your mom leave you."

"Is that what happened to yours?"

I nodded. "Yeah, she was depressed or something, I guess; she was always moody. She just up and left one day, almost ten years ago. She was weak," I said, feeling snarky, still angry at her for abandoning us. "What kind of mother leaves her husband and children?"

It was Sybil's turn to shrug. "I don't know. Maybe she had her reasons."

"Maybe, though what I can't imagine," I said. "My dad is weird most of the time, but he's done his best."

As we walked up the front steps, Sheriff Vincent came out through the automatic doors, and he tipped his hat to us. "Mr. Laurent, Ms. Hughes. Shouldn't you be in class?"

Sybil mumbled under her breath, "None of your business."

"Excuse me?" he turned around, holding his ear out.

"Just on lunch break, sir," I answered, covering up her comment.

He smiled, looking at me. "You are looking *much* better today. I hope you are staying out of trouble and have learned a lesson in all of this. I understand Rachel is still unresponsive?"

We both nodded.

The sheriff stood there, looking back and forth at us both. "I don't suppose either of you knows anything about kids running around my house last night? Or a dog?"

This time we both shook our heads quickly in unison.

"Be sure and let me know if you hear anything at school, please? Someone was sneaking around, but no damage was done," he said, as we started into the medical center.

"Yes, sir," I answered. "We will keep an ear out."

"You do that, Mr. Laurent," he said as he turned and

walked down the steps.

I wasn't sure about Sybil, but my heart was beating fast. Did he think it was us? Did he know?

I hated hospitals. And the smells inside seemed extra strong now with my newer . . . senses. And that eerie quietness. It was never like it was in the movies, the halls bustling with people and action. At least this one wasn't. It smelled like death and old people.

Mrs. Denning was inside Rachel's room, reading a book, when Sybil knocked and opened the door. Mrs. Denning smiled when she saw Sybil, but it turned to a scowl when she saw me behind her. "What's *he* doing here?"

"Teavan wanted to say hi to Rachel, that's all," Sybil answered, and her body stiffened. I could tell there was more to the scene than I was aware of.

"Sybil, I told you. I do not want that boy near her," she hissed.

Sybil shook her head. "I know, I'm sorry, but he really had nothing to do with this, I told you."

"Whether he did or didn't, he's trouble, and I want nothing to do with him."

Trouble? Me? That was the first time I'd ever been accused of being trouble. The worst thing I'd ever done was stealing a gummy bear from the corner store back in New York. Maybe a detention or two from passing notes. Possibly some harmless hacker fun.

"Mrs. Denning, please," I said. "I just wanted to see her, but I'll go; I don't want to cause any trouble."

She stood and pointed away. "Then go."

Sybil looked at me. "Sorry," she whispered. "Wait for me

outside?"

I nodded and left the room.

Fifteen minutes later Sybil came out, and her eyes were red. "Sorry about that, my aunt is still a little upset."

"Not your fault."

"I know, but, sucks when you know the truth and can't tell it."

We headed in the direction of the school. I'd eaten my lunch on the steps while waiting for Sybil.

"So, I've been thinking all morning," Sybil said as we walked side by side. "Are you still meeting with Mrs. Leclair after school? At the diner?"

"Yeah, why?"

"Well, I'd like to join you, I want to talk to her as well. I agree now, Bruno has to be stopped. And I've decided I'm going to do it."

My mouth went dry, the blood draining from my face. "What?"

She looked at me; her cheeks were red and her gaze serious. "I know all that I need to know. He needs to be stopped, and I still have the three bullets."

"You want to shoot him? Are you crazy?" I said, though I knew she was right.

"Yes, and no. What stops him now from coming after me? Or Jermaine? Or Kevin? He knows who it was last night. I think we are better off striking first, or we end up in the hospital. Or worse."

Once again, my heart was beating through my chest. I had considered something similar all morning as well, but Sybil doing it?

"You have a better idea?" she asked.

I shook my head. "Not really. It's just that . . . despite what he did, who he is. It's murder, Sybil. You can't do that."

She scoffed, "Not if I'm defending myself."

"You just wanna walk up and shoot him. And that's not murder?"

She rolled her eyes. "No, idiot. He needs to change first and come for me. Then I shoot him. It's self-defense . . . and I'd feel much better about shooting an attacking beast than a ninth grader. I couldn't do that."

We shuffled quietly down the sidewalk. It would never work; he wouldn't even need to change to beat her, to kill her with his bare hands. And he had enough control that he could stay human.

"It won't work," I said. "He won't change unless you wait until another full moon, which isn't for a month. And any other time, he can hold back, not change. It will only make things worse; he'll know the plan if you are standing there with a gun."

Sybil was quiet as she digested that. "You have a better plan, Wolfie?"

"Wolfie? Again? Seriously?" I asked.

For once, Sybil smiled and let out a small laugh. "Sorry, but I did arrive early enough last night to hear you . . . howling."

My face went red at the thought of all of them listening outside the door. "Please don't call me that."

"Okay. Do you have a better plan, Dingo?"

I ignored the jab this time. "You need help; I'll do it. And maybe the guys and Suzanne?"

She shook her head. "I don't want them knowing I'm gonna kill Bruno. They already think I'm nuts."

"Well, you can't do it alone. Not even you and me; too much can go wrong. And . . . they saw what you saw, they know what we know. We are all in this together."

Chapter 33

Afternoon class was painfully slow, but the bell finally rang at three dismissing everyone for the weekend. Jermaine, Kevin, and I met Sybil outside her locker.

"We need to talk," I said, looking at the boys.

They nodded, but Jermaine replied, "I can't right now. I promised my mom I'd come straight home after class today since I had a sleepover and all last night. And speaking of sleep, I need some."

"When then?" I asked as we walked out toward the bike racks.

"I dunno, I guess I can't even text you. When you gonna get a new phone?"

I shrugged. "Who knows. My dad told me to get a job and stop playing online games when I told him it broke."

They groaned.

"I like how he thinks you're just a gamer," Kevin said. "Not that I understand that crypto stuff, either."

Few people understood that 'crypto stuff', but I wasn't going to cash in my investment for a new phone.

"Why don't I send Suzanne a text?" Jermaine asked.

At that moment my pulse quickened when I saw a group of kids out front, gathered around Jed McGregor and Mike Thompson. They sat on the bike racks casually, smirks on their faces as we came into view.

"Dang," Kevin muttered. "Should we go back in the school?"

Across the street, Bruno sat on the grass beside the sidewalk and smiled when our eyes met. There was a weird unspoken threat in his look.

Shaking my head, I said, "There's no point. They'll just wait for us." I didn't mention that the sight of Jed and Mike actually got me a little *excited*.

I walked in front of our little foursome as we made our way over to the bike rack, the kids there making way for us. Expecting us.

"Well, well," said Mike. "If it isn't the four biggest losers at Redwood."

My blood started to boil, and the hair on my neck bristled. I walked closer to Mike, looking him straight in the eye. "Didn't you learn your lesson last time, Mikey?"

His face turned red and he hopped onto the ground in front of me. Instead of looking up a few inches to him as I had a few weeks ago, he was just a tad shorter than me now. I brought my face close to his.

"You sucker-punched me last time, Laurent," he said, our faces just inches apart.

Jed jumped down off the bike rack and held his hands between us. "Now, now, ladies. First things first," he said, looking at me then Sybil. "Whose is this?" he asked, holding up a grubby, white, rubber phone case.

Grabbing it, I turned it over in my hand. "I don't know," I said, genuinely unsure.

Sybil shrugged as well.

Jed pointed at Kevin. "What about you, *Jap boy*?"

Kevin's face went crimson. "I'm Chinese, not Japanese, you redneck."

"Redneck? Why don't you come closer and say that?" he growled, puffing his chest out.

Kevin backed down. "No thanks, Jed. I know you'd like nothing more than to use your tae kwon do on my head like a practice bag."

Jed smiled at the perceived compliment, then turned to Jermaine. "How 'bout you, dipstick?"

The circle around us closed in as everyone waited for something, and Jermaine's fists and teeth clenched. "What did you say, you inbred hillbilly?"

This time the crowd hummed at Jermaine's insult, and Jed turned red.

"Listen, boy, you call me *Mister Jed*. Never address me by anything else," he said with a smirk.

Jed was trying to get a rise out of one of us, but now it was my turn. "Jed, why does Bruno keep sending his *henchmen* here to do his dirty work? His *simpletons*?"

He spun around to look at me. "I ain't nobody's henchman, Laurent. He just wants to know whose phone case this is. Someone was at his house last night and dropped it. We just want to return it, and the phone, to the rightful owner."

It was Sybil's phone case. Hopefully she had a passcode on the phone.

"Well," I said, getting out the key to open my bike lock. "You can just let your boss know it doesn't belong to any of us and be on your way."

Jed scowled that no one was taking the bait. "Well, that's just fine then. Maybe I'll slip into Rachel's hospital room and see if she knows who it belongs to?"

In an instant, Sybil snapped and lunged at Jed. She tackled him backward into the bike rack, and they tumbled over onto the ground as she screamed at him. He did his best to shield his face from her blows, and was able to flip her under him and pin her down. "You *dare* hit me, you psycho redhead?" he spat down in her face, spittle flying in her eyes. She gritted her teeth and struggled, but he was too heavy.

I dropped my backpack and grabbed Jed by the neck, dragging him off her. The crowd was going wild as they made the circle bigger.

With extreme self-control, I forced myself to let him go and then pointed across the street. "Just leave!" Bruno was standing now on the sidewalk with his arms folded on his chest. He was clearly enjoying this but was forcing himself to stay put for whatever reason.

Jed's feet thrust up in the air, and then he flipped them down and stood up in one smooth move. He cracked his knuckles and rolled his neck around to stretch it. Everyone was watching.

Inside, I needed to remain calm and breathe. I couldn't lose my temper, since I was not sure of what could or would happen if I did.

Jed ran over and I held up my fists, ready for him; only he jumped and spun in the air. His outstretched leg and foot cracked me in the jaw before I even saw it coming.

The unexpected blow sent me spinning to the ground, though it didn't hurt nearly as much as it should have. I rolled and got onto all fours, but he charged and kicked again, right in the stomach. The strength of his kick lifted me off the ground and knocked the air out of my chest and I gasped.

"Get up, boy!" he yelled.

I realized that I may have been stronger than I used to be, but I still had no idea how to fight. As I looked over, I could see him bouncing around with his fists up, like a professional boxer. Everyone behind him stared at me on the ground. Jermaine came running over, telling me to stop, but I blocked out his voice and glared at Jed with venom in my eyes. I spat out a mouthful of blood. "I'm ready this time."

He smiled and came in lightning fast, his long leg kicked up to my head. Only I was ready now, and I held my arms out and blocked him, focusing on his moves. The miss angered him, and he attempted another roundhouse.

I caught his leg in mid-air and twisted it hard. Jed squealed in pain and flopped to the dirt, writhing in agony while holding his the leg that I might or might not have broken. I tightened my fists and prepared to jump on him to finish it.

But once again, Sybil saved me from myself and stood between us, her face inches from mine as she grabbed my shoulders and hissed under her breath. "Teavan, stop! We *need* to go. *Now.*"

At that moment, I wanted to toss her aside and finish what Jed had started. I wanted him to bleed, to beg for mercy. And I wanted Bruno to come to his rescue. To try and stop me. Everything was red; my ears were ringing. But Sybil held me tight. "Teavan . . ."

I was breathing heavily through my nose, but then slowly

the redness of the scene began to evaporate as I met her eyes. "Calm down," she whispered.

Trying to look past her, I could see Jed squirming in the dirt with Mike kneeling beside him.

"But, but, he *needs* to pay!" I hissed, trying to take a deep breath.

She looked me straight in the eye, trying to keep my attention. "He has paid, Teavan. Look at him. We *need* to go; just listen to me, okay?"

I nodded, some calmness finally settling in. Kevin tapped me from behind. "Bro, let's roll." He held my bike and backpack out.

I grabbed the bag and reluctantly got on my bike, with Sybil continuously keeping herself between me and Jed. We rode off with the crowd making a wide berth for us to leave, excitedly talking amongst themselves. Mrs. Patello, the physics teacher, was running over to the crowd as we left.

Jermaine looked back at her, then whistled. "That was close. I gotta split, you guys. Where you off to?"

Sybil looked at me, still uncertain about my next move. "We're going to meet Mrs. Leclair at the Galaxy Diner. Kevin, can you come with us? We'll drop Teavan off at home after, make sure he's . . . safe?"

He nodded.

Was she worried about my safety? Or that I'd go back?

As we pulled out of the school parking lot, Bruno just stood there, seemingly unconcerned about his injured friend. He watched me with his beady eyes and gave me an evil grin. I gave him the finger, but he only smiled bigger.

Jermaine waved to us as he pulled off a few blocks later and yelled, "I'll call you guys in a bit!"

We rode fast to the east side of town and pulled up to the Galaxy Diner.

Inside, Mrs. Leclair had a booth to herself in the far corner of the casual restaurant. We sat down and updated her on what happened after school. She gave me a disappointed look for snapping so easily.

"You need to control yourself. Don't you see? He's baiting you. You *have* to walk away, even though it's frustrating," she said.

Not as easy in the heat of the moment.

Kevin was on his phone, then looked up. "Okay, your sister and Jermaine are on their way. Maybe twenty minutes. Jermaine lucked out and his mom isn't home."

We shared our thoughts with Mrs. Leclair on what needed to be done, and of course she agreed enthusiastically. Eliminating Bruno had always been her only option.

"Just remember, dear, we have only three silver bullets. And I'm afraid I have no idea how to make more. That was something Luc did," Mrs. Leclair said.

Three chances.

It seemed easy enough, especially if we could get him in mid- or late-stage transformation as he twisted about on the ground.

"It won't be easy in the chaos of the moment," she added. Kevin was quiet through our chatter; he wasn't nearly as enthusiastic.

I looked at him. "You okay with this?"

He shrugged. "Not really. But I don't see what else to do, other than leaving the country. I . . . I can't be the one to pull the trigger, though. Just so you know . . ."

Sybil squinted. "That's okay, Kevin. I'm happy to take the lead."

The waitress kept interrupting, asking if we wanted food, and I was happy when Mrs. Leclair ordered some wings and sodas for everyone.

Suzanne and Jermaine arrived, and we shared the tentative plan with them. They both had the same reservations but agreed it seemed to be our only option.

We needed to get Bruno alone, without Jed and Mike. As much as we hated them, they didn't deserve death and certainly couldn't witness it

"But how do we get him to change?" asked Suzanne, looking at Mrs. Leclair.

"Without a full moon, he needs to either want to or to lose control," she answered.

Kevin smiled. "Maybe we all attack him at once, beat him to a pulp? That oughta get him angry."

Jermaine returned the smile. "True. But he might beat all of us to a pulp first. And Sybil needs to be ready with the gun, so she can't help."

The group remained quiet, and I thought of myself and keeping control and how I'd nearly lost it again today. Anger. Hatred. But how did we get him to lose it? What would make him snap?

A light flickered on in my brain and I shared the idea. It was the best we had. Sybil had an idea for getting him alone. Saturday night. *Tomorrow*. We couldn't afford to wait or drag this out.

We ate quietly and agreed to meet at Mrs. Leclair's the next day, rally together, and make our way to Bruno for the final stand.

Chapter 34

"You've been quiet; what are you thinking?" I asked Suzanne, pushing my bike beside her as we walked home from Mrs. Leclair's. Mrs. Leclair had volunteered to drive us to her place with my bike in the back of her truck. The sun was setting; the sky was a fiery red and orange in the west.

"What am I thinking? What am I *not thinking* is more like it," she said, shaking her head in disbelief. "I just keep pinching myself, hoping I'll wake up from this bizarre dream. And I've had some nasty dreams lately, but this one takes the cake. Can you wake me up?"

Leaning over, I yanked on her hair.

"Ouch! What was that for?" she barked, swatting my hand away.

"Just seeing if you are asleep," I said with a smirk.

Suzanne tried to suppress a smile but it snuck out. "Good try," she said with a laugh. "I just keep thinking of the chain of events that led us to this point. Why the heck did Dad have to drag us across the country to live here? Did he really think he could become an accomplished writer by living in the country?

Isn't New York the literary capital?"

I shrugged. "So they say."

"And Grandpa. Why did he have to have us living here as a condition of his will? Why would he want us to be in this environment? Did the thing between him and Dad involve us, too? Why would he do this to us?"

The same questions I'd had. "Maybe he knew I was going to change and thought it would be better here than in the city."

She looked over to me. "And you. What are you going to do? About . . . this thing? Even without Bruno around, your *situation* is messed up."

I stopped pushing the bike as we rounded the bend. "Honestly? I have no idea, Suze. Thinking about the future has not been at the top of my list this week. I'm just trying to get through each day, doing my best to come to terms with what is happening. And like you, pinching myself every so often, hoping to wake up. I mean, I have a trig test on Tuesday. I can't even remotely think about school, let alone studying for a test. Will we even be in school next week? Will we be alive?"

Suzanne pulled her curly hair back out of her face. "I hope so, Teavan. I hope so."

Neither of us spoke the rest of the walk, and we arrived home just in time for some overcooked pork chops with mushroom soup. For once, however, I thoroughly enjoyed Dad's chatter about his novel, since it had nothing to do with my current life predicament. And despite being a little bland and overcooked, there were no leftovers. My appetite was still enormous.

No surprise, I couldn't fall asleep that night. I tried to read, but my mind wasn't really taking in any of the information. I kept rereading whole pages at a time, not retaining anything that was happening in the story.

Honey whined once in a while, maybe sensing my uneasiness. She jumped off my bed periodically and left the room, patrolling the house. She'd return and jump back up on the bed, leaning her head on my leg.

I reached over and scratched her behind the ears. "You okay, girl?"

She closed her eyes, enjoying the attention, and stretched her legs out further. I kept scratching her, worried about tomorrow, full of dread. But then I'd picture Rachel, lying in the hospital, and my anger and willingness to proceed would boil up again. Then I thought of Suzanne, wanting her to be there, to guide us. To support me. But also not wanting her to be anywhere she could be hurt.

Then there was Sybil. Frigid, ball-busting Sybil. She could take care of herself better than anyone, and she was easily the most confident of all of us. But I worried she had no real idea of what she was up against. This wasn't just some wise-ass class clown that needed a verbal whipping.

This was real.

"You need what?" my dad hollered from his room the next morning as I cleaned up from breakfast.

Nervously, I shouted out, "Shoes."

"I bought you shoes a few days ago!" he said, coming back into the kitchen after breakfast on Saturday. "I mean, I know you are in a growth spurt, but this is ridiculous. You're going to eat me out of house and home if I don't publish a book!" he said, half serious but half laughing.

My dad looked me up and down. "I can't believe how much you've grown in the last few weeks. I had growth spurts, too, but none this quick. Maybe this clean country air is really agreeing with you."

I nodded. "I think so, too, Dad. My body is used to smog, and it's thriving here." This was obviously not true, but I knew he was sensitive about how we were dealing with the move. I *really* needed new shoes again and would feed him whatever compliments were necessary.

"Maybe we can stop by the mobile store and get me a new phone, too. I'd love to post some pictures of the beauty of Santa Isadora," I said, trying to slip it in while the iron was hot.

He spun around. "Don't push your luck. I haven't had the luxury of new shoes in almost two years. If you didn't waste so much money with your online gambling you'd have enough for a new phone."

"It's not gambling, it's investing."

"Buying online computer cats is not investing. I may not be an expert, but I know that much."

I groaned. "Dad, I've never put a dime into those stupid things. Give me some credit, crypto currencies are gonna be big. Some are garbage, for sure, but the future isn't paper currency."

He rolled his eyes. "Maybe you should spend your time finding me the next great tech stock."

I am.

Chapter 35

New shoes and a few hours with my dad was a good way to pass the time on an otherwise long day of dread.

He retired to his office after we got home, and I was eating a late lunch when the doorbell rang. Cautiously, I pushed the curtain aside and peeked out the window, not expecting anyone.

It was Sybil.

I opened the door. "Hey."

She had sunglasses and an old white Raiders cap on, pulled down low. There was a duffle bag slung over her shoulder. "A bit early aren't you? You look like you're ready to rob a bank," I said.

She kept her head down. "Is Suzanne home? I called her."

My sister made her way to the front door. "Hi Sybil, come on in."

Moving aside, I let her in, though I didn't quite understand why she was so early. They made their way down the hall to Suzanne's room and quietly shut the door.

"Yeah, nice to see you, too," I said to no one in particular.

I walked down the hall and knocked. "What's going on?" I

asked through the door.

Suzanne opened it. "Can you just give us some privacy for a few minutes?"

"But . . ."

"Everything isn't always about you, okay?"

I nodded. "I guess."

Why would she come early and keep it a secret? Were they planning something about me? Was there a part of tonight's plan that I wasn't included in? My mind was racing to all the possibilities.

After half an hour I knocked again, convinced they were going to shoot me, too.

"Can I come in now? Please?"

The door opened, and Suzanne let me in. Sybil was sitting on the bed, her hat off now but facing the other way, looking at a magazine. As I pulled out the chair to the makeup table, my elbow knocked over a hairspray can that tipped some other bottles onto the floor.

"Teavan!"

I grimaced, trying to pick them up and arrange them again. "Sorry," I said, thinking that I'd been knocking a lot of things over in the last few weeks. Growing four inches and gaining twenty pounds in a short time takes its toll on your dexterity.

"What's the deal?" I asked. "You guys planning something I don't know about?"

Suzanne shook her head, snorting a little. "No, nothing about tonight."

Oh.

"Is this some kind of *womanly* issue?" I asked, not really wanting to know but still a little paranoid.

When Suzanne understood what I meant, she laughed this time and shook her head. "No, not that." She went over and sat beside Sybil. "He's going to find out either way," she said to Sybil, touching her shoulder.

Slowly and reluctantly, Sybil turned around.

The blood drained from my face.

Her eye was black and a little swollen. There was a cut on her lip.

The heat started to rise inside. "What happened? Did Bruno come to your house? I'm gonna kill him."

Sybil shook her head, looking down silently. "No."

"Jed? Mike!?"

She shook it again.

I was confused. Surely she hadn't just gotten into a fight this morning. "Who would hit you?" Who *could* hit her and walk away besides Bruno?

Her hand raised up to her face, and she carefully wiped a tear away from each eye with her index finger. "It's nothing, Teavan. I tripped."

What a joke. She tripped?

"Come on, what is this, 1950? What really happened?" I asked, surprised she'd think I'd believe such a stupid lie. That was what women used to say when their husbands abused them, and she wasn't even married!

More tears welled up in her eyes as she looked at me.

Then it hit me, and I felt sick to my stomach. "Your . . . dad?"

"I don't want to talk to you about it," she said.

Surprised, I asked, "Why not? You'll talk to my sister about it but not me? I'm not some stupid jock at school, Sybil. I'm your friend, I'm not like that."

"I know you're not like that," she said quietly.

Sybil broke eye contact and looked down at the bed. "When I told him I was doing another sleepover tonight, he went off on me. About not visiting Rachel enough or supporting the family enough, and thinking I was up to no good on sleepovers. It just kinda got out of hand is all. It's fine, really."

The heat returned to my face. "No, it's not fine," I hissed, wanting to pay a visit to Mr. Hughes, or at least call Social Services, or whoever dealt with abuse.

The vision of her father yelling at her for something she didn't do and knocking her around enraged me. Here she was, about to risk her life to avenge Rachel and keep others safe in town, and her dad thought the worst of her. Deep in the pit of my stomach, I could feel the black mass trying to grow, and immediately I breathed deeply to calm myself. It went away.

Feeling a little dizzy, I sat down on the carpet. "Has this happened before?"

She shook her head. "No. Like I said, it's fine, really. We have a big night ahead of us, and we need to keep clear heads. Okay?"

I wrinkled my nose and shrugged. What could I do? When I glanced at Suzanne, she had the same look.

"But you need to tell someone, Sybil; this is wrong. We should call the police," I said.

"Yeah, I know, I know, Suzanne already gave me the third degree. Trust me, I get it. First off—it's fine, he doesn't do this often. And second off, my dad is all I have. I can't jeopardize that. School will be over in a few years, and I'll be outta here.

Trust me, I can handle it."

Three years?

"Why not move into Rachel's house? Would they take you?" Suzanne asked.

She shook her head. "It's not that simple. But listen, I didn't come here for a pity party or a counseling session. I just needed to leave the house and couldn't get stuck at my aunt's. Can we please just drop it?"

Suzanne and I were both quiet, looking at each other uneasily. There were much bigger issues to be dealt with today, and so we both nodded. I made a mental note to follow up after this was all over. If we were still alive.

Suzanne held her phone up. "Kevin texted: We're all set. We arranged for Bruno to go to Ava Murphy's place at nine tonight to watch a movie. We'll intercept him on his way."

I looked at Sybil. "Huh? That was your plan? How in the world did you convince her to invite him over?" I asked.

Sybil smirked a little. "By promising her two things. One, that he would get a better offer and never actually show up."

"And two?" I asked, seeing a mischievous look on her face.

"Two, you are taking Ava to a movie next Friday," she said with a strange look.

Ava Murphy!?

"Come on, are you serious?" I asked, not believing her.

Sybil shrugged. "Well, I mean, she is pretty cute. The boys all love her, even Bruno. And, for whatever bizarre reason, she chatted with me and seems to have a thing for you. So the stars just kinda aligned."

My face turned beet red. They both noticed and laughed. At least the mood was a little lighter in the room, even if it was at my expense.

"Come on, Teavan, she's a babe. And, unlike my cousin, she's not a choir girl; she's perfect for you," she teased.

Now my face was really turning red. I shook my head. "No thanks. Plus, doesn't Kevin have a thing for her?" I breathed out. "But I guess if that's what it takes."

She lifted an eyebrow over her good eye. "Really?"

Momentarily confused, I stammered. "The movie—I mean. If that's what it takes to make this work, I'll take her to a movie."

A flash of relief almost passed over her features, like she was testing my feelings for Rachel. "And popcorn. You have to share a popcorn with her."

"What? That was a condition of hers?" I asked.

"No," she said with a laugh. "But it would've been funny if I could keep a straight face."

Suzanne's phone beeped, and she looked down; then her eyes widened, and she smiled. "It's your aunt. Did you give her my number? She says Rachel's awake!"

Sybil's mouth dropped open. "What!? Yes, sorry, I gave her your number since my phone is gone. I . . . I need to go see her."

A lump caught in my throat and a huge sense of relief as I exhaled. "Can I come?"

That same awkward look showed on her face. "I'm not sure. You know how my aunt is."

Suzanne stood up. "Listen, why don't I drive; it'll save time. Teavan and I can wait outside while you visit. It'll give us something to do, it's only one thirty."

Sybil sprang up, a genuine smile on her face, until she

looked in the mirror. "*Ugh*. What do I do about . . . that?" she said, pointing to her eye. "All I know how to use is Chapstick."

This time Suzanne smiled and spun her makeup chair around. "Leave it to me, we'll have you looking better in no time."

Chapter 36

The girls spent half an hour in the makeup chair, and I let Honey out for a run. I waited on the front step, wearing a pair of shoes that fit again.

They finally came out, and I was stunned at the change in Sybil. Her eye problem was still visible, but much less so, and the lipstick mostly covered up the cut on her lip. She actually looked kinda cute, but I dared not say that for fear of a fist in my mouth.

"What?" she asked, looking at me.

"Oh," I said, fidgeting. "Nothing, just not used to seeing you with makeup or your hair done. Your eye looks much better now."

She sneered and pulled her cap back on.

Suzanne tried to protest. "No, leave it! Your hair looks beautiful!"

"I just want my hat on, I'm sorry. Plus, I'm gonna look weird enough with makeup. If my hair is all fancy they will really be asking questions," Sybil answered.

The scent of mango mixed with my sister's familiar perfume wafted off her as she walked by. "You smell nice, too." I smiled.

Sybil spun around, clenching her fist to strike. "Shut it, Dingo."

After parking and walking to the medical center's front steps, Sybil turned and asked us to give her a few minutes inside. Suzanne and I sat down.

There was strong smell of fire in the air as we waited. "Can you smell the smoke?"

Suzanne looked around, but there was nobody nearby. "No? I don't see anyone."

I shook my head. "No, not that kind. Forest-fire smoke. I can smell it; it's getting stronger. I think the fires are far off, but it's in the air."

She rolled her eyes. "Oh, so now you have super smelling senses?"

I shrugged. "Kinda? Not as good as when I'm . . . you know, changed. Then, it's like, crazy strong. It's weird."

We both sat quietly for another minute.

"Suze, you know, you don't have to come tonight. I'd almost be happier if you just stayed home and watched out for dad," I said, looking over at her.

"What?" she snapped, glaring at me. "Of course I'm coming? Why wouldn't I? This involves me, too, you know."

"Well, yes and no. I'm just kinda worried about you is all."

"Listen, I may not be a wolf boy, but I'm still older, smarter, and wiser than you. And just because I'm not a sports star doesn't mean I can't take care of myself. Teavan, this is big. Really big. You can't know how upset I'd be if something happened to you."

"I guess," I said, feeling warmed by her open kindness.

"Well, if you change your mind, I'll be just as happy if you watch out for dad. Just know that, okay?"

She nodded. "Sure."

A few minutes later Sybil came out, beaming. "Come in! She's awake!"

We jumped up and followed her inside to Rachel's room. Her parents filed out of the room as we waited. Mrs. Denning's eyes were all red, but she looked happy.

"Steven, I owe you an apology," she said, shifting uneasily as Mr. Denning sat down on the bench in the hall. "Rachel told me that you saw her home safely, like a gentlemen. Again, my apologies. It's just been a difficult time . . ."

"No problem, Mrs. Denning. I don't blame you," I said, unsure of what to say.

Luckily, Sybil grabbed my shirt and pulled me from the awkwardness into the room. Rachel gave us a half smile as we entered. She had white bandages on her face and arms, but she was sitting up.

"Hey, Rachel," I said, surprised at how pale and weak she looked.

"Hi yourself," she whispered in a raspy voice. "Thanks . . . for coming."

"Well, I would have come earlier but I wasn't really allowed near you," I said and then laughed.

"Sorry about that. You know—protective moms and all," she said, and then coughed.

"So, can you tell us what happened?" I asked. Suzanne stood quietly behind me, and Sybil was on the other side of the bed.

"Well, there's no big mystery, though it seems like everyone was expecting one. Even the police have been in already to talk," she wheezed. "After you dropped me off, I changed into my pajamas and went to the family room to watch TV. The doorbell rang, and when I opened the door there was nobody there. Our garbage can was knocked over in the grass, and the lid was a few feet away. I walked down the steps to fix it when I heard a growling from behind me. A dog—a big dog— jumped at me. A German shepherd or a husky or something," she broke into a fit of weak coughs. "It all happened so fast . . . it was so scary. I just tried to protect my face and curled up in a ball, praying for it to leave. Next thing I knew, I woke up here," she explained.

Sybil was holding her hand, careful not to knock the drip lines going into it.

Rachel's face contorted as she looked at me, trying to see my feet. "Is this bed super low, or are you wearing platform shoes? And your cheeks. You eating cupcakes for breakfast?"

My face went red as I shrugged. "Growth spurt."

Her eyes went wide. "I'll say. You look . . . big, much bigger. Even your chest and arms. I've never seen anyone grow so fast."

Suzanne leaned forward. "Talk to my dad; it's a common thing in our family for the boys. He's already had to buy Teavan two pairs of shoes!" Her attempt at changing the focus was welcome.

"No kidding," Rachel said, looking at me almost suspiciously, but visibly in discomfort.

"So, when do you get outta here?" I asked, shifting the subject.

Rachel shrugged. "I think tomorrow or Monday. They said as long as I'm stable, I'm okay to go home."

A knock on the door sounded from behind us; it was the nurse. "Time to let her rest, she's been with people for the last few hours and she needs a break."

We nodded.

Sybil leaned over and gave Rachel a big hug, and both their eyes were a little moist after. Then Suzanne did the same. Rachel looked at me next and held her arms out, mindful of her IV. As I leaned in, her smells—both her alluring scents and opposing sickly ones—overwhelmed me, and she pulled me in tight. My face was buried in her dark hair that was sprawled on the pillow. She drew me in tighter when I gently tried to pull back, so I held still.

She whispered in my ear, "Wow, you're hot."

I could feel the blood rushing to my face again.

Rachel loosened her grip and I sat back. "Huh?"

"I said you're hot, like you have a fever or something. I'm freezing with these covers on, and you feel like you're burning up. Are you okay?" she asked.

"Oh, yeah, no, I feel fine. It's hot out today and I just kinda run warm all the time," I mumbled as I stood back up.

"I see," she said, smiling weakly. Suzanne was standing at the door watching, and Sybil was looking toward the hall. "Come back tomorrow?"

"Hopefully," I said, thinking of the night ahead.

"Well, *hopefully* you will," she added. I blushed again and made my way to the door, looking back to her.

"Glad to see you are awake," I said as the nurse pushed past me with some linens in her hand. Mrs. Denning pulled Sybil aside and they had a spirited conversation in hushed tones farther down the hall. Suzanne and I waited without comment.

Their discussion got louder and more serious. Eventually Sybil threw her hands up. "I have to go, I'm sorry." As Sybil brushed past us, Mrs. Denning gave her a disappointed look. Suzanne and I left and caught up to Sybil.

"What was that about?" Suzanne asked.

The front doors of the medical center slid open as Sybil glanced back. "Nothing. She's worried about my basketball injury."

"What injury?" I asked.

She pointed to her eye. "Remember? The elbow I took yesterday."

We didn't answer.

It was almost three thirty and we needed to get ready for the big night. I only hoped things would go well enough that we could see Rachel again.

Chapter 37

My dad was uncharacteristically enthusiastic that I was planning another sleepover at Jermaine's house that night. Telling him it was actually at the neighbor's house would have set off a number of alarm bells. My dad was pleased that Suzanne and I were fitting in and making friends. Suzanne made up a girl's name that didn't even exist for her excuse. And at her age, that probably should have set off some kind of fatherly alarm.

Sybil being with us for the whole afternoon probably helped, too. He had no clue.

Though as I got to know Mrs. Leclair better, I almost thought introducing them might not be a terrible idea. Dad needed a woman in his life, and for a lady her age, she was kinda pretty. Plus, her knowing my deepest secret would be about the best possible combination.

And she was an amazing baker.

When it was time, I went to Mrs. Leclair's first. The girls would come thirty minutes after.

She was puttering in the kitchen when I arrived, making pastries called *Kouign-amann*. The scent was so strong I knew what she was up to before even getting close to her house, and it set my mouth watering. She seemed genuinely happy to entertain our ragtag little gang, food and all.

"Mrs. Leclair, have you ever, umm, put a wolf *down*?" I asked, munching on her baking.

"Me? Heavens no. That was for Luc to do; I haven't the stomach for it."

I had a million questions for her, maybe more, and she was the only one who could answer them. *Most would have to wait*, I thought as I leafed through the scrapbook at the kitchen table.

"After this is over, assuming we win." I shifted uneasily. "Can I come over . . . spend some time here and pick your brain on things? Maybe you can translate some of this book for me? I have so many questions, and nobody to talk to. I feel like there is a lot in here."

"May you?"

"Huh?" I asked.

"Sorry," she smiled, "Old habits. The question should be, *May I come over*? And to answer you, yes of course. I would be more than happy to pass on what I know, and any other book I have downstairs. I imagine you must be feeling quite anxious and scared, poor dear." She came over and ruffled my hair. "Another *amann*?"

I nodded. Supper had been filling but I would need my energy.

"You should meet my dad, too. You guys might hit it off."

For the first time, Mrs. Leclair blushed a little. "I *would* like to meet your father, but strictly as neighbors. I'm quite embarrassed I still haven't invited him over after what we've been through."

I snickered to myself. It felt good to make someone else

blush for a change.

"Mrs. Leclair, do you think if things don't go as planned and I need to *transform* tonight, will it happen automatically? Is there a way for me to force it? And if I do, what if I hurt the wrong person?"

She turned around, dish cloth in hand. "Would you *please* call me Geneviève? I'm not your principal," she said with a wink. "I really don't know. How it works to make the transformation happen is beyond me. But I can tell you that your grandfather could willingly change whenever he wanted, and very quickly at that. So it is possible; I'm just not sure as to how many months or years of practice it takes.

"And to your second question. It is as I explained to you before: you must not give in completely, keep your humanity at the forefront of your mind. Hold on, keep focus, and you will be able to differentiate right from wrong, friend from foe. It will be of the utmost import tonight."

Remembering the other night, I knew what she meant now. Kind of. Only, letting it take over was much easier than holding on.

"Do regular bullets hurt them?"

She nodded. "Just temporarily."

"Do you have any?"

She thought about it. "Yes, I do. But why?"

"Well, if the gun holds six bullets, we might as well fill up the empty three chambers with something. It's better than nothing." Or that's what I figured. "And, why silver bullets? Does silver magically kill them? Why can't we just make more?"

She smiled. "Oh? Why hadn't I thought of that? Let's skip

down and make a few more silver bullets for tonight."

"No?" I asked.

She shook her head. "I wish it were that simple. Suffice it to say, constructing silver bullets is much more complicated than you might imagine. It's softer and less dense than lead, and must be heated to almost two thousand degrees to melt properly. Over the years, Luc mixed in a little lead to make it cheaper, harder, and fire straighter. Though it was less pure in form, it seemed to make no difference as to its effectiveness.

"And as for why? Well, in alchemy, gold is to the sun as silver is to the moon. Your strength is also your weakness, in some ways akin to an allergy, I suppose. In your lycan genetic makeup, after you transform, a notable blood byproduct is sulfur. And when mixed with silver it produces silver sulfide, which in a werewolf doesn't dissolve and blocks the blood vessels—effectively stopping the heart."

I was trying to understand what she was saying, but it sounded very technical. "So, it would be like a bullet made of peanuts to someone allergic to them?"

She smiled. "Yes, I suppose. If a peanut could penetrate the skin, of course. Nothing about silver, or a peanut, is dangerous on its own. How the body deals with it is a different story."

Flipping through the treasure trove of information was frustrating because most of it wasn't in English. There was a page full of photos—sepia in appearance—and looked old. One photo in particular caught my eye. It was of three young men, all in dark pants and rolled up light-colored collar shirts, maybe in their early twenties. One held a spade upright, and they were all arm-in-arm with big grins and a vineyard behind them. Each of them had slicked back hair and leather work boots.

"Who's that?"

She leaned over and squinted at the picture. "Why, that's Hubert and his brothers, if I'm not mistaken."

"Was that here? In California?"

She shook her head. "No. That would be in France. His brothers . . . they never came here. His leaving was the reason they stopped speaking; I think the family never forgave him for deserting them. As they saw it, anyway. But as I said, he wanted to change, to end the line. It was something they didn't agree on."

I swallowed a lump in my throat. "Are they . . . lycans as well?"

She pursed her lips and nodded.

"Do you know them? Their names? Addresses?"

Mrs. Leclair shook her head. "Sorry, no. He did not speak of them often."

I had family, outside of my tiny family here. And they had the same genes. *They were like me.*

I flipped through a few more pages, hoping for more family photos, but then my heart stopped.

Near the end of the book was a much older faded and yellowed black-and-white photograph, curled at the edges. It featured an elderly woman with long, white hair.

Her expression was grave and serious. With her left hand, she fingered a pendant necklace drooping over her blouse.

She was seated in a wooden wheelchair.

Chapter 38

My heart rate exploded.

"Geneviève! Who is this?" I put my index figure on the picture and stood up from the table.

Mrs. Leclair wrinkled her forehead as she focused on the picture, then a look of understanding appeared. "Oh, that is her, of course, Sabine—Sabine Martin. Near the end of her life, I believe."

Sabine Martin.

I dropped my head in close to the picture. It was her. *Definitely her.*

The photograph was blurry, but my eyes were drawn to her pendant. The same C-shaped pendant that had hung from her neck in my dream. It was also the same shape as the little ornament in my grandfather's leather pouch.

I pointed to it. "What is that? Why does she have my grandmother's necklace on?"

Mrs. Leclair studied the picture. "Her lavaliere? Why would you say it's your grandmother's?"

"Because if you look close, it's the letter C."

Mrs. Leclair shook her head and smiled. "No, that's not a

C. That's a crescent moon, a sort of sigil of the lycan. These ancestral moon pendants are passed down from generation to generation. No doubt it's hundreds of years old. Why are you so alarmed?"

Rubbing my face and pacing away from the table, I could almost hear those cackles from my dream. I looked up, crossing and uncrossing my arms. "I *know* her. I've dreamt of that woman. And I found that lycan ornament thing in my grandpa's stuff."

"Are you sure? About her?"

I nodded and flipped the book closed. "Trust me, you wouldn't forget that woman."

The doorbell rang, shattering the tension in the room, and I jumped. Our conversation had been intense. Together, we opened the front door to Sybil and Suzanne.

Suzanne gave me an odd look. "You okay? You look white. Like you've seen a ghost."

"Almost," I mumbled and then coughed as we returned to the kitchen.

It was almost seven o'clock, and the other two would be arriving shortly. We hoped to be on our way within the hour. Sybil was quiet, but Suzanne made up for it with small talk, and Mrs. Leclair showed her the photo of Grandpa and his brothers. Fifteen minutes later, Jermaine arrived.

He looked nervous.

"You sure you want to do this?" I asked.

He nodded. "No, but I will anyway. The way I see it, is if you don't succeed, he knows that I probably know. So it's just a matter of time before he comes for me. Might as well make sure.

"Plus," he continued, "the Iz only has room for one wolf man, and that's one of my best friends." Jermaine smiled and punched me lightly on the shoulder.

I felt myself blushing at the compliment. "Thanks buddy. We need you."

"Would anyone like a pastry or snack?" Mrs. Leclair asked, pouring waters all around. The girls declined but Jermaine happily grabbed a few pastries from the platter.

Sybil put her backpack on the table and unzipped it. Carefully, she removed the weathered old six-shooter pistol inside. Mrs. Leclair went down to the basement to retrieve some regular bullets to fill up the empty chambers.

"Are you sure about this, Sybil?" I asked. "I know I can't."

She bit her lip, a dark and distant look in her eyes. "Yes."

Mrs. Leclair returned and took a deep breath. "You have only one chance. The Vincent boy will be fast, strong, and presumably have no qualms about killing. You must strike first. If he gets the upper hand, you have no hope. I'm afraid his size and experience will easily overpower Teavan once transformed, so your only chance are those bullets. Follow the plan and it will work, they always do. Do your best to remain calm."

It looked like Sybil had the weight of the world on her shoulders. She had a thousand mile stare and remained silent. Suzanne shifted in her seat, and we went over the plan again. I kept looking up at the clock. It was getting near eight and Kevin hadn't showed up yet. Jermaine sent him a text.

My bag was on the floor, and I grabbed it, heading to the bathroom. I quickly changed and put on the extra clothing I'd brought, happy to have thought ahead. A loose pair of athletic shorts and one of my dad's big old T-shirts.

Inside the bag's zip pouch, I pulled out the token-shaped medallion Jermaine and I found in the cabin. That subtle, but gentle tingle emanating from it wove into and through my fingers, and although it kinda scared me, I also felt drawn to it. Much more now than in the cabin that day. With little further thought, I put the leather strap over my head and tucked the medallion under my shirt.

The doorbell rang as I reentered the kitchen. Mrs. Leclair went to the front room to let Kevin in.

"Oh crap," Jermaine sighed, still seated at the table, looking at his phone. "He ain't coming."

"Who?" I asked.

"Kevin. He texted me back, 'I'm not coming. I'm really really sorry'," Jermaine answered, reading the message.

Suzanne stood up from the table. "Then who . . . ?"

I bolted to the front room. Mrs. Leclair stood with the door open, the porch light on, looking outside. "Allô?" she called out.

There was no one there. I inhaled the crisp night air and registered what I feared.

I pulled her back in quickly but gently and locked the front door.

"It's not Kevin, he's not coming. It's *him*. It's Bruno."

Chapter 39

The hairs on the back of my neck were standing, my heart was racing, and I could smell his scent. All my senses were in overdrive.

The girls and Jermaine stood there, wide-eyed.

There was a pounding on the back door.

As I pushed past them to the kitchen and the back door, everyone started panicking. Suzanne did the sign of the cross on her chest and muttered, "Please let it not be her."

At the back door, I engaged the bolt lock. I peeked through the tiny window. Nobody was there.

"It's Bruno," I said, stepping back in the brightly lit kitchen. "Cut the lights, all of them!"

"How do you know? Maybe it's just Kevin playing a trick?" Jermaine asked as I flicked the kitchen lights off.

I didn't know how I knew, but I just did. "Trust me. He's here. He knows."

Kevin. *He ratted us out.*

Mrs. Leclair turned out the lamps in the front room and hall. It was dark inside now, giving us a better view to look out. The porch light was still on, but there was nobody on it as I approached the big picture window in the front room. Just the empty wicker lounge set.

And on the glass-covered wicker coffee table lay a cell phone. "Look," I said, pointing it out to Sybil.

"That's mine," she whispered. A chill ran through the room.

Suzanne came over. "Mrs. Leclair, w-what do we do?" Her voice was shaky, and she stuttered the words.

Mrs. Leclair looked at Sybil. "Are you ready, dear? This changes nothing. There is just no element of surprise. But he still doesn't know you have those three bullets."

Except he probably did.

My pulse quickened and I could almost feel *it* in the pit of my stomach, stirring to let loose. Maybe it wouldn't be difficult to summon the change if I needed to.

Part of me wanted to run to the basement and lock us all securely in the safe room. Part of me wanted to call my dad; he was so close, but he would be of no help. Neither would the sheriff.

We had no choice. This was it.

A vision of Rachel hooked up to medical equipment with bandages on her arms and face came to mind, and I growled. It startled Sybil beside me, and she stepped away with an incredulous and fearful look in her eyes. "Teavan?"

I shook the thought away. "Sorry. I didn't mean to do that."

They all stared at me. Had the growl been that loud?

"Can you see him?" I asked, trying to deflect their gazes.

Nobody was brave enough to leave the front room—safety in numbers. We stood away from the front window but kept

234

searching the treeline.

Then, right in front of us, Bruno jumped up, inches from the window, and banged on it with his open palms. It sent a shockwave through the still room. His face was unholy and twisted. His eyes searched the room until he found mine.

We inched back, and Jermaine and Suzanne both shrieked as Bruno pounded again more fiercely, this time shattering the glass with an inhuman war cry.

He growled and jumped on the window frame, arms held high.

Before I could even consciously decide, I ran at him full tilt and dove. Our bodies collided, and my inertia sent us over the porch and crashing through the weak, wooden railing onto the gravel of the driveway.

Bruno scared me even in his normal form; the thought of him transformed into a werewolf was much worse. As we wrestled, I thought he would expect to beat me mercilessly in his wolf form, but Sybil would shoot him before he had the chance. The confrontation wouldn't need to go any further and it could all be over in the next sixty seconds.

How wrong I was.

Chapter 40

We both rolled in different directions and leapt to our feet at the same time, arms outstretched and ready for battle. I backed up closer to the house as he eyed me, and removed what was left of my ripped shirt from our skirmish. The smoke from the northern wildfires was thicker, blanketing the yard and trees in a thin white haze.

Up above, the almost-full moon cast a red glow through the smoke. My feet felt paralyzed now with the momentary lull in action, a deep fear rising in me as my mouth dried up. I glanced back at the house; Sybil stood on the porch wide-eyed and open-mouthed. But underneath she always also had this determined confidence and anger in her eyes, and she raised the gun up.

"I'm gonna enjoy this, *Annie*. Especially you," Bruno said, breathing heavily. "I mean, I enjoyed toying with Rachel and all, but you? I'll be more . . . *enthusiastic*."

Sybil's breathing quickened as he spoke. As he finished, she cocked the gun. This was not according to our plan.

A malevolent smile stretched across his face in the red, tinted moonlight. "Oh no, Annie has a gun. What ever will I do?" he pleaded with a laugh.

She shook her head slowly and pointed the gun straight at him. "You know who's going to enjoy this? Me," she hissed.

Looking back, I could see Suzanne's, Jermaine's, and Mrs. Leclair's faces all looking out through the broken window.

Bruno laughed. "I suppose old Mrs. Leclair has put some so-called silver bullets in there? Did she mention that was nothing but a myth? Probably not, since she's hiding inside," he spat, looking up at her in disgust.

A myth? Was he bluffing?

"Silver or not, a bullet in your head will end things pretty quick," Sybil answered.

His fake smile waned. "Just try, Annie. Just try."

The two of them stared each other down, then Bruno suddenly growled and darted to his right, like he was coming for us. Just as quickly, he jumped back to the left.

The piercing crack of the gun went off as Sybil fired where he *should* have been. The bullet whined past me and punctured the gravel, creating a hole the size of a softball.

She cocked the gun quickly—shaking now—and leveled it at him again as he stood unflinching.

Bruno whistled. "Nice try. But now you're down to five bullets," he taunted.

If silver was a real defense, it was really only two.

I was worried he would fake her out again and waste another bullet before he even changed. I stepped forward.

He glowered at me. "You have something to say, Laurent? Or are you just gonna hide behind Annie and her gun all night? I'm here for you."

I nodded, hearing Sybil make her way down the steps and stand beside me. "I just want to know, how are we going to do this? How do you want to do this?"

Bruno looked a little surprised. "*Want?* Weren't you the ones with the plan? Well, I guess if I had my choice, I'd like to beat you senseless with my fists, and then finish you as a wolf. I'll dispose of the rest of the witnesses once I'm done with you. And I'm just gonna assume you've told Rachel too much, so she'll have to be dealt with as well," he said with a snicker.

Sybil sucked a breath in quickly and stepped forward to shoot again, but I stopped her this time, holding my hand up. "No," I whispered, but her eyes never left his. He was getting to her.

He was calm and in control. He had both of us upset and on edge.

"Bruno, if silver bullets are just a myth, why did my grandpa put one in the back of your brother's head? Remember your poor brother? The one rotting in the earth? Would this make him proud of you?" I asked.

His eyes narrowed quickly and snapped to mine, his jaw clenched tight. "Don't talk about my brother."

"I heard about how my grandfather put poor Grayson out of his misery. Sniveling like a rodent, begging for his life right to the very end."

Bruno gritted his teeth, his face twisted as he growled. "He did not!" His fists were balled up at his sides, and I could see the veins in his neck sticking out, throbbing and tight.

It was working.

Chapter 41

"Bruno, I'd rather pulverize you as a wolf than your pathetic little boy form. That way you can join your brother in hell. Two rats burning in a fire," I taunted.

His face contorted, shaking now. I could almost see him fighting the transformation that begged to be let out. He looked up to the red moon as he let loose an uncontrolled howl that sent a wave of goosebumps through my flesh. Bruno's arms were held up, fists tight, and his chest was expanding into his shirt as he groaned.

Just twenty more seconds.

He grasped his face and fell to the ground on his knees, grunting and breathing heavily, almost talking to himself.

He was utterly at our mercy, except he was not changing any more. It stopped and reversed. I considered grabbing the gun and ending it.

But I couldn't.

He was just a boy on his knees.

It wasn't right.

"Grayson deserved everything he got, Bruno. Just like you do," I continued, hoping to spur him again.

He held his head down, his hands on his face and on his ears. Then he stood slowly and warily, like he knew Sybil wouldn't shoot him like this.

"Nice try, Laurent. But we're doing this my way," he sneered as he took his hands away from his face. "Let's say we settle this the country way?" He held up his fists and got in a boxer's stance. "It's really your only hope. I may be a so-called mutt werewolf from the south, but you are only half a pure blood. Though you have little chance of beating me fist to fist, there is no hope you can defeat me as a wolf."

As he began to dance around, fists up and ready, he leaned forward slightly and squinted, looking at my chest. His smiled turned foul again.

"Where . . . where did you get that necklace?" he asked as he stopped moving, letting his guard down, and stood straight with a confused look. "You . . . shouldn't have that. You have no right to—"

I used the element of surprise and charged him before he could finish, or before I even knew what I was doing.

Leaning forward, I rammed my shoulder into his gut and lifted him up, with more ease than I would have guessed. Running back with him held high, I smashed him into the hood of the pickup truck. A gasp of air escaped him as his head flopped against the metal.

Bruno was lying on the hood, arching his back in pain, and I grabbed his foot and dragged him off. His head and torso landed on the gravel driveway with a thud.

Beating him up as a human wasn't part of the plan.

I wasn't really sure what to do now. It felt wrong to kick or do anything more to him while he was on the ground, but I needed to keep the momentum.

Rachel flashed in my head: Her vibrant smile with stitches across her cheek.

Reenergized, I drove my foot into his chest, lifting his body up off the ground and into the side of the truck. My temper flared at the victory so close.

"Get up!" I growled as he flailed in the dusty gravel.

Bruno looked at me, his mouth breaking into a bloody smile as he spat out liquid. "Nice one, Laurent. But you gotta do better than that!"

Lightning quick, he was on his feet with his fists on my chest, grabbing and twisting my shirt before I had a chance to get my arms up. He pushed me back with such force and speed I stumbled a few feet before crashing into the steps.

Bruno tilted his neck and I could hear it crack as he readied himself. "Now I'm ready."

I leapt up and charged him again. We tumbled to the ground, rolling around in the gravel with fists flying back and forth. Our grunts and growls got louder, and I could smell the sweat coming out of his pores. And maybe even a little smell of fear.

He hadn't been expecting my strength to match his. Nor had I.

Wrestling my way on top of him, I pinned his arms down as he writhed beneath, screaming at me. "Get off!"

This time I smiled. The taste of violence felt good; there was something about it that I liked deep down. The urge to bash him into oblivion was getting stronger from within as I pounded his face with my fists. This time, I was on top.

Blood came splashing out of his nose, and he used his free arm to shield himself.

I hit him again, harder. His lip split open, and he wailed. I no longer cared about the plan or the silver bullets or anything. Spilling his blood was my only thought. Finishing him with my bare hands seemed like a better idea.

Bruno's back arched up violently, almost knocking me off him, and he shrieked. But not from my fist this time.

His jaw was shaking and throbbing, like his facial veins had just increased ten times in size. His mouth opened in another wail, and his growing teeth were visible, turning to sharp fangs.

Bruno was changing. And fast.

His left wrist was pulsing in my palm, and I tried to catch his right arm again to pin it down, but it was flying all over the place. I could feel his wrist getting bigger within my grasp as coarse black hair sprouted from every inch of his exposed skin.

With his free hand, he grabbed my shirt and wrenched me off his chest in a powerful move that I was unable to match, sending me rolling to the side.

Looking up, I saw Sybil, gun outstretched, with a horrified look in her eyes.

"Now!" I yelled, getting back up. I was out of her way, and he was flailing about.

She pulled the trigger.

CRACK!

She was too far away or shaking too much. The bullet gouged out the ground right between his outstretched legs, but he didn't even notice as he was in mid-transformation.

There was only one silver bullet left.

I scrambled over to her. "Give me it!" I hollered, grabbing for the gun. She let me take it, her eyes wide in terror and her mouth open.

It was time to end this. End *him*.

I cocked the pistol as she had and turned around.

Bruno was standing on two legs, well over six feet tall. His black hair-covered body was much bigger and more menacing now. He looked awkward, almost like a dog standing on its hind legs, but more comfortable. His powerful chest heaved with each breath.

His head was not Bruno's. It wasn't as pointy as a wolf's, but more like a cross between a wolf's and a grizzly bear's head. His massive, exposed front teeth dripped saliva as he sucked in each breath.

His transformation had been *so fast*.

The sight of him caused me to stumble; I'd expected to have another minute. I suddenly felt weak, and my arms trembled as his eyes met mine.

He let out a deafening roar.

I turned back to Sybil, who stood behind me, frozen. "Run!"

As I spun back around, my finger on the trigger, I knew I'd only have one chance.

I squeezed the trigger just as his hulking form descended on me, and the recoil of the gun surprised me as the thunderous gunshot split the air.

Chapter 42

My body was heaved up high over the werewolf's head. His hairy, sharp claws easily hoisted me up and dug into my skin, drawing blood as the gun dropped from my hands.

The bullet missed.

Bruno tossed me, and I was airborne for what seemed like forever until I went smashing into the wooden wall of Mrs. Leclair's house. My body bounced and fell to the ground below into the shrubs with a painful thud as he let loose a roar of triumph.

Rolling over onto my knees, I tried to scurry under the porch, but his powerful claw grabbed my ankle through the leaves and yanked me out. My skin scratched through all the branches and I twisted in agony as it felt like my ankle snapped.

The Bruno-wolf dragged me across the yard, the gun just out of reach as I scraped my bloody fingers through the gravel to try to stop.

I was no match for him, unable to even slow us as he pulled my limp ankle behind him, pain shooting down my leg.

As his almost demonic form turned back to me, I used my right foot to kick him with everything I had.

There was little effect as my shoe connected with his corded thigh. He grabbed that foot, and using both ankles, he swung me around like a rag doll into the side of the pickup.

The last thing I saw was the wheel well of Mrs. Leclair's old truck approaching my face at a blinding speed before it collided with my skull.

Darkness.

Change pain.

Hunger.

My eyes opened, and my whole body was hurting, but a different kind of hurt than had been inflicted upon me by the Bruno-wolf. I was half-changed, like him.

The smell of the smoke was overwhelming.

Bruno's stench was worse. I knew it to be him before I even looked; it was everywhere. It was the smell of evil, of decay. Of rot.

I jumped to my feet in my standing-wolf form, my heightened senses in overdrive. A yearning deep down tugged on me to keep changing, to go all the way.

To go primal.

Bruno stood at the house, on the porch. He was bashing the wooden supports holding the roof up over the porch in a blind fury. Things were coming back to me now. Sybil. The gun. Bruno.

Our goal.

I needed to hold on and resist the urge to change further. I focused on the Bruno-wolf, and thought of my sister inside, scared of him finding her.

Sprinting across the yard, I leapt up onto the porch and

grabbed Bruno from behind with my outstretched claws. We spun together and went crashing through all the furniture on the porch.

He got to his feet and roared.

I returned his angry howl, reaching for his massive head, wanting to twist it. To break it off. His arms met mine and we wrestled in front of the door. Eventually I was able to throw him from the porch. He spun in the air and landed in the gravel. I was already scaling down the steps and onto him again.

With his back on the ground, his hind legs sprang into my chest as I approached, and they sent me reeling back.

The urge to change further was still tugging at me. To change and leave here. To fulfill my hungers.

But somewhere else, a voice told me to hold on, to not let go, and to finish this animal off.

Standing up, I could see Bruno was ready for me this time. The taste of blood for both of us was so close. His anger was thick, its smell overpowering.

Mine probably was, too.

He ran to the corner of the house and around the back. I chased him, rounding the corner, but he wasn't there.

I could still smell him and howled in frustration.

He was gone, and his scent went no further.

It went up.

He was on the roof. I heard a window smash from above. He was trying to get in the house.

Stepping back a few feet, I sprinted and jumped. My feet easily made it to the first floor roof over the surrounding porch.

Bruno was crawling into a window as I grabbed his leg and sank my teeth into his calf, chomping as hard as I could.

The leg kicked at me, but his skin broke, and the fiery taste of copper filled my mouth. It almost, but not quite, sated my pangs of hunger. It felt wrong; I knew that somehow.

I spat out a chunky piece of meat and yanked Bruno back out of the window's frame. Bruno was snarling and howling in pain as he tried to stand, but his ripped leg was not providing enough support on the slanted roof tiles.

I charged him, once again grabbing his massive head and pushing his dangerous jaws up to leave his throat exposed.

My vise-like jaw instinctively snapped shut on his throat, and I kept pushing him across the rooftop until halted by the stone chimney jutting out from below. Bruno's wolf skull cracked through the stone, sending pieces of the chimney everywhere.

His claws had been on my head, grabbing at my ears, before the impact of the chimney, and I could feel the jolt weaken his grip.

I bit his throat harder, blood once again filling my mouth. His pained bark echoed into the night. Using my hind legs and forepaws, I pushed his body away from me while trying to hold his throat in my jaw, to rip it from his neck. He did his best to hold me close to prevent it. His body was arched over the broken chimney, and we slipped, still holding each other tight, and rolled off the roof, through the air, and back onto the ground with a thud.

With my jaw, I could feel his neck veins pulsing as he struggled. He continued to hold me tight, effectively keeping his throat in place. If only I could pull it . . .

A boy's war cry cut the night air, and Bruno's body

shuddered. His grip loosened just enough for me to pull free with my jaw still clamped.

His body shuddered and convulsed. His lupine eyes rolled to the back of his head.

His defenses were down and I wanted *more*.

Chapter 43

I drove my snout into his neck again to finish him off. But something was wrong. His taste was off now; it was rancid. The blood was coagulating, drying up and rotting. In the distance, someone was yelling. "Teavan!"

That was me.

Pulling my head away from Bruno in disgust, I saw Suzanne standing at the top of the steps, frantically waving her arms and calling my name. I growled at her intrusion, but sensed a new form of danger. Bruno's body still convulsed, but his arms were down low; he was completely defenseless.

I turned the other way, and someone was standing behind Bruno's body.

Jermaine.

He was staring at me, backing up slowly, his eyes nervously flickering between me and Bruno.

My hunger was killing me. He looked . . .

I shook my head. *No.*

Bruno's breathing stopped and his heart was still.

Inhaling deeply, desperate for oxygen, I watched as his body changed back to its human form.

249

"Teavan!" Suzanne called out again, but my ears were ringing. I was still in attack mode, nervous with people hovering.

Mrs. Leclair came down the steps holding her hands up, her eyes bulging and unblinking. "Calm down, Teavan. Deep breaths, it's over."

Looking from Mrs. Leclair, to Jermaine to Suzanne, I tried to breathe, to let the anger go. It slowly dissipated, and I slumped to the ground in exhaustion.

Deep inside, the desire to fully transform tugged at my senses, taunting me with freedom, with food nearby to satiate the *hunger*. It would be so easy.

But also, the light. Suzanne's voice, begging to come back to her.

Jermaine.

Sybil.

My dad.

Rachel.

I willed myself to end this. To change to human form.

It worked.

It *hurt*.

As my body made the painful transformation back, I was vaguely aware of the others watching in horror until it was over.

Sweating, in pain, and hungry, I rolled onto my back in the gravel and tried to catch my breath. The cool night air felt good on my bare chest.

Suzanne knelt beside me and grabbed my hand tentatively. "Teavan? Can you hear me?" she shouted.

I winced, pulling back. "Of course I can hear you. You're

yelling."

She smiled.

"Is he dead?" I asked.

Suzanne grimaced then nodded. "Big time."

I turned over, looking for Bruno. His body was sprawled in the gravel just a few feet away. An odd-looking piece of wood protruded from his back.

The urge to vomit at the sight was overwhelming and I heaved, throwing up red and yellow bile on the ground. I tried desperately to catch my breath between waves.

Suzanne handed me a cup of water. I thankfully downed it all and rinsed my mouth at the same time. Mrs. Leclair had covered up Bruno with a blanket from inside.

At this point, I was glad I had changed my clothing earlier. The shirt was gone, but the athletic shorts were still on me. The elastic waistband had proved worthy. I pulled them up a little.

"Is that why you changed earlier?" Suzanne asked, noting my shorts. Jermaine was kneeling beside her biting his lip, eyeing me nervously.

I nodded.

"You're a werewolf, and you just killed a werewolf. And you were worried about us seeing you naked after?" she asked again, one eyebrow arched up.

I shrugged. "Wasn't a big deal to change."

Suzanne grinned, ruffling my hair. "Always thinking ahead."

Gesturing to Bruno, I asked, "What's in his back?"

Mrs. Leclair answered this time. "A family heirloom. It was part of my mother's antique silverware. I guess there was enough silver in that carving knife after all. Though I think you had all but finished him either way."

The realization of what happened now made sense as I remembered something changing. "So, does that mean I didn't . . . kill him?"

Mrs. Leclair looked at Suzanne, understood my meaning, and then looked from Jermaine to me. "Unclear. You . . . both did it. It was the silver and his wounds."

I sighed with relief, falling to my back, taking in a deep breath. The moon was still red through the darkness.

I wasn't a killer. Well, not fully. Jermaine had been there. He had my back.

"Jermaine," I said, trying to make eye contact. "Thank you. You saved me."

He was just staring blankly into the darkness, and then looked down at his hand, wiping some blood onto his jeans and shrugged. He turned to me. "You put your life on the line for us; it wasn't anything you wouldn't have done for me. But like Mrs. Leclair said, I think you had already won."

At the time, I would have happily killed him. *I wanted it*. I could still taste that want—that *need*. But now . . . I was relieved to know it wasn't all me. No wonder his blood started tasting wrong.

"Now what? What do we do with him?" I asked.

"If you can help me load him into the truck, we can dispose of him. It won't be my first time," Mrs. Leclair added with a knowing grin. Then she looked at me with her head cocked to the side. "Teavan, how did you . . . change so quickly? You transformed much faster than you should be able to at this point."

I shrugged. "I dunno. I just did. It seemed oddly . . . natural. Necessary?"

Mrs. Leclair gave me a confused look, thinking.

But then a thought occurred to me, and I sat up, panicked, and looked around. "Wait. Is everyone okay? Where's Sybil?"

We looked around, suddenly nervous. "She was here. He never got to her. She ran around to the back of the house, and then you chased him up on the roof," Suzanne said, looking a little unsure.

Jermaine added, "I'll run to the back, she's probably hiding still." He jogged into the darkness, hollering her name.

Suzanne looked weary and scared. "You okay?" I asked her.

"Me? The question is are *you* okay? I didn't just transform into a werewolf and fight another one to the death. I just watched it all . . ." she answered. "Oh, and here's your necklace thing, it got ripped off in the fight. What is it?"

She handed me the medallion. The leather strap had snapped and I shoved it in my pocket.

I shrugged. "Just something I found in Grandpa's things. But man, am I tired. And I seriously need some food. You have no idea."

"Yeah, yeah, I know. You're *always* starving."

Mrs. Leclair made her way into the house to get something to tide me over, since we still needed to deal with Bruno. As I walked shakily up the front steps, Jermaine came running back around the house. His face was about as pale as it could be.

"What is it? Where's Sybil?" Suzanne asked.

He handed us his phone, which was open to a text message:

We have Sybil. Come to the pits. One hour.

Chapter 44

The message almost threw me into a rage, except my pangs of hunger were so strong I couldn't think straight.

As quickly as possible, I ate everything Mrs. Leclair put out.

"Who are 'they'?" Mrs. Leclair asked.

"Bruno's dimwitted best friends, Jed and Mike," Jermaine answered as I chewed a mouthful of cold, leftover roast beef.

"Can we borrow your truck?" Suzanne asked.

"Of course you *may*." Mrs. Leclair nodded. "But I'm coming, too. Tell me, if they were here and saw what happened, why would they take Sybil? Why not just run?"

"It's obvious," I answered.

"Is it?" asked Suzanne.

"Idiotic revenge," I said, swallowing a mouthful of milk. "They are about as stupid as they come, and I embarrassed both of them. They're gonna regret this even if they haven't harmed her."

Mrs. Leclair's eyes narrowed. "Don't be hasty. I understand you are upset, but they are teenage boys. They make poor choices. But unlike Bruno, they should have a future."

"They may not for long," I growled.

Mrs. Leclair looked at me questioningly.

"Sorry, I'm just . . . you know—pissed off. After all this, now those two mullets had to get involved," I answered, seeing the disapproval in her eyes. "Don't worry, they'll survive. They'll just wish they'd stayed away is all."

She sat down, looking at Jermaine and me. "I'm just not quite certain what they have to gain by being involved at this point. Do you have something they want?"

We both shrugged, then looked at Suzanne for support. "Don't look at me, I have no idea. It makes no sense."

"Security? Maybe negotiating with us to make sure that it ends tonight? They leave us alone and keep the secret as long as we leave them alone?" I volunteered. "Some type of insurance? Maybe they have a video of me and threaten to go public with it if something ever happens to either of them."

"Not a bad idea, to be honest," said Jermaine. "They just don't seem sharp enough to think of something like that."

"Perhaps," Mrs. Leclair answered, looking uncertain as she stood.

Grabbing a few pastries on the way out, I jumped into the back of the truck feeling reenergized. Suzanne would drive, with Mrs. Leclair as passenger. Jermaine and I were in the bed of the truck. We decided there was no point in trying to sneak up, since they already knew we were coming. Now it was a matter of striking a deal. I was prepared to agree to pretty much anything until we had Sybil back. After that, they would have nothing on me, and I would show no mercy.

Well, maybe a little.

The crisp night air cooled my skin as Suzanne sped down

the back roads to the quarry pits. My body still felt overheated, so the dropping temperature was welcome. Jermaine huddled down against the back window of the cab to escape the wind.

As Suzanne pulled into the abandoned parking lot, she shifted the old truck into park but left the lights on, pointed at the weed-covered trailer that had once housed the quarry's management team.

"This place has been closed since I was born, but they mined granite here for almost a hundred years," Jermaine whispered.

Beyond the trailer was the ledge: A one- to two-hundred foot drop straight down to the rock bottom below. At the very center of the lower pit was a pool of aqua-colored water, visible during the day when we came on our bikes. To the north end was a utility road that meandered down to the base of the quarry.

"I hope they didn't go down," Jermaine said, jumping out of the truck bed.

Stepping forward, I closed my eyes, inhaling deeply through my nose into the breeze.

Mango.

She was here.

"Jed? Mike?" I called out. "Where's Sybil?"

Silence.

"I know you're here," I shouted, feeling even more irritated at their games. "Hand over Sybil, and I promise to go easy on you."

The moon had moved across the sky, but its red glow through the smoke was still visible. It would normally have been brighter out with a moon that full. The breeze came up from the pit and Sybil's scent blew in again, and another one. It was familiar, but I couldn't quite place it.

Far to the left of the trailer and the headlight beams, two figures stepped out from another abandoned wooden shed. Only their silhouettes were visible in the faded crimson light.

My nerves went off; something wasn't right.

It wasn't Jed or Mike holding Sybil.

The taller of the two figures hollered out, "You came."

I knew that voice, a man's voice.

Sheriff Vincent.

Chapter 45

Crap.

Mrs. Leclair stepped forward, squinting at the two figures. "Sheriff, is that you?"

"Yes, Geneviève."

"Do you have Sybil?"

"Indeed."

Mrs. Leclair continued walking over. "Let her go, William. You know she has nothing to do with this. Take me."

Racking my brain, I still wasn't sure what Bruno's father knew. He must know everything if he had been there. Watching.

"What I want, *Geneviève*, is both of my sons back!" His voice cracked and he got louder. "And thanks to you and the Laurents, I need to tell my wife that her second and only remaining son is dead." His breathing was fast and his chest heaved in the moonlight. He was holding Sybil's arm with his right hand. His unstable state of mind worried me.

"William, choices were made. Mistakes were made. Chances were given. If you know about this, then you must know the whole story?" she answered.

He grunted. "I know enough."

"Why didn't you stop him? Why didn't you get help for your son?"

"I did not think he could be beaten so . . . easily. I don't understand. He needed to learn . . ."

"William, if you have been aware this whole time about what your sons were, you have yourself to blame just as much or more than anyone else. Please, let her go, take me."

"Shut up woman!" he yelled, blinking rapidly and rubbing the back of his neck, his voice trembling. I could almost feel sorry for him as he spoke. "My son, my *only* remaining son. Murdered by another Laurent. I have suffered losing two sons now. And you!" He turned to me. "Your father will feel *my* pain. He will lose his two children, just as I have," he said, spitting through his clenched teeth.

Suddenly, I felt the need to stand in front of Suzanne. He knew about my grandpa and his other son. About Bruno. About *me*.

As I realized the gravity of his knowing, I reached out to Suzanne, but she was faster and ran around me and close to him. "Take me. I'm a Laurent; it's my family you have debts with, not Sybil's."

"Suze!" I yelled, jumping forward to grab her.

Sheriff Vincent hollered, "Get back!" and pushed Sybil to the edge. She screamed. Her arms were tied behind her back as she helplessly teetered with only his hand holding her from falling.

I stopped and backed down.

Suzanne put her hand out. "Please. Take me."

It was Sybil now who called out. "No! Either way, he's not

going to let any of—"

The sheriff cut her off with a punch to her mouth. He pulled her from the edge as the sickening thud echoed off the rocks and she stumbled to the ground. He grabbed Suzanne in Sybil's place and wrenched her arm up behind her back.

"Fine," he yelled at Sybil. "Crawl away, you filthy piece of trash."

Coughing and spitting, Sybil did her best to roll out of his way and toward us.

Mrs. Leclair crept forward. "William, *please*. Take me. These kids were only defending themselves, you *know* that. They shouldn't be here. We shouldn't be here. It's over now."

He pushed Suzanne's arm up further, and she shrieked. Mrs. Leclair stopped. The sight of her wincing in painful tears caused the black mass inside me to stir, but I couldn't let it. He had Suzanne too close to the edge.

"You know," he continued, "I thought when I arranged for you to move here things would go much differently. We didn't even think you had the gift. Bruno was having great fun playing with you, but your demise was already certain. I wanted him to end you sooner, but Bruno still hurt from losing Grayson, so I let him have his way. My mistake," he spat in anger.

Wanting to keep him talking, I said, "But you didn't arrange the move. My grandfather did."

He laughed. "Your *grandfather* did? You did the exact opposite of his wishes. He didn't want you here, he never wanted you here. However, as sheriff, I do enjoy certain privileges. Having sway with the only two attorneys in town made it easy to doctor his will."

My pulse quickened again. "You changed his will? You arranged this?"

He smiled. "Of course. Why would your grandfather want you living here . . . among the wolves, if you'll pardon the expression. Before I killed Hub, I was clear with him that I would get his son and grandchildren. You should have seen the look on his face. He worked so hard to keep you away from all this."

A deep, loud growl rumbled from my throat, and I jumped forward, coursing with anger. The sheriff pushed Suzanne to the edge with sudden speed and held her there. "Easy!" he yelled, threatening to push her over.

I stopped. "Bruno killed my grandfather, not you."

The sheriff's features softened. "He thought he did, but he wasn't strong enough. I didn't have the heart to enlighten him. Fighting you was supposed to be practice for him. He was to let you change first. To play with you. It should have been easy for him; you are only a new, weak, half blood. Things did not go as planned. I still don't understand how you bested him."

"I had help."

"I saw that," he said, glowering at Jermaine. "But you had all but finished him; he only hastened the inevitable at that point. I have to ask, who was your mother?"

My mother? "No one, she's long gone. She ran off when I was little; she had mental issues," I hissed.

"Where was she from? Was she French?"

"No, she was American," I continued. "Listen, why don't you and I settle this, man to man? Why do you need to hide behind my sister?"

He smiled again. "Your two-bit reverse psychology won't

work on me, I'm afraid. But don't worry, you will get your chance. Trust me, it's what I want as well. I want to see if the Laurent half-breed makes up in youth what he lacks in blood. You may have beaten my son, but you have no chance with me."

Mrs. Leclair said he wasn't a lycan and he didn't know about them. I feared she was wrong on both counts. Cocking my head and wanting to buy some time, I asked, "What do you mean, half-breed?"

"You are only half French lycan. The other half is your mother's American genes. You may have powerful, early pure blood in your veins compared to mine, but it's only half. You can thank your father's poor choice in women for that weakness," he said with a laugh, amused with himself.

"My dad doesn't even know anything about this!"

"Oh, I know. But he will, don't worry. It might be the last thing he sees, his very worst nightmare come to life."

Mrs. Leclair stepped forward again. "Enough!" She probably sensed he almost had my temper snapped. She spun around and looked at me and Jermaine. "Please, back away. Let me handle this?"

She walked cautiously over to the sheriff. Sybil stood up beside me; she'd managed to get her arms in front of her, but they were still constricted by the plastic tie that bound her wrists. I pulled her hands up to my mouth, still watching the sheriff, and snapped it off with my teeth.

"Thanks," she whispered, rubbing her wrists. "Teavan, he wants you to lose it, just like we wanted Bruno to. There must be another way."

I was only half listening as I watched Mrs. Leclair approaching the sheriff and Suzanne. There seemed to be no options; I couldn't risk him pushing Suzanne off the edge.

Mrs. Leclair held out her hands. "Please, William. Let her go, take me."

He looked at Mrs. Leclair, Suzanne, then over at me and smiled. "As you wish." He pushed Suzanne to the ground with such force she went headfirst into the gravel. I released a deep breath at seeing Mrs. Leclair substituted for Suzanne. We were close to being ready.

Expertly, with his other hand, he reached out and grabbed Mrs. Leclair, easily spinning her around so she faced us. She closed her eyes with an almost eerie calmness about her.

"Please, *Geneviève*," he hissed, "don't take this the wrong way, you've always been a very pleasant adversary even if you didn't know it. But if not for you and Luc, we wouldn't be in this mess. And I would still have both of my boys."

In one quick, deft motion the sheriff grabbed her head with both hands and grunted as he twisted it suddenly with a *snap*. Her head angled unnaturally, and her eyes opened and rolled up as her body went limp and dropped to the ground.

My jaw dropped and my heart stopped at the sight.

Sybil screamed.

Suzanne was also screaming now, scrambling away from the sheriff on all fours in the dusty gravel. As he let go of Mrs. Leclair, he jumped forward and grabbed Suzanne's ankle, yanking her back to the edge. "Back off!" he hollered again, as I was in mid-stride toward him.

"You killed her!" I yelled, still not believing as Mrs. Leclair's body lay motionless on the ground, her face looking in the wrong direction.

"That was for Grayson," he said through clenched teeth.

I felt like I was going to be sick looking down at her lifeless body. Only seconds earlier she'd offered herself for Suzanne. Now she was dead.

Suzanne was on the ground, sobbing, as the sheriff held one of her ankles up. I looked back at Jermaine. He was on his knees with his hands covering his face. Tears streaked down Sybil's cheeks, but she stood just behind me, trembling and staring open-mouthed in disbelief.

In my peripheral vision, to the far left along the ledge of the quarry, I saw movement. Something creeping along, closing in on Suzanne and Vincent. A creature on four legs. As it got closer, it rocketed into a sprint and jumped up in the air toward the sheriff.

It was Honey.

In mid-air, she let loose a snarl just before her canine jaws locked onto the man's shoulder, catching everyone by surprise. Using his free arm, he tried to block her, but she got him and they went down.

This was our chance.

Running forward, I first wanted to pull Suzanne clear. "Get back!" I yelled at Sybil louder than I meant to. I didn't want him to get hold of anyone else and have more leverage against me.

The sheriff was struggling on the ground with Honey, but he still held Suzanne with one arm as I grabbed her hand. "Pull free!" I yelled to her. She kicked at his grip with her other foot, but he wasn't letting go.

Suddenly, I heard a sharp whine and Honey went rolling off the sheriff to the ledge and started slipping over, doing her best to scramble back.

"Honey!" I let go of Suzanne and jumped over to reach out for her collar, grabbing it just in time. The extra help was enough for her to find her footing and get back up.

The sheriff used the opportunity and was already up and dragging Suzanne by her ankle in the other direction.

His eyes met mine, and for one instant I knew his real intentions. There was to be no negotiation.

He grimaced as his other arm grabbed for her same foot. With both arms gripping her ankle, like an Olympian swinging the hammer, he spun around and pulled her up, letting her go in mid throw.

Suzanne's writhing figure went flying up and over the ledge. Her screams echoed off the quarry walls as she hurtled the hundred feet to the bottom. Then the sickening thud of her body landing on the granite floor reached us.

"Enough!" he cried as he turned to me with his eyes glowing red.

Chapter 46

My body went stiff.

This wasn't happening. The impossible echoes of Suzanne's screams filled the quarry until they were silenced just seconds later. Honey was up and barking, running at the sheriff as I looked over the edge.

In the faint crimson light, I could see her body far below. Her legs were bent under her at a sickening angle.

Sybil was yelling.

My vision turned red, almost like a calmness poured over me. Sheriff Vincent tossed Honey away from him with an easy effort and then looked at me for a reaction.

It felt surreal.

My fists clenched, my face twisted, and then the most intense fury I'd ever known took over. I leapt and transformed instantly in mid-air. By the look on his face I could tell he was shocked. By the time I reached out to him my hands were already claws, and they gripped his shoulders with my nails digging into him. He hollered in pain.

I threw the sheriff twenty feet across the open area. His body crashed through the rotting wall of the empty trailer, creating a hole where he disappeared inside.

There was yelling all around me, but none of it mattered now.

Only his death by my hands.

I ran on my two hind two legs to the trailer. Just as I was about to jump into the hole another werewolf jumped out—bigger than me. It wore his shredded pants.

His arms reached up, and as he leaned backward he let out a bloodthirsty cry. I jumped at his open torso, using the opportunity. We both went thudding into the side of the trailer, rolling and swiping at each other. I knew right away he was stronger than Bruno, and bigger. Primal instinct told me to run, but my anger wouldn't let me. I scrambled up to his neck, trying to get my jaws around it just like I did to Bruno, but he easily dodged and pushed me aside.

We stood and circled each other. He was taller and wider than his son, with more brown fur than black. His stance was surer, more steady.

Leaping forward, I attacked again, picking him up and running him backward like a linebacker holding a running back. He used the chance to sink his teeth into my shoulder, the pain flooding my upper body and neck. Stumbling, I let go and fell to my knees, grasping my bloody shoulder. Before I could look up, he had my head in his claws, twisting it with immense power, trying to break my neck. I gritted my teeth, reaching up to pull his arms free, but he was so *strong*. Against my will, my neck was slowly turning the wrong way . . .

BANG!

A gunshot thundered through the air, so close it was deafening to my sensitive ears.

BANG!

Again.

The tension on my neck eased just enough to pull his vise-like claws off my head so I could stand.

BANG!

His arms shuddered with each shot. I spun around to face him, a look of agony on his lycan snout. His eyes were glossy and unfocused, his outstretched arms swinging wildly.

Behind him, Sybil was running the other way with the pistol. She'd used the last three bullets.

Which weren't silver.

This time, I reached for his face. I clawed it, trying to gouge his eyes out with my sharp and powerful nails. His cheek ripped open, but I couldn't quite get to his eyes before he regained his composure and tried to defend himself, blindly pushing me back. His strength grew again as the gunshots healed, and his eyes straightened out and found mine as we struggled. Our arms were locked. I used the claws on my leg to try to eviscerate him, but he brought his knee up in defense, and we both went rolling to the ground again.

This time, he ended up on top, pinning me. My strength was waning; he was too big. I turned to see Honey lying motionless in the distance. Jermaine and Sybil were throwing something—rocks—but they bounced harmlessly off my enemy. There was victory in his eyes, defeat in my soul. He let loose a final roar, his putrid, hot breath blowing in my face, and then he locked his impressive jaw onto my neck despite my struggles.

One of my last thoughts was that he would do to me as I had done to his son.

Chapter 47

Stinging pain shot out in every direction from my neck, and once his grip was locked he pulled hard. Holding him with everything I had, my neck started to give, and my grip started to loosen.

Just as my vision had almost gone dark, something strange happened. Abruptly, a dark figure came flying from nowhere, and grabbed the lycan's face. Clearly, he hadn't been expecting it, and the new intruder's claws dug into the sheriff's undefended eyes. He howled and let his jaw go loose, letting go of my throat. The smell of my blood was overwhelming, its heat spreading to the ground beneath me.

The other lycan figure was on top of the sheriff, its claws digging into his face.

The sheriff twisted and yelped before finally knocking the intruder off. My throat stung, but it was still intact as I tried to get up.

Our enemy was standing and shrieking with his hands to his face. As they came down, I could see that both eye sockets were bloody and damaged. The other lycan attacked the sheriff's midsection, knocking him to the ground.

I dove toward his top half, his own throat now exposed.

Working together, it only took us a few seconds time to finish him off for good this time.

Panting and weak, I stood, facing the new lycan. The intruder.

My rescuer.

He stood tall, though not as tall as I. We both eyed each other with uncertainty.

Sybil and Jermaine remained at a safe distance, watching. They backed farther away.

My anger was dissipating; I felt he meant no harm, and my defenses were weakening as I fell to my knees in exhaustion. The other one stepped closer, his head cocked to the side.

Right before I blacked out, his scent stirred a memory in me.

It was not immediately clear what was happening when I woke up. It was cool, my only clothing was the shorts, and the only light was the red moon that had shifted almost to the horizon.

Someone was lying right beside me. Before even looking, I knew who it was from the mango scent. She was shaking.

I startled her as I attempted to sit up. "Sybil?"

She quickly skittered away so our bodies no longer touched. "Hey . . ."

"What happened? Where is everyone?"

A shadow crossed her face in the low light. "There is no *everyone*. It's just Jermaine now, and he's gone to get food, keys, and supplies."

Sheriff Vincent. I turned and saw his naked body twenty feet away, lifeless and bloody. Then I remembered Mrs. Leclair, also dead. Honey must not have been too badly hurt, as she was curled up a few feet away.

Then I remembered Suzanne. Her death.

Tears sprang to my eyes. I didn't bother to blink them away. As if she could see everything was coming back to me, Sybil shuffled closer and laid her palm on my cheek, just staring at me as the tears rolled down.

"I'm so sorry, Teavan," she said, her body trembling. Her bare arms and legs had gooseflesh, and I realized it was the cold she was shaking from. Or at least I assumed.

I reached up and pulled her frigid hand off my cheek, but held it in my warm hands. "You're freezing."

She shrugged. "I'm fine."

Pulling her closer, she came in reluctantly and I did my best to wrap myself around her. "I g-guess I should have dressed warmer," she stuttered.

She pulled away at first, but the heat I provided must have proved too necessary because she eventually sank in, letting me wrap her in it. In the pocket of my shorts, I could feel the medallion in there squeezed between us. It gave me an unexplained relief at knowing it was still safe.

"You are so warm," she said. "I was lying against you, worried about you but also needing your heat. Waiting for Jermaine."

I didn't want to think about Suzanne. I couldn't. I tried to block it out.

"He's getting supplies? What supplies?"

She was quiet at first. "We talked, you were hurt, your . . . throat and all. We need to do something with the bodies, and thought maybe the quarry water? He's getting ropes, some food for you, and hopefully another set of keys for Mrs. Leclair's truck."

Suzanne had the other set. She was gone. Tears continued to stream down my face.

"He might be a while, since he had to walk. I didn't want to leave you here alone, so I stayed back to watch over you."

Suzanne died to save us.

A distant memory triggered. "Wait!" I was racking my brain, going over the foggy events. The memories weren't clear, but they were coming back. The *other* wolf. It helped me. It saved me.

I know that wolf.

It couldn't be.

Jumping up, I ran over to the ledge of the quarry, searching the dark bottom with my eyes.

Suzanne's crumpled body was gone.

"Look!" I pointed down as Sybil came up beside me, squinting.

"I can't see anything?"

"Exactly," Adrenaline pumped through me. "She's gone!"

"Who? I mean, I can't *see* anything, it's too dark? What are you looking at?"

I smiled. "Suzanne, her body, it's gone. That other werewolf—that was *her!*"

Sybil's jaw dropped and her eyes sparkled. "That wolf was Suzanne? Are you sure? After you passed out, it transformed into a full four-legged wolf. I thought it was going to kill us, but then it ran off. Are you sure?"

Once again, my eyes welled up, but in joy this time. She was *alive.*

I nodded fast, unable to speak; worried I'd break down sobbing. Not only was she alive and well, she was like me. I grabbed the shivering Sybil and pulled her in close, and she once again futilely tried to resist, then gave in with her cold cheek resting on my bare chest. Her arms folded up between us to keep warm. She felt so tiny and vulnerable in my grip, not like the Sybil I usually knew.

An unbelievable joy filled me, like a bubble of happiness. My sister was *alive*. The flip from excruciating sadness to an unbelievable joy took over, and I laughed.

Less gently than intended, I grabbed Sybil's face, turned it to mine, and grinned. She had a confused look as we stared at each other. I can't explain why, but this overwhelming urge to kiss her took over. I leaned in and kissed her cold lips.

Her body went even more rigid than it had been, and she pushed me back, wide-eyed. "What the hell are you doing?"

I don't know, I thought, unable to contain my joy.

My unwavering gaze continued, though I said nothing. Her angry grimace softened as she tilted her head and searched my eyes. I wasn't sure what she was thinking, but she seemed less upset. Her body relaxed, and she stopped pushing me away. Her head tilted a little more, and she reached up to me this time. Leaning down, our mouths connected again, but the feelings mutual.

Starting gently, but then becoming frantic. Like an insatiable need.

Her arms wrapped around me, and mine around her. She was cold and trembling, her body pressed tightly against mine. I'm not sure how long we kissed, but thoughts of all else disappeared while we did. Energy flowed back and forth between us, and she kissed me even more aggressively. Her tongue reached out and explored my lips, and I did the same.

In time, our mouths parted, and she nuzzled into my neck. We both remained quiet. Sybil's shivering stopped, and her grip on me tightened. It felt so natural. *So right.* Thinking of Sybil romantically had never occurred to me before. I didn't even think she liked me, let alone had feelings for me. I couldn't picture her having feelings for any guy; she pushed everyone away.

But for this moment, she was completely mine. We felt like one, with an unspoken bond and understanding.

My eyes were closed and I savored that moment for what seemed like forever.

Until I heard footsteps in the distance—shoes in the gravel. Over Sybil's head and through the dark I could see Jermaine. I could tell from his walk.

As soon as Sybil heard the footsteps, she went rigid again and pushed away. "Jermaine?" she called out, distancing herself from me.

"Yeah," he answered, holding up a duffel bag as he approached. "You okay? How you feelin'?" he asked me quietly.

Smiling again, I answered, "Great."

"Great?" he asked, appearing surprised.

Nodding to him. "It's Suzanne—she's alive. She was the *other* werewolf, the one that saved me."

One of his eyebrows shot up. "Wha? Are you messin'?"

I shook my head. "No. It was her."

"Wow, well, that's good. Dude, I'm happy to hear that, that's the best news I've had all day," he said, dropping the bag down and leaning in to hug me. "Where is she?"

"Out," I said. "She'll be back."

"I brought a bunch of ropes and ties, and there is a tarp already in the truck. I brought every keychain I could find in Mrs. Leclair's house. Hopefully one is for the pickup," he said, looking at both of us.

I shook my head. "I don't think we should sink him in that water. The sheriff—that is. Things will get complicated, and Bruno's mom will already have to deal with her son's death, then for her husband to just go missing . . . I think we leave him, let the cops deal with it. It's over. But we should bring Mrs. Leclair home; we can't leave her body here."

After some discussion they agreed, and we carefully put Mrs. Leclair's body in the back of the truck. Jermaine attempted to drive us as best he could, since none of us had a license. I stayed with Mrs. Leclair, making sure she didn't roll around.

She deserved so much more. She was only trying to help us, to mediate the situation. And now she was dead.

I'd never get all the answers she promised me.

It was still dark when we got to her house, ultimately deciding to leave Bruno as he was, all mangled in her yard. But we put Mrs. Leclair carefully on her porch. The cops could try to piece together whatever happened here.

As we cleaned out our stuff from around the house, in case they looked for evidence, I heard a rustling in the bushes. I stiffened.

"Hey!" someone whispered through the trees.

A smile came to my face, and I ran through the yard to the source.

"Don't come any closer!!"

It was Suzanne, hiding in the shrubs.

Still smiling, I asked, "Let me guess, you need something to cover yourself with?"

Her milky white face peaked through the green leaves. "Please."

Chapter 48

As I darted past the truck, I could see Jermaine inside, wiping the steering wheel and everything down with bathroom and tub cleaner we found in the house. We weren't sure, but we hoped it would get rid of our fingerprints.

The sun was almost coming up as I ran into the house in search of something for Suzanne to wear. In the kitchen, Sybil was washing dishes. We thought it would be best if the kitchen was clean and that it not look like she had been entertaining or feeding people that night.

Sybil didn't hear me as I came in softly, looking around for Suzanne's bag. She stood scrubbing, face turned away and toward the sink. Her scruffy jean shorts revealed her scratched legs and bare feet. She looked cute and almost domestic standing there with an apron on.

Tiptoeing up behind her, I gently reached for her sides and leaned my face into her messy hair. "Suzanne's returned," I whispered and kissed her head.

She was quick to shrug me off. "Huh? What are you doing?" she spat, spinning around with a scowl.

"I was just . . . saying hi? I mean, you know, after what happened and all?"

Sybil shook her head. "Don't do that again, Teavan. Things earlier . . . that was stupid. We got caught up in the chaos, made a dumb decision. End of story."

I stepped back. "Caught up? I wasn't caught up in anything. You kissed me back. You *felt* it."

She shook her head again. "Fine. *I* got caught up, whatever. This can't work anyway, and we both know it. Someone always gets hurt, so it's best to leave things. You like Rachel and she likes you. I'll never do anything to hurt her."

"Well, yeah, but things are different now. So much has happened, so much has changed," I said, thinking about our kiss and the events before it.

She turned to the sink. "So, let me ask you this. You had a huge crush on Rachel, and then she gets hurt, so you change your mind? Did you think of me in that way—even yesterday?"

I shrugged. "I don't know. But I do know something has changed between us."

"Like I said, it was the situation, the emotion of knowing Suzanne was okay. We both got caught up in things."

At that moment, Jermaine bounded into the kitchen with cleaning materials in hand. "Teavan, you'd better get out there! Your sister is here and calling for you. She freaked out when I went to help her."

Her bag was under the table and I grabbed it. Sybil said nothing, finishing up with the dishes.

"Be right back," I said.

Running across the yard toward the trees, I held the bag out. "You there?"

"What took you so long?" she hissed.

I tossed it in the shrubs. "Sorry. I'll meet you inside."

Walking back to the house, I wondered, *Was that all it was? Getting caught up in the moment?* It was definitely the wrong time for romance, and yet, as I thought about Sybil, I knew it was different. We were changed.

I liked her *differently* now. Had it been there all along?

Maybe that was wrong, given Rachel and all. Was I a bad person? It's not like Rachel and I were boyfriend and girlfriend. But we had shared a kiss that night, albeit a small one. An innocent one.

My kiss with Sybil was not the same, it was much deeper, more passionate.

That kiss felt *right*.

Suzanne joined us in the kitchen a few minutes later, looking filthy and a little worse for wear. But otherwise healthy and definitely not dead. She remembered bits and pieces from before she fully transformed, then it all went hazy as she tried to recount the last few hours.

She ate everything in the fridge, too. Well, not everything, but quite a bit. I knew how she felt.

"So, now what?" she asked, down to eating bread with peanut butter on it.

Jermaine, Sybil, and I joined her at the table.

"We go home soon, and we know nothing about any of this. I'll bike over here later, saying Honey was barking and upset about something, so I came over to investigate. I'll put a call into the sheriff's office and we'll let the police deal with it," I suggested.

"And Sheriff Vincent?" Suzanne asked.

I shrugged. "Someone will find him, and until then he'll be

missing."

Jermaine leaned in. "What about Kevin? He's been texting me apologies all night."

The mention of his name made angry. "Who cares."

"But he knows; he'll know the truth. We need to talk to him either way," he answered.

"Is he awake?" I asked.

Jermaine nodded. "I think so. I get a text every thirty minutes asking if we are okay."

"Tell him to come over then. Quick."

Kevin arrived shortly after on his bike. It was almost seven in the morning. He, too, looked like he hadn't slept much. He held his head low as he parked his bike. At the sight of Bruno's body, he started coughing and dry heaving. The four of us came out and stood on the porch. Mrs. Leclair's body was beside the wicker furniture, covered up with a blanket.

"Is . . . is that *him*?" he asked, avoiding Bruno's body as he shuffled over.

Jermaine nodded. "Uh huh."

Everyone just stood there; nobody talked. Kevin's eyes were puffy and red.

"I . . . I can't apologize enough to you guys for what I did. Bruno—he knew; he came to my house yesterday. Made me talk to him, threatened to kill my little sister if I didn't tell him something. I was so scared. For me, for her . . . for my whole family. I know it was wrong and I'm so sorry," he said, wiping tears away with the back of his arm.

Jermaine took a step down, glaring at Kevin. "Dude, you gave us up! We could've been killed. You basically signed our death warrants."

"But you aren't dead," he countered. "Everyone is okay, it all worked out. Right, bro?"

Jermaine shook his head. "Don't call me that, you ain't my brother. A brother wouldn't give you up when things get dicey. You're just a coward."

"But—"

"And," Jermaine continued, "things aren't all okay." He walked back up the steps and lifted the blanket. "If you want to apologize to someone, apologize to *her*."

Kevin's eyes went wide as they processed the corpse of Mrs. Leclair, and his hand came up to his mouth. "Bruno killed her?"

"No, but his dad did," Jermaine said, dropping the blanket back down.

We reluctantly updated a teary-eyed Kevin on what happened over the night, but left out the part about Suzanne almost dying and changing as well. He didn't need to know about her.

Even I was feeling a little bad for the guy. He seemed genuinely sorry, and I could kinda get where he was coming from. Though I still wouldn't have squealed.

"What can I do?" Kevin asked, looking to each of us.

"Not much you can do now," I said. "Just go with the story and keep your mouth shut. Hopefully this will all be a memory in time."

"And . . . us?" he asked, looking at everyone but particularly Jermaine.

Jermaine shook his head. "Dude, there is no *us*. We were here—together—we ended this. You? You gave us up, left us for dead. That's all there is."

Kevin's lip quivered, and tears streamed down his face again. "I know, trust me, I know. I wish I could take it back."

"Easy to say now," Jermaine said.

Jermaine and Kevin had been friends a lot longer than I'd known either of them, so the hurt probably ran a lot deeper between the two of them. They stood staring mostly at each other.

"F-fair enough," Kevin stammered, getting on his bike. "Well, if there is anything I can do, call me. And I hope one day you guys can forgive me."

And with that, he rode back down the lane as quietly as he'd come.

I noticed tears glistening in the morning sun on Jermaine's cheek as he watched Kevin ride off. Suzanne, Sybil, and I said nothing as we walked back in the house.

We decided to leave a short time later, not wanting to get home too early, but not wanting to be there in case the police showed up. I wanted to crawl into my bed and sleep for a week.

We said our awkward goodbyes and took the covers off both bodies. Jermaine and Sybil headed back into town, while Suzanne and I went to our place with Honey limping quietly beside us.

"We should talk," I said as we tiptoed up our front steps, hoping not to wake Dad if he was still sleeping.

"I know," she said. "But not now; I'm so tired I could sleep in the grass."

I knew how she felt.

Nodding, I opened the front door. The house was quiet, and my dad's bedroom door was closed. He was still asleep.

We retreated to our bedrooms in silence, and I crawled under the covers and quickly drifted off.

Although I didn't know it at first, the same dream returned that morning, though a little different than before. There was knocking at the front door, and the wind howled outside the house.

I got up and noticed Honey wasn't there, but thought nothing of it as I stumbled down the hall to answer the door.

As I approached, old dream memories returned and I knew I was in a dream. I *knew* who was outside without even looking. Fear filled my body as I backed away from the locked door, and the knocking persisted. The old woman's cackles could be heard above the wind.

However, when I turned to hide, Suzanne was standing behind me, motionless. "You're home?" she asked.

"Uh huh." I nodded, wondering if she'd had the same dream. "You are too, finally."

The outside screen door opened, and the pounding started on the inside door, sending icy shivers down my spine. Suzanne joined me in the front entrance.

"Should we just let her in?" Suzanne whispered, keeping an eye on the door.

Outside, the winds suddenly stopped blowing right as I came to the same decision.

But then the screen door slammed shut and it was quiet.

In the distance, someone was calling my name.

As Suzanne unlocked the door, I saw the old woman was

gone.

We had already let her in. Getting in our house had never been what she was after.

"Teavan!" my dad said, shaking me awake from the dream.

Blinking, I looked around my sun-filled room, confused. "Dad?"

He smiled. "Rise and shine! It's past two in the afternoon! What is with you?"

I looked at the clock, it was 2:17.

Shrugging, with one eye closed, I answered, "Tired Dad, real tired. We didn't get much sleep last night."

"Evidently your sister didn't, either," he answered as he walked out into the hall and knocked on her door. Honey stood up and lay directly on me, licking my face with her gross dog breath.

"Honey!" I yelped as I hid my head under the pillow, but enjoying her loving attention.

Time to face the world.

Chapter 49

Over our late breakfast, my dad shared some terrible news with us. The sheriff and his son had been mauled by a wild animal. Or a pack of wild animals. Turned out maybe my friend Jermaine had been right about wolves, he reluctantly admitted.

And even worse, our dear neighbor to the west, Geneviève Leclair, had also died, possibly of a heart attack, but the police weren't sure yet. The county was under an immediate curfew until the animals responsible could be contained.

"I want you close to home, and Honey, too. Terrible thing. That poor Vincent woman has lost both her sons, and her husband now. And Santa Isadora has lost its sheriff."

"See Dad?" Suzanne said, with less snark than usual. "We should have just stayed in New York."

He eyed her with one eyebrow up. "There are *plenty* of murders in New York, I'll have you know. Statistically speaking, we are much safer here."

She winked at me, then poked her head back into the fridge, looking for more leftovers. "Doesn't seem safer," she mumbled.

To say I was missing my cell phone is an understatement. It was driving me nuts. I wanted to text Rachel because I didn't want to make a call or visit, and I wanted to text Sybil something because I couldn't make the call. I'd promised to visit Rachel, so I had to go, even though I no longer felt right about it.

We told Dad I forgot some textbooks at Jermaine's, and Suzanne volunteered to drive me to pick them up. Dad asked us to grab some ground beef for dinner while we were out.

Suzanne and I had so much to talk about on the short drive. We were both sickened by what happened to Mrs. Leclair, and even Bruno and Mr. Vincent—though that was necessary. And I was probably more excited than I should have been now that I knew she was a lycan as well. Not being alone in this journey felt oddly reassuring, especially now that my only mentor was gone.

Though we had no one to talk to about it, at least we had each other.

As we drove through town to the medical center, I asked her to make a quick stop.

"Here? Why?" she asked, wondering what possible reason I had for stopping at the lumber supply store.

"Just gimme a sec."

Running into Timberland Lumber gave me second thoughts, but I continued to the front help desk. It was loud, busy, and smelled like fresh cut wood inside the industrial retail space.

"Is Mr. Hughes working today?" I asked.

The lady at the front desk looked up. "He's in the back, through those staff doors. Just poke your head in and holler."

Dodging a small forklift, I walked to the back of the store and pushed through the marked double doors, looking around. "Mr. Hughes?"

A man was cutting plywood. He turned the saw off, lifted his goggles to his forehead, and turned around. "Eh?" he said.

"Mr. Hughes?" I asked again.

He nodded. "What do you want? I'm not working on the floor right now."

Trevor Hughes was not a small man: probably six feet tall and over two hundred pounds. He had tattoos on his bare arms, and his head was shaved bald, but he had a full black beard. My second thoughts returned.

He put the goggles on the table. "What's up, kid?"

"Are you Sybil's father?" I asked.

His previously neutral demeanor disappeared. "Yeah, why? What's she done now?"

Stepping forward, I said, "Nothing. That's the problem."

Despite a bit of a belly, I could tell he had once been in good shape. His neck muscles tensed. "What the hell do you want?"

I hesitated. "Don't ever hurt her again, got it?"

His face crinkled. "Excuse me?"

"You heard me."

Mr. Hughes took off his gloves now, sizing me up with a smile. "What, are you her boyfriend or something? Is that where she tramps off to? You think you are some tough guy 'cause you're captain of the football team?"

I shook my head. "No. She doesn't even have a boyfriend, but that's not the point. I'm just saying, don't touch her. *Ever*. And she's about as far as they come from being a tramp; I only wish you could see that."

Quick as a flash, he grabbed and pushed me back, bending me over the bench, spittle flying out as he barked, "You little pissant. How dare you come to my place of work and threaten me."

My back hurt as the corner of the table gouged into it; his full weight was pushing me down. It was what I wanted.

The feeling was coming, deep down in the pit of my stomach. I pulled on it just a little, and let loose a deep-throated growl as I glared up at him.

His eyes jumped open from anger to surprise, and I pushed him off me easily.

It was my turn.

He stood, momentarily confused. Before he could react, I grabbed his thick work shirt and thrust him against the wall, my face just inches from his. I growled—loudly—and lifted him up against the wall, about six inches off the floor.

My voice was guttural and raspy, full of anger. "I *said* don't ever touch her again, or I will come back, and I will *end* you. Understand?"

The terrified look in his eyes alerted me just seconds before the smell of urine did that he understood. As I lowered him back to the ground, into a small puddle around his boots, I mockingly straightened out his shirt and industrial apron.

"She's a good girl; don't forget it. Just appreciate it," I said, almost politely.

I turned and left the room. Mr. Hughes said nothing further.

Pissant.

"What was that about?" Suzanne asked as I got back in the

car.

"Nothing," I said, putting on my seatbelt. "I just had a quick talk with Sybil's dad about his treatment of her."

"Oh no," she said, shaking her head. But then she smiled. "And?"

I grinned. "I think we have an understanding."

Rachel's parents stood when I entered her room.

"You two can visit. Dad and I will run home for a few minutes, okay?" Mrs. Denning asked Rachel.

She smiled weakly. "Sure," she said, then looked at me. "Hey big guy."

"Big guy?"

Her laugh turned to a cough. "Sorry, couldn't help it."

As I stood there awkwardly, she patted her bed. "Sit."

My eyes looked down at the spot she patted. She looked a lot better today. Her hair was done perfectly and held back in her customary headband. She even had a little makeup on, more color in her cheeks against the white bandages.

But being here felt *wrong*.

Not only because of my changed feelings, but because of who I was. *What* I was. I remembered her saying something like 'if there is divine good in this world, there must also be evil.'

Was that me now? It may not have been me that harmed her, but it was one of my kind. An evil abomination.

"What?" she asked, tilting her head. "Are you okay?"

I shook myself out of it. "You look better today, that's all. Healthier."

She turned red. "Thanks. I *feel* better. They let me have a

289

proper shower, and I could finally comb my hair. I can't wait to get out of here tomorrow, I hate hospitals. Did you hear what happened last night?"

I nodded. "Yeah. I can't believe it. My poor neighbor."

"It's scary, Teavan. Whatever did this to me . . . it's getting worse. And now they're calling for a curfew for the whole county. This doesn't seem right. It doesn't seem *natural*. I'll bet you never had issues like this back in New York."

I shook my head. "Nope. But we had shootings and muggings to deal with. Nah, I think things will be okay. I'm not really worried, to be honest."

Her head tilted again. "Not worried? Some rabid mountain lion or werewolf killing people near your house and that don't worry you? Because it should. I keep having nightmares . . . I drift off so often in this bed, and the attack replays itself over and over. It makes me sick to think it's still out there."

"I know, but I just have this feeling that everything is going to be okay. You don't need to worry anymore."

She grabbed my hand, holding it in both of hers. "For some reason, against all logic, I almost believe you. You have this weird, reassuring presence. Has anyone ever told you that?"

"No." I tried to gently pull my hand back. I was a fake. I *was* her nightmare.

"It . . . it makes me feel safe."

It shouldn't.

Rachel was staring at me intently, and I at her, but not for the same reason. I had to snap myself out of it. "Has anyone ever told you that you have this weird, super positive and happy presence?"

She laughed. "Well, not in so many words, but Sybil has mentioned it. Though for her, I'm not sure it's necessarily a good thing."

"Well, it is," I said, and I meant it. Her positivity was infectious, and her quiet nearness made me feel calm. Her hands on mine felt cool.

There were these impenetrable walls around Sybil that made me want to get through them. It was like a challenge. But with Rachel, she let me in; let me see her as she was. It was a nice change. With Rachel, it wasn't a constant battle. It was easy and comfortable.

Except Rachel didn't know what evil lurked inside me. Sybil did.

"Teavan?" she asked.

"Huh?"

"You looked like you were trying to stare into my soul."

I was staring into my own. "Sorry. Just lost in thought, I guess."

"Are you okay? You seem . . . different today."

Not only am I your worst nightmare, I'm also in love with your cousin. I'm a fraud.

"Just tired."

I needed to leave.

Her eyes flicked up to the door and her face cracked into a grin. "Come in!" she waved with her free hand. Sybil was there with a small bag in her hand. She had been watching. Slowly and discreetly, I tried to pull my hand away, but Rachel tightened her grip.

"My two *favorite* people." Rachel smiled, patting the other side of the bed. "Well, besides my parents."

Stiffly, Sybil sat down and passed Rachel the bag. "Here is the stuff you wanted."

"Thanks," Rachel said, putting it on the bedside table.

Sybil and I nodded to each other, but she said nothing.

"I should let you two catch up, have some alone time," Sybil said, not looking at me. "We've already had our visit today."

"No! Stay! You can both stay, this place is so boring, you don't know. And I love my parents and all, but they aren't that much fun after a while. Did you bike here?" she asked me.

"No, Suzanne drove me. She's in the waiting room, said to say hi. I actually don't have that much time, she said to make it quick. Homework and all."

I just wanted out of this hospital.

Rachel frowned. "I wish that was my biggest problem—homework. For once, I'm really sad to be missing school. Hopefully I can return next week.

"Enjoy it while you can, you'll be back in class before you know it," I said, trying to lighten things. "But I really should be going. So you're checking out tomorrow?"

Rachel nodded. "Yes, that's the plan."

"How about we talk then?"

"Okay. Don't forget."

"I won't," I said. "Sybil, can I talk to you for a second? Outside?"

Sybil scowled and looked annoyed. "Umm, I guess? Can it wait until school tomorrow?"

I shook my head. "No, it's about the trig test," I lied.

"Fine," she mumbled, getting up. "Be right back, Rachel."

Rachel held out her arms for a hug, and I leaned in

reluctantly. She smelled much better today, her sweet scent now masking the smell of the hospital.

I probably smelled of evil. Of murder. If she only knew what I'd done not twelve hours before.

"See ya, *big guy*," she said with a wink.

I tried to join her in laughing, but it felt fake, and I slipped out of the room.

In the hall, Sybil stood with her hands on her hips. "What?"

"Are you . . . mad? This whole thing, it's awkward."

"Mad? About what? Everything is fine," she said, doing her best to look me in the eye.

"Just this weird triangle thing and all. I'll tell Rachel once she's feeling better, that things won't work out between me and her. Even if you don't want any part of me. I promise."

Sybil smiled, looking forced into something she didn't often do. "Teavan, there is no triangle. There is me, and there is you and her. Trust me, it's all good. See you tomorrow in class." And with that, she went back into Rachel's room and closed the door.

As I walked into the waiting room, Suzanne looked up from her phone. "Ready to go?"

"Yep."

Chapter 50

The drive home was quiet at first.

"Anything you want to talk about?" Suzanne asked.

"Not really."

"Woman trouble?"

"Kinda."

"Tell me about it."

I was quiet, not used to opening up about my feelings.

"Come on, little brother. We have a lot more between us now than we ever have, and this is relatively small."

It didn't *feel* small. "Well, just this whole Rachel-me-Sybil thing."

"I see. That is complicated. Do they both know? Feel the same?"

"Yes and no," I said, rubbing my face. "Like, first I was really attracted to Rachel, and we clicked, and it was awesome. She's *so* awesome. And not just because she's super pretty. She has a heart of gold and I really like her." And I meant it.

"But then with Sybil, she *knows* about my secret. And even though she's so difficult, we kissed last night. Like a deep, serious kiss. There was this insane connection between us. Like we knew each other's souls. She knows my darkest secret, and yet, she kissed me so deeply. We've been through so much, and when I woke last night, it was *her* with me, taking care of me in the middle of the night."

Suzanne looked over at me as she turned down the rural road where our house was. "I wondered what was happening. Besides the obvious chaos, there was something very odd between you two this morning. I noticed you kept trying to get her attention and she avoided it. So, you had a crush on the school sweetheart, but now you have serious feelings for the hard-to-get girl."

"No, it's not like that."

"No?"

"It's not because Rachel is a sweetheart. And not because Sybil is hard to get. It just turned out that way."

"I mean, I like Rachel and all, she's great from what I know. But now . . . given all this, she doesn't seem right for you. And with Sybil, maybe it's just because it was your first real kiss? "

I shook my head. "No, that's not it. And it wasn't my *first real kiss*, I'll have you know. It's more than that, but I hear what you're saying. That's pretty much what she said."

"So she doesn't want to pursue it?"

"No, she doesn't. But I think it's because of Rachel. It's complicated."

"So it appears," she added. "You know, I like Sybil. *A lot*. I mean, she's rough around the edges, but these last few days with her . . . I don't know. I like her. She's real. But maybe there's something to what she's saying. I mean, the timing isn't great. It's not even good. You've got a lot of stuff to deal with after last night—I know I do. And with who we are, *what* we are . . . maybe it's the exact wrong time to complicate things by pursuing a relationship with anyone."

I closed my eyes, thinking about last night. Mrs. Leclair. Bruno. The sheriff. My brain hadn't even really acknowledged events yet.

"You're probably right."

"Hey, last night," she asked. "Did we answer the front door together for that woman in the wheelchair? In a dream? Or was it just something I dreamed?"

My pulse quickened at the memory. "That's right! I forgot about that. Every time I've dreamt of her, you're never there."

"Neither are you," she said, smirking. "Who is she? She's scary for senior citizen in a wheelchair."

"Tell me about it. She's Sabine Martin. There was a picture of her in Mrs. Leclair's scrapbook."

"But . . . how?"

I shrugged. "Beats me. How is *any* of this happening?"

Suzanne leaned over and ruffled my hair with a smile. "Who knew just a few short weeks ago that you would become a werewolf, then I would, and then you would be juggling two girls that are not only cousins but best friends?"

That ridiculous thought actually made me almost laugh. "Right? Man, things seemed so much simpler in New York. Speaking of, how are *you* feeling about this werewolf thing?"

She pulled up to the house and parked, but left the car running. "Honestly, I've barely had time to process things today. No offence, but this really sucks. My whole life— everything—is not going to be as I planned. Marriage. Kids. New York. You name it." She leaned forward with her eyes closed and put her head on the steering wheel.

I rubbed her back. "It's not that bad, Suze."

She looked over, her eyes welling up. "No, it is *that bad*. I can never be normal, Teavan. I might have to live near you forever, so we can look after each other."

"Gee, thanks."

"You know what I mean. I'm no longer free to do whatever I want with life. I'm bound by this freakin' curse," she said with a sniffle.

"There are positives, you know. Remember what Mrs. Leclair said, some of the most successful people have the gene. You'll be better at almost everything."

"I don't want to be strong. I just want to be normal." With that, she turned the car off and got out, head down, and walked quietly up the steps.

It was nearly six o'clock, and the thought of school in the morning just seemed impossible given the events of the weekend.

Suzanne and I spoke very little during dinner, but my dad made up for it. He said the game wardens had been by earlier, and they warned him about wild animals in the vicinity and about keeping vigilant.

As he spoke, I kept going over every event of the weekend in my mind. I longed to crawl into bed. I was exhausted, but at the same time dreaded Monday morning. The sooner I closed my eyes, the sooner the alarm would go off to wake up. Though getting back to some type of normal would be refreshing. Maybe I just needed to be *sick* tomorrow . . .

Honey was under the table, and she suddenly jumped up

and ran to the front door, barking. Moments later, the doorbell rang.

Two tall, clean-cut men in dark suits stood at the door, with a black Suburban parked in our driveway. They introduced themselves as Officer Davis and Officer Miller of the California Department of Fish and Wildlife.

"Someone was already here from the Game Department," Dad said, a little surprised.

Officer Davis stepped forward. "We are in a different division, a higher priority subdivision, if you will. We specialize in large predators that have caused harm to people, unlike our counterparts who also do fish, waters, plants, hunting, etcetera."

My dad nodded. "I see."

Davis motioned to the sofa in the living room. "May we come in?"

Chapter 51

We went over the events of the weekend, and got similar warnings from these two as Dad had from the officers earlier.

"Santa Isadora has had more than its fair share of *incidents* over the years. This isn't the first time we've been here. As a matter of fact, we had an unofficial alliance with your father until his untimely passing," Miller said. "My condolences on your loss."

"Thank you," my dad said. "But he wasn't a warden. He didn't even hunt, did he?"

"No, not really. But he loved this area and he was passionate about wildlife. We can't really have officers in every county, so we have volunteers here and there to assist and tip us off as necessary," he said. "But the events here this weekend are obviously particularly disturbing and worrisome."

"I'll say," my dad said. "Three deaths! What can we do?"

"Follow the curfew and be aware. Don't leave food or garbage outside if you can help it. And please, report anything you see or hear," Miller added, handing my dad a business card, but looking at me.

"Rest assured, Mr. Laurent," Davis said, breaking the awkwardness as he leaned forward, "we *will* be monitoring this area very closely now. And if necessary, we won't hesitate to come back and institute a rigorous predator culling program. Once the animal gets a taste for human blood, it's best to have them put down. It's unfortunate, but it's the reality for everyone's safety." Officer Davis turned to me. "How about you? Do you have anything to add? Or any specific concerns or questions?"

I shook my head. His gaze gave me an eerie feeling. "No sir."

He leaned over, keeping his eyes trained on mine, and handed me a card as well. "Don't hesitate to call, son. We want to ensure the safety of the citizens of this town. It is our first priority. Understand?"

I nodded quickly.

My dad stretched his arms over his head. "Well, you definitely have our support. This is scary, and I have these two kids and a dog to worry about. I'd rather you find this thing now and cull it."

"We'll try, Mr. Laurent," Davis said, standing up to leave. "But for now, please watch yourselves, follow the law, and be alert."

They both gave me an odd look as they put their shoes on.

"You have yourselves a nice evening," Davis said as he opened the door and they left.

My bed had never felt so welcoming. So warm. So soft.

Though I dreaded class the next morning, I also craved life to get back to normal. And I really needed sleep. Honey was curled up at the foot of my bed.

It was only nine o'clock, but my eyes were so heavy I

wasn't even sure I would be able to read anything before falling asleep. I wondered if updating my reading lists to include Bram Stoker and Stephen King might be a good or bad idea, given the turn of events in my life.

The game wardens' visit threw me off. Were they giving me a message? Did they know? Were they the so-called lycan police Mrs. Leclair talked about, the Gencara? Or was I just being paranoid? Suzanne and I would have to be careful and cautious, but not about what was roaming outside.

From what was *inside*.

Tap.

Something hit my window, and Honey and I both looked up.

Tap.

Honey barked and jumped off the bed.

I cupped my face against the glass, looking around, then down. Sybil was standing below, staring up as I opened the window. "Hey," I whispered. "I'll go to the front door."

Honey ran ahead and waited expectantly. When I opened the door, she leapt outside. Sybil stood at the bottom of our steps with her arms crossed. It was dark, but the moon was still close to being full, providing enough light to see she had been crying.

"What are you doing here?" I asked as I skipped down the steps, excited to see her. "Are you okay?"

She squinted in the dark, and her lips were pursed. "Did you threaten my dad?"

Nodding, I looked down, suddenly embarrassed. "Sorta."

"What did I say?" she asked, her voice angry.

"To stay out of it—"

"—and you go to my dad's work and *threaten him*? Was that 'staying out of it'? What is wrong with you?" Her voice was cracking now, on the verge of tears. "Did you think that would make things better? Or did it just make you feel better?"

I hunched over, kicking some rocks lightly as I put my hands in my pockets. "I don't know actually—"

Whap!

Her open palm slapped my cheek. I almost hoped she'd do it again if it made her feel better. Her lip was quivering, and her eyes were red. "What did you say to him?"

"I'm sorry."

Whap!

She slapped me again. Harder. Her face trembled.

Her arm shook as she held it up again, and I waited for the next blow. But then she lowered it, and her glassy eyes closed. She began to sob. She pulled her hands into the sleeves of her sweater and held them up to her face, struggling for control. But the tears wouldn't stop.

I stepped forward and pulled her into my arms, half expecting a knee to the groin, but was happily rewarded with silence and consent for once. She was shaking and she burrowed into my shirt and cried.

We stood there for what seemed like forever.

When she finally calmed, I convinced her to come inside.

"I'm a complete mess," she said with a sniffle.

"Suzanne's asleep, and my dad is in his study. Come on, it's fine."

I led her through the house and into my room. She sat on the bed, wiping her eyes, stooped over.

"Do you want some water or something?"

She nodded quietly. "Do you have something to eat? I . . . I never ate dinner, and I've been out walking for hours. I ran out when my dad came home . . ."

"Of course, gimme a sec."

I sped to the kitchen and made a little tray of cheese, crackers, and olives. I felt horrible about what I did, and what she probably had to face when her dad got home. What was I thinking? Was she right? Did I do it only to make me feel good?

When I returned, Sybil was curled up on my bed, fast asleep. I put the food on the bedside table and pulled the covers up over her. She had never looked so quiet, peaceful, and unguarded before. I grabbed a spare pillow and some blankets from the hall closet and nestled down on the floor next to my bed with Honey. The moon was just visible in the sky from where I lay. It looked a little whiter, almost silver, tonight.

Where all of this would lead us, I did not know. I was happy Sybil had come here when she had nowhere else. However, Suzanne's advice about keeping things simple between us bounced around in my thoughts.

As for being a lycan, I felt confident that Suzanne and I would have control. The wardens wouldn't ever need to return to *cull* anything. At least going forward, we would face things together, my big sister and me. Well, she was smaller now, but still older at least. Maybe this turn of events would keep her from moving back to New York.

Though she was right that many doors had been closed for us, many had also been opened. A smile spread across my face as I considered those possibilities.

In the end, as bizarre as it sounded, maybe moving to Santa

Isadora was for the best. I couldn't imagine what would have happened had I unexpectedly transformed in Manhattan without having any knowledge of what was going on.

And now? Well, I might have a girlfriend, but probably not. But I did have a great friend in Jermaine, and possibly Kevin if I ever forgave him.

And Suzanne and I were closer than we'd ever been. I was sure that bond would only strengthen going forward.

And family. We had family—out there. Far away, across the ocean. And they, too, were lycans. Suzanne and I needed to find them.

Our future held infinite possibilities.

Outside, the almost-full moon held my attention. Like it was calling me. The urge was there, buried deep . . . but there. I longed to transform—*all the way*—and simply run.

And eat.

And discover.

And explore this new and exciting world.

AUTHOR'S NOTE

If you enjoyed this novel, please rate or leave a review on **Amazon**, **Goodreads**, or whichever platform you visit, it would be very much appreciated!

R. A. Watt is a dedicated husband, father, and new author based in the gorgeous Okanagan Valley of British Columbia. *AS SILVER IS TO THE MOON* is his debut novel.

www.ryanawatt.com

CPSIA information can be obtained
at www.ICGtesting.com
Printed in the USA
LVHW111919160419
614426LV00001B/17/P